EVELYN M. MAYS

# Blueberry
# *fi*elds

*A Three Bridges Novel*

PRAIRIE CREEK
CHRISTIAN PRESS
Ben Wheeler, Texas

**Blueberry Fields**
Copyright ©2012 Evelyn Mays
All rights reserved.

Cover Design: Steven Peterson
Interior Formatting: Ellen C. Maze, The Author's Mentor, ellencmaze.com
Author Website: http://www.evelynmays.com/

Prairie Creek Christian Press
Ben Wheeler, Texas
ISBN-13: 978-0615804477
ISBN-10: 0615804470
Also available in eBook publication

Unless otherwise indicated, Bible quotations are taken from the New International Version. Copyright © 1973, 1978, 1984 by Holman Bible Publishers, Nashville, TN.

PRINTED IN THE UNITED STATES OF AMERICA

# Acknowledgments

Writing is a lonely job with only a computer as companion. At times when working on the *Three Bridges* series, I felt as if I were writing in a vacuum. At the completion of this book, I realized that I was never ever alone, but the experiences shared with family and friends throughout my life were with me through every page of this book.

Thank you to everyone—and you are many—that have listened to me talk about the Three Bridges series of books and especially Blueberry Fields. I particularly thank those of you that have read, and reread the emerging manuscripts. Your kind words of praise have fueled my energy to complete the task.

A very special lady that lives on the hill has contributed so much by reading and correcting those early manuscripts. Her proofreading skills and words of enthusiastic encouragement made the writing easier. But the greatest gift she gave me was friendship. I thank you, Wanda Morris.

As I finish each manuscript, I am reminded that whatever success and achievements that come my way are the blessings of God. I am overwhelmed by His love and mercy.

*This book is dedicated to Bob, my husband and encourager and to my ever-patient son Ed.*

# $\mathcal{P}$rologue

**Welcome to Three Bridges, Texas. This small town in the** heart of East Texas was founded around 1880 on the *other side* of a small meandering stream that masquerades as a river in springtime, and took its name from three bridges built by feuding immigrant farmers trying to establish their boundaries and build their future.

By mid-1930 only one bridge remained—a new structure built when a tornado cut a wide swath through the town destroying the old bridges. Still, the name of Three Bridges was firmly in place and the town grew steadily, spurred in part by the discovery of oil in East Texas. No wells were drilled in Three Bridges, but the newly rich became enchanted with this growing town.

Today if you wandered off the interstate and crossed Compromise Creek, Main Street would take you to the heart of Three Bridges. The Bank of Three Bridges is on the right, and City Café across the street. On River Road, beautiful Victorian and Craftsman style homes stand proud, and on the edge of town, Community Baptist Church welcomes the residents of this small town. Three Bridges may be quiet looking to the observer, but if you lived here . . . well you'd know that there's always something going on.

# $\mathcal{O}$ne

**It's hot, every morning, always stinking hot. I pulled a ratty** old kitchen towel from my jeans and took another swipe at my brow. Nine years . . . no ten. Every summer for the past ten years, it's been the same routine. Up with the chickens and work like a field hand. When you combine East Texas heat with the ever-present humidity—well, femininity just doesn't stand a chance.

I tucked the sweat dampened towel back into the waistband of my faded denims, and tried to focus. I moved my foot one step higher on the ladder and continued to pick berries.

I can't reach the top branches without a ladder. I'm short. And tired. Tired enough to be granny old, but I'm only thirty-two. I picked and plucked until I had removed all the ripe berries that I could reach and then climbed off the work scarred aluminum ladder.

I moved it to the other side of this huge plant and started picking again with that familiar rhythm. Pluck a handful of plump berries, drop them into my bucket, and repeat. Every few minutes, I'd swipe a hand across my face, removing the sweat, and leaving stains and dirt. These rhythmic actions were accompanied by a question racing through my mind the same way it had every morning for a while now.

*Why? Why am I working in this blueberry field?*

It's early. Not much past dawn and the East Texas sun is already scorching hot. I don't have to be out here helping with the daily blueberry harvest. I have a full crew of skilled workers to do what I'm pretending to enjoy. And the other reason that I shouldn't be out here picking blueberries is this: I have a real job that starts in two hours.

I'm here because I own Anderson Farms. It was an inheritance from my grandmother, and since her passing, I've tried to fill her shoes. I've tried to continue with the same work ethic that she brought to fields, and to the rest of her businesses. I've tried, but I think I'm falling short of the mark.

Everything was fine and I was managing pretty well until Clarke Watson died five months ago. Since that day, the joy of being a banker has faded. Now, I take no pleasure in changing from my worn-out denims into the tailored clothing of a banker.

To some folks, my title might be impressive. Julie Trahan, Executive Vice-President. However, I'm no longer impressed or even thankful to have that title. My *real* job doesn't fill me with those warm fuzzies as it did in the past. It's just what I do until the day ends and I go home to sleep and start the routine again the next day.

During June and July, I jump out of bed every morning at four o'clock and arrive at the farm about forty minutes later. I pick blueberries until a quarter after seven. Since Clarke's death, I open the bank at eight o'clock every banking day. It's a tight schedule, but so far it's worked.

"Julie, Miss Julie." I smiled to myself at the sound of that voice. That voice has called me "Miss Julie" since I was a child, visiting during the summer with my brother and older sister. Even after I grew up and moved to Three Bridges, she still calls me Miss Julie.

"Miss Julie." The sound was closer and I looked to my right to see the matriarch of the Salazar family making a beeline for me as fast as she could shuffle. I handed my morning's work to

Marcus Salazar and stood with a frown on my face as she approached.

"Hortense! Why did you walk all the way out to the fields? It's almost time for me to quit. I was coming in soon."

"Now Julie, don't fuss, I just wanted to get out for a bit before it gets too hot. I came to tell you that someone called for you a few minutes ago. This call, it was strange. The man asked for Juliana Elizabeth Trahan. Is that you?"

Juliana Elizabeth Trahan. That was me all right. But why would anyone around here know that name? I've always been *Julie* to everyone. I folded up the ladder, laid it down on the ground and then cautiously sat on the upturned edged. I'd done this before and only toppled over a time or two. I looked at my watch, ten minutes before seven.

Who would be calling me so early at the farm and asking for me by a name that only appears on legal documents? I stood up and tried to shake the creepy feeling off. I've had too many surprises in life and I didn't need any more.

"Come on, Hortense, let's go back to your kitchen before you get too hot. It's going to be another scorcher today."

We started the long trek back to the offices of Anderson Blueberry Farms, but Hortense wasn't willing to let go of the mysterious phone call.

"What about the phone call, Julie? Who do you think it could be? I didn't recognize his voice, and nobody calls you *Juliana.* But that's not all. When I asked if he would like to leave a message, he sort of growled and then muttered something that sounded like—'Tell Little Jet that I'll catch up with her sooner or later. 'Tell Little Jet—I'm certain that's what he said. Julie—do you know who this could be?"

I stumbled on a clod of dirt and almost landed on my face, but Hortense reached out a hand to steady me. "Are you okay, Little Julie?"

"Little Julie, Little Jet, why were these words reaching out with cold and clammy fingers, making it almost impossible for me to breathe? I thought I'd put my past firmly behind me. *Little*

*Jet* was a name I hadn't heard since high school—and I didn't want to hear it now.

By now, we'd reached the barn that housed all the activities related to our commercial baking. Even though I'd eaten a big breakfast—and suffered a shock with the message Hortense gave me—the enticing smell from the bakery made my knees weak and my stomach curl up with hunger. Something in the oven filled the room with the aroma of blueberries, vanilla, and cinnamon.

I speculated that Hortense was working on another version of blueberry pound cake—she was constantly striving to improve something that was already perfect—in my opinion.

This kitchen was the place that Hortense loved the best. It was her comfort zone and her territory. Even though I was running short on time, I sat at the kitchen table and put my feet in another chair. This action by anyone else would have been chastised, but Hortense always catered to me—just like another grandmother.

"Julie, I know you're tired, but I've got one other bit of business to discuss. There is a new restaurant opening in Tyler, and they want to carry our blueberry muffins and a few deserts. What do you think about adding another customer?"

"I thought the kitchen was running at full capacity now. Can we handle another account?"

"I don't know if we can add another customer without hiring more girls and we really don't have any more workspace. What do you think we should do?"

"Oh, let's think about it for a while. We haven't had a great year, our overhead is too high, and our profit—well, you know about that. I don't think we should hire anyone else now. Maybe later if things continue to pick up. And, this new business might fold and we'd be stuck with new employees that we may not need. Let's pass for now."

"Okay, you're the boss lady. Your job is to figure out what works. My job is to cook, and I'm running behind in my job. You need anything before you go?"

"No, just going to wash off a little and then head back to town."

I unbuttoned the long-sleeved cotton big shirt that I wore to the fields, pulled it off and walked across the room to a deep sink that was part of the kitchen setup. Wearing a tank top and the extra full raggedy denims, I turned on the spray faucet to wash down my arms and couldn't resist the pleasure of rinsing the sweat off my face. Thank goodness, it was probably too early to run into anyone I might know, and besides, I really didn't care.

"Hortense, if that man calls back, ask him to leave his name and number. Gotta go, it's going to be a really busy day at the bank."

I left the comfort of Anderson Farms kitchen and drove back to town—almost twenty miles—but my mind was not on the road I was traveling.

*"Tell Little Jet . . .*

*"Tell Little Jet . . .*

*"Tell Little Jet . . .*

Those innocent words sent shivers down my spine. Not very many people called me by that name. Certainly not anyone I knew currently. And probably not more than three people in the world would think of calling me Little Jet so many years after high school.

Only one person continued to call me by that nickname long after high school and I certainly didn't want to hear from him now.

*Little Jet* was the nickname given to me by my basketball coach. I was really too short to play, but I had such determination and speed, Mrs. Leonard took pity on me and let me play at least part of every game. When I managed to hit the basket on occasion, the stands would roar with that silly name.

*Little Jet!*

Life is so difficult now with the situation at the bank, and worry about turning a profit at Anderson Farms that I truly wished I could score some points—but I didn't want to do it as *Little Jet.*

# $\mathscr{T}$wo

**Half an hour later, I drove my aging SUV up to a beautiful** Victorian house, graceful and elegant, perched in the middle of two acres with its back facing the west. White paint glistened in the early morning sun and brought the deep green shutters and roof shingles into glowing contrast. Broad concrete steps rose to meet the wide porch with newly painted grey floor boards. Almost eighty years of footsteps had worn a path to the leaded glass entry door.

The porch followed the lines of the house, cornering to span the entire north side. Between each section of the intricate porch railing, lush green ferns were gently swaying in the morning breeze. The house still looked the same, even though Grandmother has been gone over three years now. I am proud that I have been able to keep it looking so good.

I was home. I parked in an old garage toward the rear of the property, and looked around before going in through the kitchen door. Compromise Creek runs thru the rear of the property and separates us from acreage that serves no purpose except to grow an assortment of trees, mosquitos, and feral hogs. I glanced past the two houses to the north, and I could almost see the remains of the first bridge that spanned the creek but now stands rotting and ignored. We never walk in that area. It's overgrown and creepy, although rumor has it to be a good fishing spot when the creek rises.

The creek usually rises when the skies open up and rain falls so quickly that the drought hardened soil can't absorb it. That can happen any time of the year, but mostly in the spring, and many days I've stood with Grandmother in the safety of the back porch, watching as the rain fell in buckets. We would watch in awe and debate how high the water would rise.

I moved here at the age of twenty-two, and I had no plans to stay. The real story is that back then I had no plans for anything and I didn't want any plans, but Grandmother changed all that. She made me work hard, and she taught me to fight for my survival, but she also taught me how to love life. She's been gone for over three years, and I miss her.

I told myself to stop this woolgathering and get in the house, but before I could reach the back steps, a golden fur ball with four big feet ran to greet me. I share my house with this very cheerful dog of questionable ancestry that appeared on the back porch one rainy morning and has never left. After Grandmother went to be with Jesus, Goldie was sometimes the only comfort for my pain.

I refilled water and food dishes as my puppy continued to wag her tail so fast that she stirred up a small breeze. With so much energy, the poor pup never gave up on wanting to play.

"Later, Goldie. Be a good dog and hold the fort today. I am gonna be late for work if I don't hurry."


I don't have a lot of clothes, but my years with Grandmother had taught me to shop for quality rather than quantity. A few minutes later, I made a quick assessment in the mirror. Working in the fields had given me a tan most women would get in a tanning bed, but my tan was earned with hours of berry picking.

My summer darkened skin complimented my dark brown naturally-curly hair, and brown eyes. A sleeveless coffee brown linen dress and my latest splurge, a pair of dark brown leather shoes—Gucci shoes—completed my banker wardrobe for the day. I was a monochromatic study in brown, offset by gold jewelry. And that was as good as it would get this morning.

∽᠍᠍᠍᠍᠍᠍᠍ᢙᢙ

The Bank of Three Bridges is one of the oldest businesses in town, founded in 1920 by John Jefferson Watson, Sr. I now work for Jeff Watson, great grandson of the founder and the first "reluctant" Watson ever to sit in the president's chair. I wondered if he would show up for work today.

I pulled my old SUV into the parking lot behind the bank and began my morning trek through broken concrete that gave birth to a mixed variety of weeds, and finally stepped onto a sidewalk that had seen better days.

My workday started as I opened the original oak and glass doors, circa 1930, and entered The Bank of Three Bridges. I had worked three hours already, but my real job was beginning.


"Morning Jessie, did you have a good weekend?"

"I had a great weekend, Julie. We had the grandkids without any parents, so we did whatever the kids wanted to do. It was fun, but I was also rather happy to see the kids go back home."

Jessie Baker was the backbone of this bank and she'd been head teller for most of my life. "Oh, Jessie, you are too funny."

"I wasn't joking about the kids. I'm too old to run around playing games, but it was nice for a few hours. Okay, gotta get the coffee going so the vault will open. Sounds silly, but I know there's a connection."

Mondays are tough in any business, and banking is no exception. A weekend of unexpected expenses, surprising opportunities (which involved spending), and assorted other financial needs brought an increase in banking activity. As usual, we were inundated with withdrawals, transfers from one account to another, and loan applications.

Small town banks are no different from big city banks, just fewer customers, and fewer bank personnel to serve those customers. When our first customer of the day came in, I was in the storage room opening a box of toilet paper for the ladies' restroom. Julie Trahan, Executive Vice-President, Bank of Three Bridges, and part-time janitor. Some of my duties are more pleasant than others, and today, my first customer was a doozie that made thoughts of being a janitor seem pleasant.

Before I had a chance to speak any words of greeting, Miss Maddie Wallace fluffed her bright auburn hair, straightened her slightly stooped frame, and struggled to rise to her full height of five-feet-four inches. Since she was now almost two inches taller than I, she opened fire with a voice that could be heard in any corner of the bank and I was her verbal target. Lucky me.

"Well, Miss Julie Trahan, it's about time you got back to your desk. This bank has just gone to pot since Clarke Watson died and left that incompetent son of his in charge. And just where is he, may I ask?"

"Come on in to my office, Miss Maddie, perhaps I can help you with your banking today."

Miss Maddie wasn't alone, and that fact did nothing to improve my agitated state. She was accompanied by her friend, driver, and personal interior decorator. Odie Marshall wears many hats in Three Bridges. I didn't want to think about any other layers of their relationship. However, to the casual observer, they seem to be a perfectly matched set despite the age difference.

Odie Marshall and Miss Maddie Wallace are the sort of people that try my patience and test my Christian attitude. They are contentious and disagreeable, either by nature or by choice, but I think their pictures should be in the dictionary to further define the word *challenge*.

My first customers of the day. Not how I would have chosen to start this day, but I am a professional.

"How can I help you, Miss Maddie?"

"You didn't answer my question. Where is that young man that's supposed to be running this bank? Why isn't he here?"

"Jeff has a lot of obligations just now, Miss Maddie. I can

help you or you can call later and make an appointment with him. I'm sure he'd be happy to meet with you."

"Well, I suppose you can handle this. It's simple enough that even a clerk could take care of it. I want to add Odie Marshall as a signatory on my checking and savings account."

I inadvertently shook my head. Good bankers shouldn't let the customers see their gut reactions, but I had no chance to cover my mental lapse. I deliberately avoided eye contact with Odie Marshall, but from the corner of my vision, I could see him twist in his chair and lean forward in anticipation. I sat straighter and further back in my high back banker's desk chair and straightened my professional banker shoulders.

"Now don't look at me like that, Missy. This is purely a business arrangement. I need someone to take care of my affairs when I'm away. As you know, I occasionally leave the country."

"Certainly, Miss Maddie. You have the right to add whomever you wish to sign on your accounts. I'll be happy to assist you."

I said the words. I said them in a calm and straightforward manner, but I *was not* happy to assist her. In a flash, an idea popped into my head and I committed an outright sin. I lied.

"Please excuse me for just a moment. I see that one of my tellers is trying to get my attention. I won't be but a second." I scurried out of my office and across the lobby.


"Jessie, you know that under normal circumstances I never ask anyone to lie, and if you don't feel comfortable doing this, I understand. This is just a little thing and I'll explain everything later. Can you think of something that you might need to ask Odie? I need to get Miss Maddie alone for just a little while."

"Not a problem, because I do indeed have something to ask him. Let me finish up here and I'll be right behind you. Don't worry, this will not be a lie. I can handle this."

I straightened my spine, put a pleasant and totally insincere expression on my face, and returned to my office.

"I'm sorry, something needed my attention. Now, Miss Maddie, you were talking about traveling. Are you planning to travel out of the country?"

Jessie tapped lightly on the door before she could answer, and I hope I looked sufficiently unhappy at the disturbing knock.

"Pardon me Julie, sorry to interrupt. Odie, could I see you for a moment? This is important. Sorry to interrupt, Miss Maddie."

Odie looked at Miss Maddie with a pained expression, got up and walked out of my office. Jessie quickly closed the door behind him. I couldn't hear her words, but I could see that he wasn't happy with the conversation. I needed to talk fast.

"Sorry about that, Miss Maddie. Now then, are you certain, without any doubt that you want to do this? It's somewhat unusual for anyone other than a spouse or a very close relative to sign on an account."

She didn't answer for a moment then fairly exploded with righteous indignation.

"What an incredibly tacky thing to say. Of course I want to do this. Young lady, I trust that dear man with my very life. Odie is much, much more than a friend. He's been such a great help to me. We understand each other so well I feel as if he's my soul mate. Yes, a soul mate. Isn't that what you young folks all say today?"

It took only a moment for me to answer. "Miss Maddie, I've never had a soul mate on this earth, and honestly, the only soul mate that I want is Jesus."

I must have shocked her into silence, so I plunged on before she could think of a retort. "Just one more question. Do you want to put any restrictions on your account, a maximum dollar amount for withdrawal, or anything like that?"

She had no chance to answer that question as Odie, obviously disconcerted, rushed back into the room, and practically threw himself into the client chair across from me.

"Julie, could we just sign the cards? I've got another appointment soon. You know how busy I am with this festival just a few days away. We're behind on everything because we couldn't get enough qualified volunteers this year, and everyone is overworked, especially me."

I knew this remark was aimed at me because I had refused to accept any role in the Three Bridges annual Blueberry Festival. My plate was full this year, and I didn't have the emotional energy to work with Odie Marshall after putting in my sixteen hour summer-time work days.

"That subject is over and done, Odie. I'm just too busy this year. I don't have time to serve on the Blueberry Festival committee. Okay, let's get those cards signed."

I hastened to accomplish the task, and then walked Miss Maddie Wallace to the front door of the bank. I hope I exuded polite charm as I held the door and said goodbye, but I was still thinking that Odie Marshall was a good one to keep under a watchful eye and out of your checking account.

# $\mathscr{T}$hree

**To work off the tension from dealing with Miss Maddie and** Odie Marshall, I cleaned my desk. Three large stacks of bank documents were separated into six smaller stacks, and then most of those were put out of sight.

I have my own system. The lower right hand desk has hanging file folders with specific captions: Today's Work, Tomorrow's Work, and ASAP. It works for me.

My desk was cleared, leaving a refreshingly clean desktop, but only for a moment. Soon it was filled up with a smaller stack of papers.

"Julie, here are your messages and those new accounts I opened last week."

I was interrupted from my rambling thoughts by the voice of another long-time bank employee, Vonda Sue Gunderson. Clark Watson had assembled a small but loyal staff to help him run The Bank of Three Bridges, and Vonda was an important part of this process.

She's about ten years my senior, and has been working at the bank since she graduated from her two year college course. Tall, plain, and quiet, Vonda was known primarily for her unique style of clothing. She didn't follow the trends, but still dressed in those flowing styles of several years back—actually many years ago—but the casual style seemed perfect for her quiet personality.

Instead of dropping her head and slipping from my office as she normally did, Vonda hesitated a moment and then walked closer to my desk, almost leaning on it.

"I know it's none of my business, but I couldn't help but notice Odie and Miss Maddie. What's going on with them?"

"Oh Vonda, you know I can't comment on that. Are you still seeing Odie? Oops—forget that I said anything. I can't talk bank business, and you don't have to answer personal questions."

"I really wouldn't mind answering your questions if I knew the answer. Odie was at my house last night, talking tough and acting important, but what's new?"

The frown on her face gave Vonda the appearance of a woman scorned. It was a look that didn't flatter her less than attractive features. She and Odie had a long history together, a long-term and typical on-again-off-again romance. Mostly off on his part.

We both realized there was nothing left to say on this subject so she turned and walked out of my office as I attempted to go back to my banker duties.

I looked at the new account cards and tried to memorize the names of the two new families that had opened accounts with us. Our little community was beginning to grow. I made a note on my calendar to write welcome letters to these people. I tried not to think about the fact that Jeff Watson should be having that pleasure.

At two o'clock Jeff Watson walked through the door of my office. "Miss Trahan, I need to see you in my office."

For a moment I didn't move, merely reflected on the arrogance of this man, among other things. Actually, if my thoughts could have been mapped, it would look similar to the big city traffic maps television stations show in the morning traffic reports—lots of streets stacked up with traffic. My thoughts were running in many directions at a frantic pace, and like those angry drivers in rush hour traffic, those thoughts tended to border on unchristian.

Sometimes my thoughts crossed the border. Sometimes I talk to myself. Sometimes I talk to myself in an audible voice. This was one of those times. "I can't afford to miss another Wednesday night prayer service. My attitude could really benefit from some intense prayer."

I took a deep breath and walked into the president's office.

"Have a seat, Miss Trahan. As you know, things have been very difficult these last few months. I want to thank you and all the bank staff for handling things so well."

He paused, but I didn't fill in the gap of silence. I wanted to be nice.

"Miss Trahan, I guess I really should call you Julie. My dad thought the world of you. He said that you were exceptionally bright and capable. I trust that proves true."

Again, I wanted to be nice and so I didn't respond. But I did sit a little straighter in my chair. And waited. While I waited, I made a mental assessment of the man sitting behind his father's desk.

I knew that Jeff was four years older than I am because his father had often commented on the fact. I also knew that he was an architect in Santa Fe, New Mexico, with a successful business. And even though he loved his mother dearly and was heartbroken by the death of his father, he didn't want to be a banker in Three Bridges, Texas.

I continued my assessment. Young, physically fit and even to my angry eyes, very handsome. Jeff was also probably a foot taller than I am. Sun bleached blonde hair curled low over his collar, and intelligent, cold blue eyes seemed to be taking a similar assessment of me. Finally, he broke the silence in the room.

"Julie, for the past few weeks, I've tried to close out my business in Santa Fe, and I just can't do it by long distance.

There are several things that demand my physical presence, so I'm flying out late this evening."

Still, I didn't respond, using this time to think of an intelligent and respectful response. My soul wanted to cry out in anger. *Grow up, man up, take ownership of your responsibilities.* I remained silent.

"Surely you have something you'd like to ask me?"

Yes, there were things I wanted to say, but I restricted my comments with something approaching a professional response.

"First, how long will you be gone, and second, who's going to be in charge? Is your mother coming out to Three Bridges every day?"

"Fair enough questions. I'll be gone as long as it takes, two or maybe even three weeks. And no, my mother will not be here in Three Bridges. Julie, I believe your title is Executive Vice-President. You will be in charge. Think you can handle it?"

"I'll do my best, but your dad handled all the major decisions. I just did as he told me. Jeff, I don't know that I have all the skills to keep this bank going by myself that long. What should I do if I run into a problem?"

He looked at me as if I had antennae sprouting from my head. "Oh, come on Julie, nothing ever happens in Three Bridges."

For the remainder of the workday I must have answered a dozen phone calls, visited with at least that many people—some who had banking business and others who just wanted to visit. Finally, the banking day neared closing time and I began to clear my desktop. As I was rearranging stacks of paper work on my desk, I found the annoying little yellow forms and discovered another call for *Juliana Elizabeth Trahan*. The busy flow of traffic through the bank was probably the reason I never got very far into the stack of phone messages Vonda had delivered earlier.

I looked at the form again. No message and no number for a return call. No mention of 'Little Jet"—and nothing but a mystery that I really didn't want or need.

*Dear God, I don't need this. You know my plate is full to overflowing with things to deal with. I have no room in my life for mysterious callers. Lord, help me get through this.*

The day was over at last and I took my attitude from a line spoken poignantly in a famous movie about the south, "I'll worry about that tomorrow."

I checked the vault, took a cursory look around the bank, then locked the front door, and started home. Jeff Watson's words kept echoing in my head. "Julie, nothing ever happens in Three Bridges."

I went home to an uneventful evening, and woke to another day and my familiar routine.

From Monday through Thursday, my day job in the banking world and my early morning job at Anderson Blueberry Farms proceeded without incident. This morning, Friday, I reached the farm just as the sun cleared the horizon, and made a beeline for the kitchen to sample whatever delicious food Hortense Salazar had just taken from her oven.

I saw a pan of bar cookies on the counter that had just been cut. I put a couple of cookies on a plate, added sliced peaches fresh from our orchard, and took extra napkins to wipe up the peach juice. Lastly, I poured a cup of coffee and sat at the kitchen table.

"Delicious, Hortense, these are some of the best peaches we've grown. If you have a minute, I'd like to talk to you before I go to work."

Neither of us enjoyed the financial discussions, but neither did we avoid them. I pulled out a folder and laid it across the end of the table.

"I printed out our expenses and income from the first six months of this year. Something is different from the past years. I can't explain it, but we're hardly breaking even. If I hadn't been so consumed with the bank, I would have picked this up sooner. Something is very wrong, and we've got to figure out how to fix it."

Hortense was staring at the report as if it were written in

*20*

ancient Greek. Her time worn Hispanic face creased with worry as she ran a trembling finger across each line. Finally, she stopped and looked me in the eye.

"Why are our vehicle expenses so high? Each month is higher than the last. I don't understand what's going on. I know the insurance has gone up on the workers and the property, but what is with the truck expenses?"

"I don't know. I thought you would have an explanation for that. I don't have backup receipts for most of those expenses. I was hoping you had them."

"No, I don't think so. No one has given me any receipts, but I will certainly look, and more certainly, I will ask. If this continues, we won't break even next month. Miss Julie, what have I done wrong?"

"I don't think it's you, Hortense. Most of these expenses are related to the equipment and the delivery trucks. Do we have a new person on these trucks? There has to be some explanation. Last month we had almost five thousand dollars in expenses and I don't have all the receipts, and these large amounts aren't backed up with a work ticket. We've got to get to the bottom of this."

"Marcus always has work tickets to back up any maintenance expense. I wonder if he knows what's going on."

"You're right, Marcus keeps very good records of everything. I think he doesn't know that this is going on."

"Your sainted grandmother would never have let this happen. I feel ashamed that the Salazar family cannot do the job as we should. Miss Julie, do you want someone else to run this farm?"

"Hortense, my grandmother had faith in you and your family and so do I, but sometimes things happen. Sometimes people change. Think about how my mother has behaved these last few years."

I got up and started to leave, but I was still searching for some magic solution to this problem.

"I can't run this farm without you in charge. You and your

family have worked hard to make Anderson Farms the success it is today. We need to figure out what's going on, and we need to solve this. I hope there's a good explanation. Talk to Marcus and let me know."

I went to the fields, but my feet and my enthusiasm were dragging. I grabbed a ladder and a bucket and went to work. When I reached the end of the row of bushes that I was picking, I noticed one of the younger Salazar's heading out to meet someone driving up in a black car with a lot of shiny chrome and dark windows. He spoke briefly to the driver and then hurried back to the fields.

I worked at picking berries for another hour, but probably left as many berries on the trees as I picked. My mind was a whirlwind of problems. I picked berries and worried about the bank, the farm, and my life. Finally, it was time to hand over my morning's work and head back to Three Bridges and my other job. My real job.

# *Four*

**This old Victorian house has been my home for ten years** now, and I'm still in awe. Tall ceilings, an abundance of windows, and space. Lots of space, such as this huge closet and dressing area. I was tucked away inside, multi-tasking with one hand holding a hair dryer, blowing out my newly showered curls while the other hand moved hangers about, trying to find another appropriate garment for work.

When my decisions were made, I dressed hastily, then sat down at my vanity to finish the morning ritual. Finally, with shoes in hand, I returned to the bedroom just in time to hear the last ring of the phone as the call went to voice mail.

Was this another call for Juliana Elizabeth? Did I really want to answer that call? Did I really want to hear that voice say my name—any name? The thought was annoying and worrisome. I shivered at the thought of that unnamed person calling for Juliana—or more truthfully—*Little Jet*—but now there wasn't an extra second to retrieve the message. Thankfully, the bank was waiting.

Driving to the bank, I couldn't get those phone calls off my mind, but then I suppose this was the desired effect the caller wished to achieve. Of course he wanted me to think and wonder about who was calling, or he would have left his name and a message.

No, this person's intent was to worry me, to keep me feeling on edge, as he played this clever game. True, there had been only one mention of *Little Jet* and that in the first phone call, but I knew this caller had an association with the most painful years of my life.

I thought those years had been laid to rest by Grandmother's old fashioned work-therapy, but four or five anonymous phone calls had brought past memories to mix with today's worries. Well, these phone calls were something that I had no control over—at least not now—and I shouldn't let this fear of unexpected calls from strangers drive me crazy. No point in pondering the identity of the anonymous caller. There was only one person who would be calling for Juliana Elizabeth— *Little Jet*—and I didn't want to talk to him. Ever.

*Get over it, Julie, let it go. There are too many real things to worry about—like those unexplained truck expenses.*


I threw myself into the daily routine at the bank, and tried to keep the personal problems in the background. Much of today's work was a breeze, especially since Maddie Wallace and Odie Marshall had been absent from the bank all week. Also, I didn't hear anything from Marcus or Hortense by closing time, so that problem would wait a while. It was Friday and my work week was over. I was most happy to lock the doors, hurry home, and change into jeans, a tee shirt, and sandals. I like to be comfortable when I eat.


I parked in the rear of the lot adjacent to City Café. The moment I opened the car door, I could smell grilled onions and frying fish. I spoke to a few people already leaving and another couple going in for the all-you-can-eat catfish supper.

City Café has been on this corner for as long as I can remember, and nothing has changed, especially Henry, the owner and chef. He would be best described by a fading plaque hanging on the wall near the cash register. He points to it anytime someone comments on his ever expanding girth. *Never trust a skinny cook.*

If I'm down, my spirits always pick up when I enter this place. On the right side of the room, a mirror runs the entire length and is now covered with signs, posters, and favorite quotes from certain patrons. In front of this mirror is a long counter with round padded stools bolted to the floor. This counter space is usually taken by those guys who just want a cup of coffee and a friendly visit with a buddy.

The booths are covered in red leather-like fabric and most have seen better days. The tables are topped with glass so old that each piece has a unique set of scratches and chips. Tucked between the aging glass and the table top are favorite snapshots—some dating back to the earliest days of Three Bridges. City Café is a place for the locals, but strangers always feel welcome. I headed for the last booth on the left side.

"Hey, girls, you're all here before me today! How did that happen, Marlene? Cynthia, how are you? Why Martha, it's so good to see you. It's been a while."

The exchange of hugs and enthusiastic greetings between friends continued until Geraldine, a long-time employee of City Café, interrupted.

"Everybody except Marlene drinking sweet tea tonight?"

After the drink orders were placed, she asked as always, "Y'all gonna have the seafood tonight? Thought so, I'll be right back with the tea."

I looked around the table at these friends I had made in Three Bridges. I was the youngest of the group and still in my twenties when our bond was formed. Cynthia—a few years older—was also shy of thirty, but Marlene and Dr. Martha admitted to being thirty-something back then. We don't talk about our age now, because we are just friends. Unique friends that have been through a lot together.

After a few months of Friday night suppers at City Café, someone decided that our group should have a name. It wasn't long before we found the right name—The Three Bridges Social Club.

"Hey, Julie, I heard that Jeff Watson left town. What's up?"

"How do you keep up on all the town gossip, Marlene? You work in Tyler, but you know everything, and usually before I do."

"I have my sources. Okay, I'll 'fess up. Actually, I was waiting for a client at Tyler airport and Jeff was waiting for a commuter flight. Smart girl that I am, I put two and two together and came up with an answer. Julie will run the bank and Jeff will run away, right?

"Well, it's true, he'll be gone for about three weeks. His physical presence is required in Santa Fe. He told me not to worry, that nothing ever happens in Three Bridges."

The spontaneous laughter filled the back corner of The City Café, and as usual drew more than a few looks, but most were friendly. We tend to be a little raucous. Sometimes we might even get loud, but most of the customers are tolerant of our enthusiasm.

We seldom see each other during the week, but most Friday nights we are usually in our favorite booth indulging in food— deep-fried, loaded with calories, and more soul satisfying than most meals at a four-star restaurant.

Chatter flowed around the table. We discussed the weather, the upcoming Blueberry Festival, and other tidbits of gossip when suddenly Dr. Martha put something on the table.

"Hey, girls, look at this. My car is in the shop, and I'm driving a brand new car—courtesy of my dealer. This gadget opens the door and I sure hope I don't lose it."

I looked at the gadget for moment, then picked it up and examined it closely. "I need a new car. My old one needs tires, and something isn't right under the hood, but I'm afraid to take it to the shop. Things aren't going too well at the farm this year, but maybe in the fall, I can afford a new car."

Martha grabbed my hand and spoke to me in her doctor voice. "Julie, when are you going to accept the inheritance from your grandmother? You know she wanted you to have that money. She would be heartbroken to know that you're struggling along, living paycheck to paycheck."

"Ah, Martha, you know how it is. There's still so much bad blood between Mother and me. She keeps threatening to proceed with the lawsuit, although time is running out on that."

I took a healthy bite of hush puppy and another sip of tea.

"Here's the deal. I'm afraid to spend a lot of money, because I may have to do repairs to the house. If mother should happen to have the will set aside, it could be very difficult for me financially. Whatever happens, right now I'm living just one day at a time."

Tired of that topic, I changed the subject.

"Marlene, you saw Jeff at the airport. Does that mean you were meeting Mr. Right?"

"No, but looking for Mr. Right is still more fun than anything going on around here, right, girls?"

We responded to this with shrieks of laughter and giggles and other silly comments that might be more commonly associated with teen-agers, but at times like these, we seem to forget our mature status. And again the nearby diners' heads were turned and smiles exchanged.

"Hey y'all, look over there, Odie Marshall is at the counter. He must be waiting for a takeout, but he can't stop looking at us. Actually, I think he's looking at Julie."

We turned in the direction that Marlene pointed, trying to be inconspicuous and most likely failing. Odie was sitting at the counter, but at an angle, so that he could stare in our direction.

I allowed only a small glance, but even so, his look was intense and threatening, making a shiver run up my spine. Even Dr. Martha commented on his behavior.

"What's going on with this guy? If looks could kill, at least one of us would be dead by now."

Cynthia ventured another look at Odie and then pushed her plate aside. "I told you the other day that he was crankier than ever. How in the world Vonda has put up with him for all these years beats me."

"Well, I'm speaking out of turn, but I think she's beginning to see the light. Sorry to change the subject, but I should go home. I need to be picking blueberries when the sun comes up tomorrow."

"Wait up, Julie, I walked up here this evening but I really don't want to walk home. Can I get a ride?"

"Of course, Cynthia, you know you can. Why'd you walk up here?"

"Oh, you've heard it all before. When these things bother me and I can't shake it off, I've found that walking helps. I highly recommend it if you've got a good meal waiting at the end of the walk."

"And a willing neighbor to hitch a ride with? Come on, neighbor. Let's go home."

☙❧

When I got home, I picked up the telephone and checked those voice mails, wishing once again that I had caller ID. Another thing that I really need to take care of—when I get time. I listened impatiently to the two phone calls from telemarketers, and erased them before they played through. No other calls, except the one from this morning—and that was merely the sound of a disconnect when the call reached voice mail.

# $\mathscr{F}$ive

**Next morning the blueberries were waiting for me, but I** couldn't get going. I wanted to cover up my head and stay in bed, but then I remembered Grandmother. She was always up at four-thirty, ready for the fields and a full day's work. So I stumbled out of bed and made a mad dash for the coffee pot and thanked the good Lord for technology.

So simple. Fix the pot at night, set the timer and wake up to a fresh brew. Delicious. Unlike most people my age, I am addicted to coffee and have been for many years. After all, I grew up in South Louisiana.

My routine is to have breakfast with Hortense, but this morning, the wonderful blueberry muffins were served with scrambled eggs and bacon and a large dish of trouble.

"Miss Julie, I didn't sleep last night, worrying about the farm. What is going on? Who is stealing our money? Whatever way you look at it, something is going on, and it looks like some sort of thievery to me."

"Let's don't go there yet, Hortense. Right now, we don't know the reason for this, but I agree—it looks like someone is stealing from us. We need to go through this and figure it out."

There was something else I wanted to say, but I wanted to choose my words carefully before I continued.

"Yesterday, I noticed something that got my attention. A new black SUV drove up to the edge of the fields and one of the younger boys went over to talk to the driver. I couldn't see who was driving because of the tinted windows. Have you ever seen a car like that out here before?"

I've read many books and I've seen the expression, "he (or she) withered before my very eyes," but that is the only way to explain her reaction to my question. She seemed to pale and wither before my eyes. I reached my hand across to her, urging her to sit down.

'What's going on, Hortense? Who drives that SUV?"

"I don't know, but that must have been Rudi going to meet him. He's Marcus's youngest son, and I'm ashamed to say, he's a troublesome young man."

My heart broke for her sorrow. I thought I had recognized the person crossing field, even though I didn't want to believe it was Rudi. He'd always been a good kid, but the harsh truth remained: someone was stealing from us and we had to get to the bottom of this problem.

"Miss Julie, somehow I will make this right. If Rudi is involved in this theft, I will personally repay whatever he has taken from this business."

"Let's wait on that for a while, Hortense. We have to find out what is going on before we can do anything about it, but whoever is at fault, we will work it out."

With those words ringing in my ears, I started towards the fields. The berries were calling to me, offering work to wipe out the worry.


While I picked blueberries, I watched the other workers in the fields. More than once, Marcus could be heard speaking to Rudi, urging him to pay attention, get back to work, and other such parental scolding. From where I stood on my ladder, it seemed that the comments were received with a sullen smirk, and basically ignored.

Trouble had definitely come to Anderson farms like a wild summer crop. How could we save this young man before he bankrupted my business?

I worked until almost noon and then went back to the kitchen to tell Hortense that I was leaving. Not only had I eaten like a field hand, worked like a field hand, I also smelled like one. My hair was a rat's nest from getting caught up in the twiggy little branches that bore those little orbs of bluish-purple fruit that everyone in East Texas craved this time of the year. Thank goodness blueberry season would end in a few weeks and life could return to normal. Well, almost normal.

I showered for a very long time to get off the sweat and grime of the blueberry fields. Then I slathered on lotion, dried my hair, and added makeup. From a shelf in the closet, I pulled out a pair of white shorts and added a blue and white tee shirt and thongs. My nails needed to be done, but there was no time for that, because I have to be at the bank all day. That responsibility should have been shared between the bank president and me, but he had other business that was more important than banking.

I didn't want to think about the bank, but I did have other things to sort through. Four years ago, or maybe a little longer, our little group began helping people anonymously. It began when a fire destroyed a home and killed the wife and four children. The father was at work and the youngest son was having a sleepover at a friend's house. It was devastating to that little community, and the local resources were small.

We saw needs that weren't being met and we provided them. Only Judge and Grandmother were aware of this philanthropy. Several times a year, we act when there is a need, and also, we make donations to small churches that have programs to provide funds for senior citizens that need a little financial assistance.

Two years ago, Judge called us in for a meeting. He'd not done that before, and we were all anticipating any number of problems. He greeted us with a big smile on his face, and seemed to beam with pleasure. He had great news.

He wouldn't reveal any details, but someone had provided funds for our group to receive quarterly payments to continue our work. The gift came with some rules, which we followed diligently. We are obligated to spend most of that money each quarter, keeping only a small percentage for expenses.

The second quarter had just ended, and we had money that had not been spent and only a few days grace period to donate or spend the money. We had to find a way to use the money or we'd forfeit the next anonymous payment. This afternoon we will meet to determine how to proceed.

Our little seat-of-the-pants philanthropic venture had turned into a rigidly organized business. Still, we were thankful for the ability to help others, and none of us ever stopped trying to figure out where this money came from. I heard car doors slam and I wondered at their timing. Always consistent, not running a few minutes behind as I sometimes did.

"Hey, girls, come on in out of this July heat."

"Well, Julie, it may be hot summer, but those ferns look wonderful. They make me feel cool even if it's a hundred-plus degrees. Which it will be soon."

"Right, Marlene. I wish it were cooler so we could sit on the porch, but let's try the sunroom. It's air conditioned."

We were friends of long standing, and no one stood on ceremony. As soon as we were in the kitchen, everyone took charge of her own drink choices. We live in the south, we never meet without refreshments of some sort. Today chips, dip, and a few fruit slices filled the goody tray and everyone was soon comfortable in the sunroom.

Marlene brought us up to date on our giving, and Cynthia listed a few options to spend the remaining funds from last quarter, and they were all good causes. I had an idea to put forth, but Dr. Martha beat me to the punch.

"Girls, I have a need. Someone, actually someone from Three Bridges, still owes a substantial amount for services received at Tyler Trauma Center two years ago. I have kept this out of the legal department as long as I can, but very soon, they're going to be forced to file suit to settle this account."

"Can you tell us the person's name or not?"

"I can, Marlene, and you may not be surprised. It's Krystal Kelly. You know the circumstances. A no-good husband walks off and leaves her to care for her child. And the police never determined how she was injured, only that someone must have hit her with a car. It was life and death for a time, but that little doll pulled through."

"Yes, I remember it well. Krystal certainly earned my admiration after she divorced that loser she married. How in the world could she take care of Jim's son? He's a handful."

I couldn't believe it. Krystal Kelly was also past due on a loan with the bank—a loan with a rather high balance. Perhaps this could all be worked out as a package deal. We moved from the comfort of the sunroom to the kitchen table for some working room. With pads and pens and a few calculators, we worked out the details.

By the time we finished it was getting late.

"Whew, I'm glad we got this all worked out. Tyler Trauma Center and The Bank of Three Bridges will be happy also. Great work, girls. Now we have time to get ready for our Saturday night dates."

As I said before, our group can be loud and cheerful. They were still loud and cheerful as they headed home for a lonely evening. None of us were dating. Oh well, in God's time.

I should have gone to bed. I was so tired that I should have been able to drop to sleep standing up, but my mind was going crazy. I went out to the wide porch and walked from one end to the other, thinking and checking on the ferns. Some were really dry and in need of a thorough watering, so I pulled them from their hangers and carried all twelve of them to a spot in the backyard, near the water hydrant. I don't like pulling that heavy hose around.

Of course the moment I began watering, Goldie came romping up, wanting to play. She loved running through the water, so we played her silly game for a while and I managed to get a little water on the plants.

I picked up one of the plants, heavy with water, and decided that I'd leave them in the back yard until tomorrow. The tiredness had settled on me like a thick blanket and I said goodnight to Goldie and walked back into the house with heavy footsteps. I heard the last ring of the phone the moment I opened the kitchen door.

For only a moment I thought about checking the answering machine, but I decided to ignore it. If the call was truly important, the caller would call again. Even though I'd had a shower after coming in from the fields, Goldie had managed to get me pretty messy with the water spray games that she loved to play so I headed back to the bathroom.

Two hours later, I was still awake. The shower must have been too invigorating, or perhaps the worries were too intense. I went to the kitchen and made a cup of instant hot chocolate, then headed back to the sunroom. I sat in darkness, sipping the warm cocoa, and praying.

Finally peace and the urge to sleep settled in at the same time.

# $\mathcal{S}$ix

**After an unremarkable weekend and rather calm Monday, I** changed my routine. Tuesday, I slept late and didn't go to the farm, but went to City Café for breakfast instead. Simple changes, but at least I was stepping out of the rut and getting away from the boring routine of my life. Surely, a thirty-two year old woman should have something in her life besides work? Or maybe not?

I was sitting in a booth, midway back from the front of the café and enjoying a quiet breakfast when Cynthia slipped in across from me.

"Want some company, or is this quiet time?"

"Sure, have a seat. What are you doing here?"

"I didn't eat supper last night and woke up hungry. Went to the kitchen and discovered that I was out of coffee. This Blueberry Festival is driving me crazy. Odie Marshall is driving me crazy. I need coffee."

We finished our breakfast without many comments. Cynthia was lost in her anger toward Odie Marshall, and I was lost in the labyrinth of problems at Anderson Farms. We paid our breakfast tab and each walked out with a cup to go, on the house from Henry, the chubby café owner.

I settled down in my office and took a hard look at the calendar on my desk. One week from today would be July fourth. The bank would be closed, and perhaps it would be a good day to try to work out some of the problems at the farm. Perhaps. But before I could attend to banking business and earn my paycheck, I had a call to make.

"Hortense, I have so much work at the bank that I won't be working in the fields for a while, but I think I've figured out where our money is going. Have you got a minute to talk?"

"Yes, certainly Miss Julie, we need to figure this out."

"I've done some checking back on the charges, and it seems that we have replaced a truck motor, overhauled a transmission, and purchased ten oil changes. There were some other things, fill-ups for gasoline, but these are the biggest."

"I don't know about any motors or transmissions. Maybe Marcus knows, but he usually tells me about everything going on with the equipment. Ten oil changes and gas fill-ups? That can't be right. We usually change the oil and keep the tanks filled here. And repair all our trucks if we can. What's going on? Is it Rudi?"

"It looks like Rudi is involved, but someone at the garage is in on this also. Two more charges came in overnight, and I called the garage."

There was no answer, so I continued.

"Hortense, I really hate to do this, but I need to call the sheriff. If this is Rudi, I'm sorry, but the stealing has got to stop. I hoped that you and Marcus could work this out."

"Little Julie, do whatever you think is right. Somehow, Marcus and I will take care of Rudi, if he'll let us."

There wasn't going to be a good solution for this mess, but I had to stop this. I cancelled all our credit cards. Then I called the only garage in town and told them that all charges had to be approved by me until further notice. I followed up with two nearby businesses that sometimes worked on our equipment. I didn't call the garage that had submitted the fraudulent charges. I wanted to see if they tried anything today. There was nothing we could do except wait.

❧❧

More than thirty years ago, my grandmother bought the property that is now Anderson Blueberry Farms. She was smart and savvy, and she could bargain with the best. The farm took a while to become established, but within a few years, Hortense

Salazar, her daughter and her three boys came to work the fields. Grandmother and Hortense made a formidable team, two widowed women that succeeded in a man's world, and they did it by hard work and perseverance.

I still marvel at the exceptional efficiency of this operation, a system that was tweaked and changed and improved as the years passed until Anderson Blueberry Farms evolved into the successful operation it is today.

Some of our berries are sold as they come from the fields and others are frozen for our future use. Berries that are saved for future baking are picked, sorted, washed, and dried before freezing.

Anderson Farms is a diversified business and has extensive acreage that produces blueberries, peaches, a few blackberries, and ten acres of vegetables. The commercial kitchens operate year-round but the seasonal fruit is the basis of our extensive offerings.

We make and freeze peach pies, in several sizes and under several labels, and during the summer, we offer the best peach ice cream available. The main focus of the commercial bakery is the blueberry muffins, and the ever changing additions.

We make pies, cheesecakes, pound cakes, and bar cookies. Actually, we make all things blueberry. Our customers are local hotels, restaurants, coffee shops, and several private clubs. Even a few large companies purchase our blueberry muffins for special occasions. The income from the bakery keeps the business going, as long as we watch the expenses. Last month we didn't do so well, and that has to change.

At The Bank of Three Bridges, all credit card activity is contracted to a clearing agency. I had set up a flag on this account and around two o'clock, I was notified when a bogus charge was attempted at a garage in a town about twenty miles away. I called the sheriff's office and got the standard reply,

"Thank you, ma'am, we'll have someone check this out. Where can you be reached?"

I called the farm and waited.

To keep my mind away from the farm business, I dug into bank work, including calling Jeff Watson. He may think he could just walk away and forget us, but I needed his authorization on a few matters.

"Jeff, how are you? Can you talk? I have a few questions."

"Sorry, Miss Trahan, I am with someone at the present time. If you have a bank issue, just use your good judgment. After all, my father said you were exceptional in all matters of banking."

I sat at my desk, holding a telephone that wasn't connected to anything except dead air. What was going on with that man? He sounded . . . could he be jealous? How stupid. I was only a bank employee, Jeff Watson was the heir to the throne.

I looked up from my busywork when someone tapped on my office door. I smiled at the red-headed man standing at my door.

"Hey, Rev. Peppers, come in. What brings you to the bank?"

"Julie, I wanted to chat with you a minute. I thought perhaps you could use a visit from your pastor. I heard that you've been left with a load of responsibility that you didn't ask for, and I wanted you to know that I'm praying for you."

"Thanks, Preacher, I need it. So far, things are going okay, but still I feel so tied down. I haven't gone out to the farm this week because I have to be here for ten hours a day. Sorry, I shouldn't complain, at least I have a job."

"Yes, you have a job, but you also need a life. Julie, you are too young to shut yourself off from the possibility of romance. And I pray for each of you young ladies in the Three Bridges Social Club. Yes, Judge has told me that's what you call your group."

"It was a joke, sort of a slap at those social clubs that were so popular a while back. Laughing at ourselves is sometimes all the fun we have—at least for the last few months."

"God bless you Julie. I just wanted to stop in and say hello. I need to run to Tyler and check on a couple from my old church.

Some ties are never broken. Remember, if you need anything at all, call me."

As he walked out of the bank and left me thinking, *what a nice man.* Before I could stop my thoughts from spiraling into the past, I was remembering how kind he'd been with grandmother. Rev. Peppers was new to Three Bridges when she became ill, but he was there with us every step of the way. While others had made promises, Roger Peppers didn't promise, he just did.

I turned my desk chair around and faced the rear wall of my office. With my head leaning on the headrest, I spent several minutes taking stock of my problems, and thanking God that I had good friends like the Three Bridges Social Club, and a caring pastor who understood the needs of his congregation.

Odie Marshall was in the middle of a private melt down and the second floor of The Flower Box was bearing the brunt of his anger. He had planned to renovate this area into the living space of the original store, but today his only intent was to wreak havoc on the nearest objects.

Odie never considered that a customer, or his manager would be concerned by all the noise he was making. His mind was not accustomed to considering others, so he continued to lash out in anger.

He kicked a wall that separated two of the planned bedrooms. He kicked and pushed and then picked up a sledgehammer and totally demolished that wall and started on another.

Women. What was he going to do with the stupid women in his life? His phone was ringing constantly with unwanted calls from either Vonda or Maddie Wallace. And now, Maddie said that she wanted to rethink loaning him the money for this renovation. After all he'd done for that old woman, things that even Odie Marshall would not have done only a few years ago. Well, at least she had not cut him off from her bank account—

yet.

Maddie was driving him crazy, Vonda was acting strange lately and on top of that, he had to deal with *The Annual Joke*. That's how he thought of The Blueberry Festival, a joke that came around much too often, and this year he didn't have the time or the energy to take care of everything. These stupid ignorant backwoods people didn't appreciate all that he did for this town, and no one wanted to do any work. It was as if they expected him to do everything.

Exhausted, with tears streaking down his face, Odie Marshall fell to the floor. *God, I don't know how much longer I can take all this pressure.* Extreme tiredness overtook him and he slept—and slept till long after the store closed and his worried manager went home.

✎✎

Thirty minutes before the bank closed, Jessie waved the telephone in my direction and signaled line two. Jessie had her own style, which was usually blunt and to the point. I went to my office and punched the second button and put on my professional personality.

"Julie Trahan, how may I help you?"

"This is Deputy Troy Humble. I'm following up on a complaint about credit card fraud. I believe someone from Anderson Farms made the complaint. Is that person there or did someone from the bank make this complaint for Anderson farms?"

"Deputy Humble, I made the complaint. I own Anderson Farms and I'm also the Vice President of The Bank of Three Bridges. Do you have any information for me?"

"Yes ma'am, I do. I need to talk to you in person. Where can I find you in about an hour?"

"I can be at Anderson Farms about that time, or shortly after that. Depends on how long it takes to close the bank today. Do you know where Anderson Farms is located? We're south of town and about twelve miles on County Road 470."

"I'll find you. I think we may have solved your problem."

# Seven

I left the bank about twenty minutes past six, and that was earlier than I had expected. The closing went smoothly as we balanced each tray. My car was blistering hot when I got in, but that was to be expected, also. Texas summers are hot, always and I was several miles down the road before my cranky air conditioner began to cool the car. That was another thing on my to-do list. I really must start car shopping.

Perhaps I could get a root canal instead.

Without anesthetic.

Or walk on nails, barefoot.

Through a jungle filled with angry natives.

The next eight or nine miles passed quickly as I added to the list of things I would rather do than shop for a car. Like jump into a frigid lake in the middle of winter. But car shopping might be more pleasant than what was facing me right now.

I pulled up to the back door of the old farmhouse and went in. Hortense and Marcus, minus Rudi, were sitting at the table. She'd been crying and he wouldn't look at me.

Tires scrunching on the gravel driveway caught my attention. Surprisingly, it wasn't a white cruiser, but a smaller black SUV that had pulled off the driveway and parked facing the roadway. The door panel bore the recognizable lone star symbol and was labeled *Elbamarle County Sheriff*.

"Well, I suppose this must be Deputy Humble." I

backtracked and opened the kitchen door. Both Salazar's seemed to lack the strength or the inclination to get up from the table.

"Deputy Humble? I'm Julie Trahan, we spoke earlier. Come in."

He followed me into the kitchen without saying much more that a brief hello. Since Hortense hadn't looked up from the table, I took two glasses from the cabinet, filled them with ice and offered tea or water. We both opted for sweet tea and I drank thirstily. Someday I really must learn to act like a lady. Someday.

I pointed to the table and introduced Hortense and Marcus.

Again, the greetings were brief, businesslike, nothing more than, "Deputy Troy Humble, Elbamarle County Sheriff's Department."

I pulled out a chair near Marcus and Hortense, sat down, and waited. We all waited for the dreaded news. Deputy Humble remained standing.

"Miss Trahan, you are the owner of this farm? And these people work here?"

"Yes, I own the farm and Hortense is general manager. Marcus Salazar is her son and our foreman. We've all worked together for a very long time."

"I see. Do any of you know a Rudi Salazar?"

Hortense began to cry again and Marcus hung his head, but managed to answer.

"He is my son."

"Mr. Salazar, I'm sorry to inform you that your son was arrested a few hours ago, trying to commit a fraudulent credit card transaction. It seems that he and a few buddies had developed a system for stealing a little drug money and I think they got a little greedy."

"He called, but we spoke only briefly. Where is my son?"

"He and his friend were apprehended near Tyler, so he is in the Smith County Jail. He'll be arraigned tomorrow and you can most likely make bail then."

He took his eyes away from them and looked at me. "Miss Trahan, our department was notified when you reported a suspected credit card fraud was being perpetrated on your business. Now, I have a few more questions for you folks."

Just as I warned Hortense, this didn't end well. My heart was breaking as I witnessed the grief and embarrassment of a father and a grandmother. For the first time ever, I realized that being a parent is difficult. Perhaps I am more blessed being single and without children.

According to Deputy Humble, Rudi and his friends got a little too greedy and much too dumb. Several fake transactions had been charged at a garage about twenty miles from us, a place that we didn't normally use. Everything worked fine in the scam until the credit card was declined. As luck would have it, the garage owner returned four days earlier than expected and was there to handle the declined card. He called the police.

When the owner was out of town, the boys made fraudulent charges, and then took cash from the daily deposits. Sometimes more than the credit card charges, sometimes less. The scam was doomed to failure from the beginning, but the end came more quickly because I watched our account so closely.

I reached over to Hortense and gave her a big hug, but she just continued to sob. My heart hurt for her pain, but I felt she needed her own space.

"Hortense, we'll get Rudi back on track, somehow. Now you try to relax and have a good night's sleep. I'll call you tomorrow."

"Deputy Humble, if you're ready to leave, I'll lock the door behind us."

We walked to our cars, or rather, he followed me to my clunker and opened the door. For the first time, I looked at the man wearing the uniform. Wow!

Tall, fair-haired, very muscular, and young. It appeared he was also checking me out, but he had to look down to do so.

"Miss Trahan, I may have a few more questions, but I'm

technically off duty. If I follow you back to Three Bridges, will you have dinner with me at City Café?"

Double Wow! This handsome deputy was asking me to have dinner with him. Would that be a date? Probably not, but he said he was technically off duty. Well, I was technically available and also hungry.

"I think that would work, Deputy. Since you'll be following me, I'll try not to speed."

He laughed. Loudly.

"If you can make this car go over the speed limit, have at it. Miss Trahan, you own this farm and you're a big wig at the bank. Why are you driving this rent-a-wreck?"

"Very simple answer. I hate car shopping. See you at City Café. And call me Julie."

If a deputy sheriff hadn't been driving behind me, I would have dug my cell phone from the bottom of my purse and called Cynthia. I still wasn't certain that having dinner at City Café was actually a date, but it was close enough. Especially since I had not been on a date in . . . four years? Pathetic.

Even if this wasn't a real date, I was going to boost my sagging ego and claim it as a real date. *Julie, get a grip. It's just a meal. With a deputy sheriff. A handsome deputy.*

Clouds had moved in and the morning was dark and threatening when I arrived at Anderson Farms the next day. No one was in the fields yet, but a few of the guys were standing around the tractor shed. Some were drinking coffee and others were just squatted down, waiting for the weather to decide if this would be a rain-day, or a work-day.

Hortense was in the kitchen absently stirring something on the stove. Marcus was sitting in the same chair as yesterday, leaning against the table, and looking no better than he did when I left last night.

"Hey Marcus, how're you doing? Did you get any sleep last

night?"

"No, Julie, I walked the floor all night, listening to my wife cry. Finally about three o'clock this morning, she managed to go to sleep. I came on over here, and Mamá was up. I'm more worried about her than I am Janna. Rudi has broken his grandmother's heart and shamed this family."

We were speaking quietly, and Hortense was in her own world of sorrow and shame. Marcus was a friend as well as a co-worker, but I could do little to console him. Instead of mouthing words, I went to the cabinet and poured a cup of coffee.

As usual, blueberry muffins were on the table, so I nibbled on one while I drank the coffee.

"Are you going to the arraignment today? Have you got a lawyer and is there anything I can do to help?" The questions finally burst forth but Marcus could only shake his head and shrugged. Hortense turned to me and answered me.

"Yes, we are going to Tyler today, Julie. Marcus and Janna will go to pay their youngest son out of jail. We will bring him home and pray that he will turn from this criminal behavior. We have to try."

I got up and hugged Hortense extra hard and for a moment I thought she was going to give in to the pain, but she straightened her shoulders and pulled away. Soon she was drinking a cup of coffee and picking at a muffin, forcing herself to eat, and I was struggling to make sensible conversation.

"I wanted to see everyone this morning, so I came out early. I guess there won't be any berry picking if the rain comes, but that's farming." I walked toward the back door as a bolt of lightning struck not very far away.

"I need to run before the storm really hits. Call if you need anything."

I drove back into town, fretting about our situation. If Jeff Watson was back in Three Bridges where he belonged, I could take a few hours from the bank and go to Tyler for the arraignment. But that wasn't going to happen.

I once heard a rising young musician described as having an *old soul*. I think I share the same trait, or gene, or whatever thing within that makes me different from others my age. Deputy Humble broke a four-year pattern in my life when he asked me to have dinner with him. Should have been over the moon today, right? Well, didn't happen. Last night, I discovered that I have an old soul, a very old soul.

I was still lamenting that fact that Deputy Humble and I didn't hit it off when Cynthia walked into the bank around noon with a sack of food from City Café. Henry had made spaghetti just for us, and the aroma of garlic and tomato and special spices filled the air.

"Well, Julie, let's get caught up on all the news. Now, I heard that Rudi was arrested, and that Marcus and Hortense are heartbroken. Why do the cutest and brightest kids mess up their lives like that?"

"I don't know, but you certainly described him to a *T*. A few years ago, I worked in Sunday school with his age group, and he stood out from the rest. I don't know how this will end, but maybe he'll straighten up. What's new with the Blueberry Festival?"

"I don't know how to say this, but something's not right with Odie. He's always hard to deal with, but now he flies off the handle if someone asks even a simple question. Some of the committee have been talking, and next year, Odie Marshall will not be the chairman."

We sat for a while in the break room of the bank, enjoying our lunch. Between meals prepared by Hortense and Henry's special treats for Cynthia and me, I'm gonna be porked up in no time.

"Julie, I've been waiting for you to tell me about your hot date."

"How did you know that I had a date? Forget I asked. I know that gossip fuels all the energy in this town."

"Well, tell, what was he like?"

"Very simple to tell this story. Deputy Humble and I may be two ships that pass, but we're not even in the same ocean. I'm older than him by three calendar years, and light years older in maturity."

"So sorry. I thought perhaps one of us would have some excitement in our lives. Perhaps I'll bring a TV to my office and watch the soaps. I need a life."

"Cynthia, we both need a life, or at least a little vacation."

# $\mathscr{E}$ight

**The Salazars were grief-stricken and shamed by Rudi's** conduct. I wasn't able to attend the arraignment, but I know Marcus well enough to know that he was ashamed and embarrassed to bail his son out of jail. Rudi is home, and I haven't gone back to the farm since Tuesday evening. I think they need their space.

The last half of the week was slow at the bank, and allowed us to catch up on our work. I juggled the schedule so that Vonda and Jessie both had afternoons off, and I took an extra two hours this morning. Of course, because I wasn't in the bank, I found a small list of telephone calls waiting for me.

I looked at the first *While You Were Out* form. Another call for Juliana Trahan. Well, at least this time, whoever called, left off the Elizabeth. Somehow, I had the feeling that this person was playing with me, testing me, with these anonymous calls. All of them so far had been at very early hours of the day, most before banking hours. Today, the call came in at nine thirty, and usually I would be at the bank.

Still, there was no name and no call back number. I don't like games. I flipped through a few more calls that I would handle later. Then I saw the last call.

The call from Jeff Watson came about fifteen minutes before I got to the bank. "Vonda, did Jeff want me to call him back? Did he leave a message?"

"No, he just asked for you. Actually, he had very little to say. I thought . . . well, he seemed distracted. I told him that you'd be in at eleven today and then asked if he wanted to speak to Jessie. He said he'd get back with us later."

"This has been some week. I'll be glad when six o'clock comes and we can have a few days away from the bank."

Those feelings carried over until the doors were locked shortly after six and I crossed the street to The City Café for our usual Friday evening meal. When the evening ended I went home and crawled into bed at nine thirty, but not before I prayed for a better week for all of us, especially Hortense, Marcus, and Rudi.

≪≫

"Vonda, open up, I've brought breakfast. Come on sleepyhead, time to rise and shine."

*Oh no, what is he doing here?* Vonda struggled from the bed, still tired from a restless night when sleep was so long in coming. She went through the kitchen and opened the back door, but didn't give him much room to enter.

"Odie, what are you doing here so early in the morning? You know I like to sleep late on Saturday. Oh, my gosh, it's not even seven o'clock. Odie, what are you up to ?"

Odie shoved her aside with a brief kiss on the cheek and walked into the small kitchen and placed the takeout from City Cafe on the table.

"Hey, ol' girl, thought you'd be glad to see me. I know I've been busy, but I thought maybe we could go to Tyler and fool around for a while, maybe eat lunch, see an early movie. How about it?"

She ignored Odie, but against her best intentions, she succumbed to the tantalizing aroma of coffee. She grabbed one of the cups and took a sip of the coffee, and then another sip before she sat down at the old oak table that had been in this kitchen all her life. It was one of the things she really liked about this house. For some reason, sitting at this table gave her a sense of comfort.

"Odie, I don't know why you're here. I've seen you maybe three times in the last month. When I call to invite you to dinner, you're busy. Lately, the only times I see you are when you're cashing checks on Miss Maddie's account. Does Miss Maddie really know you're taking that much money from her?"

"Vonda, don't worry your little pea-brain about that. Miss Maddie knows what I'm doing. She thinks we're going on a trip, maybe around the world. That old girl is something else, and she sure likes your Odie. Come over here and give me a kiss, Vonda. You know you've been missing me."

He stood with his arms out wide, an invitation for her to come running as she had done so often throughout the years.

Vonda looked at Odie and heard the same words that she had responded to so many times in the past. As she looked at him, a cold reality took control of her heart. *Not now, not today, and hopefully not ever again. It's time to move on with my life and forget Odie Marshall.*

"Odie, why don't you just get your takeout breakfast and go see Miss Maddie? I'm not interested in hearing about her, or lunch in Tyler, or an early movie, or anything else right now. I'm concerned about what you're doing with that old woman's money. I don't like her, but it's not right that you should have access to all that money. Look Odie, I'm tired and I'm going to bed. Alone!"

Without another word, she slammed out of the kitchen, down the short hall and locked the bedroom door. There was a time when Vonda thought she loved Odie Marshall, a time when she would have done whatever he wanted, anything just to get his attention and to keep him around.

Something within her very core was changing, something she had no understanding of, but this morning she felt stronger than ever before. Maybe she was just growing up, finally. The last thing she heard before drifting off to sleep was Odie slamming the kitchen door.

❦❦

I opened my eyes to bright daylight filtering through the blinds. I scrubbed my face and shook my head to whisk away the remnants of sleep that lingered still. I reached to the bedside table and picked up my watch and shook my head again. I'd slept almost twelve hours without waking. I turned over and thought about the day before I hit the ground running as usual.

I couldn't think without my morning coffee. I hadn't set the timer on the pot last night, so I pushed the button and waited for it to drip. I fed Goldie and then took my coffee and toast slathered in butter to the porch. I sat in the swing and thought about the farm.

For several days now, I hadn't worked in the berry patch. I looked at my hands and they seemed to look younger and softer already. Perhaps I would someday have nice hands if I didn't have to work at picking berries.

Did that really make a difference? At this point in time, there wasn't likely to be someone reaching out to hold my hand. Drat. I went back inside for another cup of coffee and a little Saturday housekeeping.

I ran through the house, doing a few chores while trying unsuccessfully to ignore the deepening layer of dust on every surface. I promised to find someone to clean for me very soon.

Around noon, I went out to the farm, anxious to see Hortense. The mystery of the fraudulent charges was solved and Rudi and his friend would be duly punished, but his family was punished also.

I didn't realize how much she had suffered until I sat across from her in the kitchen for a while. She told me that she hadn't cooked since Rudi was arrested, that she had turned the kitchen over to her two oldest granddaughters.

"Miss Julie, perhaps I'm too old to do this. You've trusted me to run this farm and I messed up. Maybe you'd better look for someone else."

"Oh, I don't think that's necessary, but why don't you just rest for a while, and let the girls take over. They can run things.

I'm going outside for a while. I caught a glimpse of the flower garden and I want to smell some flowers today."

I pushed my chair under the table and walked slowly to the back door. I stopped, and asked a question.

"Hortense, I think I'm going into Tyler next week to that wholesale grocery outlet. I need to buy a few frozen cheesecakes and other desserts. Do you need anything?"

I heard nothing but the door slamming behind me. Nothing but dead silence for a while and then a sudden clatter of pots and pans and cabinet doors being opened and shut. Then I heard her voice again, talking to me through the screen door.

"Julie Trahan, what has come over you? Frozen cheesecakes! Your sainted grandmother would turn over in her grave. I'll make your cheesecakes and anything else you want."

I was standing outside the kitchen, looking at a small flower garden and admiring the Bougainvillea that had twined around an old abandoned clothes line. But really, I was just waiting for Hortense to come out. I knew she would, and soon I heard the screen door open with its uniquely rasping squeak and then I felt short, chubby arms circling me from the back and I accepted her hug.

"Julie, you're a smart one. Thanks for jumpstarting me, I needed it. I let my mind become the devil's playground because of Rudi, and I quit caring about everything else. I'm ashamed because I know God is big enough to handle this. He can take care of the big stuff and I can bake. When you come out again, I will have enough food to fill up your freezer."

Odie had indeed followed Vonda's advice and gone to Maddie's. He'd waited for her to dress and they drove to Tyler. They had brunch at one of her favorite places, and then drove around town for a while. He suggested a matinee, but she declined and asked to go home instead. For some reason, she didn't enjoy Odie's company as much as she had in the past.

Maddie was now in her luxurious bedroom suite with nothing but memories surging up from all sides. Thoughts of the past, even further back than the last few months seemed to take over her mind. She walked from her bedroom and around the third floor family room, to the large windows that looked out to the rear of the property. It was beautiful, even in the hot summer. A winding creek cut through the land, and trees that grew along the edge of the creek leaned inward, creating a leafy covering for the shallow stream.

The gardener had tried to plant a few shrubs and annuals down there, but so far nothing had done very well except a few wildflowers, and this late in the year, they were mostly gone. But still it was pretty and one of the reasons that she and R.J. had chosen this particular place.

Back then, they had been young enough to walk along the creek bank for miles, searching for treasures that weren't found. Except for a few silly things, like small stones with unique color or shapes, or a bunch of wild violets in the spring.

"R.J. is gone, and I'm getting old. Odie Marshall is the only comfort I have now. I guess that makes me a miserable old woman who talks to nothing but a creek that I can only see through a window."

❦

Odie walked through the kitchen at Maddie's and was surprised to see a new chef standing near the stove. When had Maddie hired this woman? She usually discussed everything with him.

"Hi, I'm Odie Marshall, Maddie's friend. How long have you been working here?"

"I'm Denise Hougan, and I've been here almost a month. I've cooked your supper several times and also your breakfast. I guess you just don't notice the hired help."

He looked at the woman. She was mid-forties, very plain

*54*

looking and heftier than he liked. He looked at her face again and saw beautiful grey eyes, but pale skin and lashes. With a little cosmetic help and a good diet, she really wouldn't be so plain; she might even be pretty.

But why was he thinking those things? After all, it was like she said. She was hired help. He left the kitchen without saying another word.

# $\mathcal{N}$ine

**Most bank holidays correspond with government holidays,** and usually fall on Mondays. This year, the Fourth of July is on Tuesday, and that makes for a strange work week. I'm not complaining, because I need a break.

July third started with a bang, just like most Mondays, only worse. One of the first customers of the day was not a happy camper, but there was nothing different about that. It was Odie Marshall. He was seldom happy.

"Well, Julie, I guess you know this just messes up my week, having to be here today to cash a check when I really need to be working on the festival."

"We understand your concerns. Odie, we're just abiding by the rules like everyone else. What can I do for you?"

I closed the teller drawer and shuffled a few things around on the counter, trying to work off my anger in the few seconds he took to assume his favorite domineering posture.

"I need to cash a check, and I want it all in big bills, you know, hundreds. Count it twice and make sure you don't short me on this."

I didn't cringe or throw anything at him, but I wanted to. Very badly. I merely accepted the proffered check for five thousand dollars and looked it over carefully. Then I keyed in the account on our computer, to check the balance, knowing it was unnecessary. The check was drawn on Maddie Wallace's account. I locked my drawer and started for the vault because we don't keep that amount in big bills in our drawer.

"Hey, where are you going, Julie? I'm in a hurry here. Get on with it. Bring on my Benjamin's!"

*Dear Lord, fill me with grace and a kind heart. Don't let me sink to his level. Give me grace, Lord.*

The prayer was uttered in deepest sincerity. If I responded in my own impulsive manner, I would have throttled this obnoxious man.

"Odie, I have to go to the vault because we don't keep that much money in the drawer. Go get a cup of coffee and calm down."

I really wanted to tell him that if he hadn't interfered, I'd be much closer to finishing his transaction, but obviously *grace* prevailed. I went to the vault and withdrew a strapped bundle of hundred dollar bills, presorted by the Federal Reserve Bank in amounts of five thousand dollars per bundle. I signed in all the correct places and returned to the window, wondering just how much money Odie had taken from Miss Maddie's account in the last week.

This is why I wished Jeff were here. It would be good to pass this problem to someone else. That was my wish, but for now, I was the one in charge. I finished the transaction with Odie and handled a few more before Jessie appeared at my side.

"Hey, young lady, let me have my job back. I know you'd rather be out picking blueberries in this heat than working the teller window."

"Got that right and thanks for coming in early. You're not scheduled for another hour. What's going on?"

"I had a twinge of conscience and decided to rescue you, so now you owe me lunch."

"Thanks, friend. Lunch is on me. By the way, what are you doing tomorrow? Are the kids coming out?"

"No, Donald and I are going to Ft. Worth to Jason's house. Bobbie Anne and Robert will be there too. Thank goodness I don't have the cleanup to do this year. Those little ones can make a mess, even though I love each one of them dearly."

Jessie's children were all grown and had children of their own. My friend and co-worker was a wonderful woman. From what I could see, her good core values were instilled in their children, but I didn't really know her husband very well, even after all this time.

☙�

For the last few years, I have invited my friends out to Anderson Farms to celebrate Independence Day with a mid-morning brunch. Everyone loves coming out to the farm.

I like to think that we are very much up to date with our equipment, and the four-wheelers and ATV's parked in our equipment shed proved that. Usually the guys use them to get from one field to another, but on this day, they have been cleaned and shined up for my friends to use.

Since Judge and Rev. Peppers don't feel comfortable driving these vehicles, they each rode with one of the girls in the two-seater vehicles. Today, our small parade of four-wheelers headed out to the various fields intending to pick all they could carry. Eventually, everyone had buckets of berries, peaches, and produce. Even Judge managed to pick a few tomatoes and pull a few onions.

When we finished, we sat down to a wonderful meal. After Rev. Peppers blessed the food, the six of us enjoyed a delightful meal provided by Hortense and a few of her girls.

It's always a challenge and a battle to get her to agree, but in the end I win. I pay her extra for this, and any other meals that I ask her to provide.

When no one could eat another bite, we made hurried excuses to leave, to get back to town. Anderson Farms is twenty-one miles from the city limits of Three Bridges, and most of that mileage is over ill-kept, narrow, and difficult to travel farm roads.

As we prepared to go home, the first rolls of thunder could be heard in the distance and it looked as if this extreme July heat might soon be alleviated by a cooling summer rain. To me, the winds, rolling thunder and stabs of lightning across the sky were far more frightening than the thoughts of continued heat.

After everyone left, I stayed a while to chat with Hortense and pick up the previously promised load of baked goods. While we visited, the rolling thunder came a little closer and became lot more worrisome.

I ran to my car with my arms full of the pastries from Hortense's kitchen and then realized that I didn't have my purse. From the yard, I could hear the phone ringing, and for some reason my internal alert system activated. Back in the kitchen, Hortense was waiting for me.

"Miss Julie, that man is on the phone again, asking for Juliana Elizabeth Trahan. Do you want to take this call?"

I answer phone calls all day long, every day except on the weekend. For some reason, this call for *Juliana Elizabeth Trahan* set my nerves on edge. With a lot of trepidation, I picked up the phone.

"This is Julie Trahan, may I help you?" For a brief moment there was no sound on the line. Nothing. Just when I was about to hang up the phone, I heard the intake of breath as the caller prepared to speak.

"Little Julie—I thought since you were all grown up that maybe you were using your given name. I remember it well, Juliana Elizabeth Trahan. I also remember your other name— *Little Jet*. My, my, *Little Jet*, how is it that someone as lovely as you are still single? I thought by now you would have two or three rug-rats running around. What gives?"

I sat in silence for several seconds. Almost ten years had passed and I still recognized his voice, but just the sound. There was something there that I did not recognize, a terribly hard and taunting quality. I took a deep breath and finally spoke.

"Ryan Daigle. This is Ryan, isn't it? How did you find me and where are you calling from?"

"Julie, you don't exactly sound happy to hear from me. Yes, of course it's Ryan. I'm calling because I thought we could get together, maybe talk about old times. How 'bout it? I could be in your little town in about ninety minutes."

"Ryan, you've caught me at the farm, and it isn't convenient to talk now."

I almost hung up the receiver. I'd already started moving the phone from my ear to the cradle when I had a second thought.

"Ryan, you've been out of my life, by your choice, for a long time. I have no reason to want to see you or to talk about old times. I think you should just forget about whatever you have in mind."

"One question before you hang up. I know that's what you're wanting to do. Are you with someone, are you seeing someone? Is that why you won't see me?"

The arrogance of this man. How dare he ask me anything about my life? I wanted to throw the phone across the room. I wanted to lie and tell him I was in a long-standing and permanent relationship with a Dallas Cowboy defensive lineman. I searched for any words that would ward him off. From nowhere, I found an appropriate response.

"Ryan, I'm not in a dating relationship. However, I do have someone in my life, *someone* that I've given my life to and right now there's no room for anyone else, unless God directs the relationship. I don't believe this is in his direction. Bye, Ryan."

✍✎

My weather forecasting skills are minimal, but the years I've spent in Texas have given me a fair amount of understanding about our weather patterns. A beautiful day can turn stormy in only minutes, or as this storm, move into an area with deliberate slowness.

Three or four miles into my homeward journey, the color of the sky deepened and offered an eerily strange darkness. The wind blew with increasing strength. Dust and debris were flying through the air, creating a weird and ever changing mobile. Nature's art was being created right before my eyes.

The weather had been hot and dry for several weeks, and now, there were a plethora of small limbs that had dried up and fallen or pushed to the ground by gusting winds. The ever present wind also harvested dead leaves and other rubble that could and would be picked up and hurled across the fields and onto the roadways.

I was anxious to get home, but as I drove, I was fascinated by the rainstorm moving closer. It began as a line of silvery raindrops hitting hard against fields and blacktopped road, marching toward me like rapidly advancing foot soldiers until suddenly I was in the midst of a tremendous downpour, complete with strong wind, lightning, and hail.

I never can decide what I fear the most, the storm itself or the accompanying sound of thunder and the incessant staccato of big drops of rain hitting the ground, buildings, and cars. My ancient SUV was taking another beating. The hail was beginning to hit and I had no place to go except those overhanging trees in the entrance to Miss Maddie's estate. If I could make it another two miles I might find some shelter.

Her house was on a private road and entry to the estate was through ornate gates of white wrought iron. The gates were tall, with blossoms and trailing vines across the rounded top. They were electronically controlled and sat well back from the road.

Just ahead, I recognized the giant oak trees that marked the property line and I stopped on the road, and then reversed my car into the private driveway. I parked under the trees, well away from the gates, feeling pleased that I had a degree of safety from the elements.

# $\mathcal{T}$en

**I forced myself to calm down, breathe deeply, and regain** my composure. Then I began to pray for my safety from the overhanging limbs and for my friends as they traveled home. I sat hiding from the storm, but my mind was processing the telephone call from the past. My ex-fiancé, Ryan Daigle.

Ten years ago this summer he disappeared from my life, leaving me grieving and broken in spirit. In only a matter of days, I had sunk into an extremely depressive state, with only my very wise father to help. For whatever reason, known only to her, my mother had gone on one of her trips. Those trips were frequent and the explanations were seldom logical.

The details of that time are so painful that even today, I don't want to go there. Thankfully, my very wise father, a physician, knew how to deal with my emotional state. He brought me to my grandmother.

Hard work, good food, and sleep do wonders for depression, even when it results from a broken heart. A praying grandmother with boundless energy and wise in all things, can work miracles. Eventually, I began to heal. I seldom looked back, because the looking-back is so very unpleasant.

A huge gust of wind took my mind off the memories and for other fifteen or so minutes, I alternately prayed for safety and feared the force of the wind. The big live oak trees began to sway, to dip and bend first toward me and then immediately shake their leafy limbs in the other direction. As my car rocked with the power of the storm, I began to question the intelligence of putting myself between and under these very large trees. The rain continued, but at least most of the hail was diverted by the overhanging oak limbs.

My hands were white-knuckled on the steering wheel. Perhaps in a few tomorrows, this might be funny, but not now. I forced my hands from the wheel, took a swipe at the side window that had begun to fog up, and then reached over to adjust the air conditioning to change the flow of air to the windshield, hoping it would clear before I had to pull back on the road. Suddenly, I heard a blast from a car horn—right in front of me.

Through the defrosting glass, I could just make out the image of a large car, a Mercedes. Oh no, it was Odie Marshall, and his hand gestures were speaking volumes. Without a second of hesitation, I steered my car hard to the left, off the asphalt drive and onto soggy ground. Surprisingly, I didn't bog down. I left the private driveway with as much speed and caution as I could muster.

I knew that before the day ended I would probably hear from Odie or Miss Maddie. She seldom offered even the merest courtesies to people, and since I had blocked the entrance to her rather large estate, I would surely hear about this.

"Odie, get control of yourself! Why are you throwing such a tantrum? You're behaving like a spoiled ten-year-old. I think you need to calm down—now."

"Julie Trahan was sitting in our driveway, blocking our entrance to the gate. She had no right to be here. What was she doing, spying on us? Trying to find out some gossip to spread with that pea-brained group of women she runs with? Something is very wrong with that picture, all those women hanging out together, and there's something wrong with her being on our road."

Maddie Wallace had seen the signs. She'd been watching him for several days now, and he frightened her. Something was going on within the brain of Odie Marshall. He seemed constantly to be in a state of near rage—anxious over everything. And sadly, she had watched this man turn from a handsome, exciting, and cheerful person into an angry and whining childish figure that was trying her patience and making her rethink some recent decisions.

"First of all, Odie, this is not *our* road, it is mine. Secondly, there is nothing wrong with women having women friends. These young ladies don't hurt anyone, and in fact, I happen to be a fan of that group. Thirdly, *even I* can offer a safe harbor in a storm."

"Maddie, you don't know them like I do. Julie Trahan was up to something and she was blocking the gate."

"Odie, you had plenty of room to go around her because she *was not* blocking the gate. Instead, you deliberately drove in front of her, trying to intimidate her."

She stopped lecturing him only briefly as the car approached the garage, and they waited for the slowly rising door.

"You behaved badly, Odie. If I see this type of conduct again, well, we just might take another look at our 'friendship'. Get the door, Odie. I'm tired, and I need to rest."

⋙⋘

Miss Maddie's step was slow as she entered the elevator and sat on the richly upholstered bench and waited to be taken to her third floor bedroom. Like the elevator and all the rooms in this mansion, the room was overly decorated, ornate, and almost garishly so. It was all those things and more, and it usually brought solace to her unhappy heart, but not today.

Odie Marshall had guided her throughout the redecorating process only weeks after R.J. died. She had wanted . . . no, she had needed a change.

She and R.J had been together for most of her life and his death had left her unsettled. Yes, she had needed a change.

There had been times when she thought she had gone too far with this room and with her life, especially in the last few weeks.

She would think over those recent events, but now she needed to rest. She didn't know why she had been so unnaturally tired lately. Her recent behavior was causing her some worry, but she was too tired to think about it.

She must have dozed, but only for a few minutes. When she woke, she took in her surroundings with a critical eye.

Indeed, this was a most ostentatious room, the likes of which were seldom seen, not even in a magazine. Antiques overwhelmed the generous space and made the room appear to shrink in size. Every piece of furniture was ornately carved, dark, massive, and very expensive. The bedding and draperies were silk, in vibrant tones of red, pink and gold. Over the fireplace at the end of the room was a near life-sized portrait of Miss Maddie obviously painted at least twenty years earlier.

The portrait flattered her. Never a beautiful woman, the artist had somehow managed to portray her with dignity and an air of something akin to grace. Miss Maddie had been very proud of this portrait. It had been commissioned as a gift to R.J. when he turned sixty. He said all the right words that day, but she sensed his heart really wasn't in the speaking. But at least he acknowledged the gift. Sometimes he didn't.

Maddie picked up the bedside phone and pushed a number preprogrammed to ring in the kitchen, pantry, and private quarters of the housekeeper.

"Yes, Mrs. Wallace, how may I help you. Would you like some tea?"

"No, Denise, just come to my rooms, please. We'll talk when you get here."

Maddie Wallace, in the eyes of this town, was an old fool. Well, she admitted to being old, and lately she had acted foolishly, but she still had control of most of her reasoning and common sense.

There was much more to Maddie than the public saw. Even in her advancing years, she was intelligent, shrewd, and capable of being manipulative. Adding Odie Marshall to her checking account had not been a spur of the moment decision but one reached after hours of coldly, heartlessly assessing her future.

In the last few weeks, she had felt listless, or lethargic, and those feelings brought on miserable thoughts of her lonely future. If she were honest, and she always tried to be honest with herself, allowing Odie Marshall to have open access to her funds was nothing more than a tool to keep him with her longer than she had a right to expect.

Odie Marshall was capricious, fickle, unreliable—however you wanted to label him. Yes, in spite of her recent actions to the contrary, she saw those same unflattering traits in him as other people did, only she had chosen to ignore them. After all, she was using him just as he was using her. These were the thoughts she attempted to process through her brain while waiting for her housekeeper. Finally, the woman knocked on the door.

"Come in, Denise, I need to speak to you for a moment. Is Odie still here?"

The woman blushed. She couldn't hide her emotions, they were revealed on her plain and unadorned face. This chubby forty-five-year-old woman had been enjoying Odie's company. Maddie was put off by the unaccustomed feeling of sympathy and understanding of this woman, a vulnerable woman. She tried for a more neutral topic.

"Has it stopped raining, Denise?"

"Almost, only a few sprinkles now and then. Do you need something, Mrs. Wallace?"

"Yes, I want you and Odie Marshall to run some errands for me in Tyler. I want you to use your car but be sure to have Odie fill it with gasoline before you leave town. When you get to Tyler, stop in at Macy's and get some of that perfume I like so well. Maybe you need to write these things down. Get a pad and pen from my desk."

Denise hurried to comply and began making notes as Maddie Wallace ticked off item after item on her spur of the moment agenda.

She looked at her watch, figuring out just how many errands she could ask these two people to run and how much time that would involve.

She listed a few other unnecessary items and then decided to send the pair for dinner.

"Oh yes, I want you to pick up something for dinner at that steak place, you know the one I like. As a matter of fact, I want you and Odie to eat dinner there. Call me before you're through eating, then I'll tell you what I want for dinner."

Maddie watched Denise write down every word, and then double-check to see if she'd gotten everything. Then she added one other detail.

"Have Odie pay for these purchases, he has my bankcard. And Denise, I want all my receipts. Make certain you get those from Odie."

She was planning her time wisely, the time when Odie would be absent from this house. Lately, that was a rare event. Again, she mentally calculated the time these two people would be away from her estate, at least several hours, and hoped that was enough time for her to accomplish her task.


Maddie watched the monitor with an unyielding gaze. Denise's car was captured by the security camera as it left the garage and drove through the entry gates. She breathed a sigh of relief and reached for the phone to call Judge.

"Rosalie, this is Maddie Wallace. I need to see Judge and I need to see him now. Is he there? Yes, I'll hold on."

While she was waiting for the answer, Maddie was busy pulling papers from her desk, looking into her purse to find her key ring, just fidgeting, anxious to take care of this issue that was putting her in an apprehensive state close to panic.

Rosalie came back to the phone, giving her permission to come immediately.

# $\mathcal{E}$leven

**He was standing near the rear of the wraparound porch,** watching for Maddie Wallace and feeling concern because she was driving the big Mercedes into town for the meeting. As usual, he was impatient, muttering under his breath about silly old women when finally the impressive black car slowly turned onto the side street and parked in the drive.

Maddie put one small but elegantly clad foot on the bottom step and grasped his extended hand with an unexpected firmness—as if reaching for a lifeline.

"Judge, I'm so glad you had time to see me today, I really need your help. I have several matters that I need help with immediately."

"Come on, Maddie, let's go in through the kitchen, and see what kind of tea Rosalie brewed for us. My Daphne had a fondness for Earl Grey and we don't stray too far from the traditional in this house, but Rosalie may have something else in the pantry if you prefer."

Soon they were ensconced in the room Judge referred to as a study since he was now semi-retired. Her visit was unusual and seemed urgent, and yet she seemed reluctant to bring the issue forward.

"How may I help you today, Maddie? Is there some serious problem? Rosalie said you seemed agitated. I noticed that you drove yourself and I thought you'd given up driving."

"No, I'm still able to drive. Silly me, I guess I was flattered to have Odie drive me around. I may have been silly about many things. That's why I'm here today."

He remained silent. His thoughts would only have echoed her words and he never wasted energy on redundancy.

"Judge, I have some concerns about . . . well . . . about my future. Lately I've not felt as well as I normally do. I don't like to admit it, but I've lived my 'three score and ten' and added a few more. All this to say, I want to write a new will. Many things have changed, especially in the last few months, and I feel a strong necessity to do this. Actually an immediately and dire necessity."

Still he waited. Maddie Wallace must make her case in her own words.

"Judge, I don't mean to sound overly dramatic. I've been dabbling with this idea for a few weeks now, and suddenly, I feel a very strong urgency about this. Can you get it done before the weekend?"

Judge rocked his chair closer to the desk and flipped through the pages of his calendar. The days of the week were firmly planted in his mind, but he wanted to consider why she had such an urgent need.

"Well, Maddie, it's two forty-five on this Tuesday afternoon. To finish this before the weekend gives us three days. Perhaps I can, depending on what needs to be done. I can give it my best shot. Is that good enough?"

"Please, Judge, do the best you can. I really want to have a new signed will as soon as possible."

"Maddie, is there something specific going on that I should know about?"

"No, most likely just some chickens coming home to roost, and I want to make certain that the henhouse is all locked up."

They both laughed at her attempt at humor, but still he wondered.

෨෬

The storm was lessening, bringing somewhat cooler temperatures for a while. I sat down in the porch swing to allow my still shaky nerves to calm down. My mind replayed the incident at Miss Maddie's gateway several times.

Even with the rain pelting down, I could see the rage on Odie's face. Or was I merely dramatizing the event? Who knows, but if I had to describe his expression, it would be maniacal. It was still frightening to remember what happened, but sitting around brooding never accomplished much, but a shopping trip might.

Before I could change my mind, I picked up the phone and called my shopping buddy.

"Cynthia, I need to go to Tyler. Want to go with me?"

"Are we shopping, or what?"

"Shopping and an early dinner. I'd like to go to that warehouse club to stock up on some things for the house. I also need to pick up a few things for the bank."

"Sounds great. It's about time for one of those delicious T-bone steak salads."

We giggled like schoolgirls all the way into Tyler, laughing at others but mostly at ourselves. The conversation turned somber when I mentioned getting caught in the storm and being caught out as I stopped in front of Miss Maddie's gate.

"Did you get an earful from Miss Maddie, or did Odie get to do the honors?"

"Not a word from either of them. It's like waiting for the other shoe to drop, which will most likely happen tomorrow when I'm up to my ears in work at the bank."

We shopped several stores at leisure, adding a quick sashay through one of our favorite dress shops, and thought we were through shopping and ready for dinner when Cynthia remembered that she was out of shampoo.

"Julie, I think I used the last drop this afternoon. After getting caught in that downpour, I had to shower and shampoo. Can we make another stop?"

"No problem, let's just go to that Walgreens close to the

steak house. I never miss a shopping experience."

I pulled into a spot near the entrance and stopped with wide-open mouth.

"Look, Cynthia, who is that with Odie? Is that Denise, and what are they doing?"

"Oh my, did you ever? First Vonda, then Miss Maddie, and now Denise. This is getting too complicated."

We both sat and stared. Odie and Denise were laden down with packages. She was looking up at him as if he were a Greek god, or a movie star. He was accepting the look and her obvious adulation with enthusiasm. We watched with jaw-dropping amazement as Odie escorted her to the passenger seat of her car and opened the door.

The shampoo purchase was accomplished with speed, my hunger was forcing me to move quickly, and Cynthia surely felt the same. We hurried to the steak house that was two blocks over and arrived to find the waiting area filled. Standing room only.

While waiting, I allowed my eyes to explore the room, looking for friends, customers, or acquaintances. My roving eyes went from couple to couple without recognizing anyone until my gaze landed on a couple next in line to be seated. I couldn't believe my eyes.

"Cynthia, look up there, standing at the front of the line. Look, that's Odie and Denise. Can you believe this? We've run into them twice tonight."

"Julie, I love you. You're my best friend, but if you poke me one more time with your elbow, I just might deck you."

"Sorry, I guess I did get carried away. Thought you would want to know."

We watched with undisguised interest as Odie and Denise followed the server into the dining room. In those few short minutes, Cynthia's sweet personality returned.

"Sorry for my tone. I didn't eat lunch today and I'm starved. The smell of that food is driving me nuts. I need my steak salad."

I could think of no appropriate comment, so I dutifully checked my elbows along with my inquisitive eyes and waited. Not patiently, but I waited nevertheless.

༻∽ও঵∼༺

The next morning, I woke to the sound of rain and a grouchy mood. I didn't want to go to work, I just wanted to stay in bed a little longer. I allowed my tired body a little extra time.

My dozing was interrupted. The ringing phone filled me with immediate hostility for Mr. A. G. Bell, but civility prevailed over rudeness, just barely.

"Julie, how's it going? Things at the bank okay? Everything cool?"

My boss, speaking in very terse questions. Is he calling to apologize for his nasty attitude the last time we spoke? Somehow, I didn't think so.

"Good morning, Jeff. Things are as you left them. Mostly okay, but we're a little stretched with so few employees. When are you coming back to Three Bridges?"

"That's why I'm calling. I'm not coming back just yet. I have some serious unfinished business over here. Think you can hold on another couple of weeks, just until I get this thorny problem resolved?"

I sat in stunned silence. I wanted to decline the request, if it was a request. It felt more like an order. An order that I wanted to ignore. I remembered his short and snippy tone in our last conversation and realized there would be no apology. Things at the bank were so different since Clarke Watson died, but what could I do? I could hear Jeff calling my name, urging me to respond.

"Okay, Jeff, I'll give it my best shot on a week to week basis. This is difficult. We don't have enough employees, and we're all overworked. Even if I could find someone to hire as a temp, I don't have time to train a new person."

Now that I was awake and given the opportunity to vent, I was going to do it.

"Jeff, I don't have the authority to handle some issues in the same manner that you do. Could you at least give me a contact number where I can reach you if I have a problem?"

"Just call Mother, Julie. I told you before, quit worrying. Nothing ever happens in Three Bridges."

If I were in a cartoon character, my image would be depicted with a huge frown on my face and steam erupting from my ears. I am not a cartoon figure. I am a mature senior Vice-President of The Bank of Three Bridges, and it was time to go to work.

My workday didn't improve very much, no doubt because of the cloud of doom that accompanied me. My fellow employees seemed to catch on quickly and except for the most necessary requirements, I was left alone in my office.

I was busy with paper work, phone calls, overdue loans, and typical banking business. Suddenly, in the midst of my oblivion, I heard a tentative voice.

"Pardon me, Julie, may I see you a moment? I only have a short time. I had Odie drop me off. I told him I needed to put something in my safe deposit box while he went to The Flower Box."

I watched with awe as this formerly abrasive woman stood in my door, meekly asking permission to enter.

"Come on in, Miss Maddie. How can I help you today?"

"Julie, I think I made a horrendous mistake to allow Odie to sign on my accounts. I spent some time with Judge yesterday afternoon, and he urged me to change this situation immediately. Can you do that for me?"

"Not a problem. I'll transfer all your funds into other accounts, it won't take long. I'll pull up you accounts and get started."

"Julie, I think there may be some outstanding debit card purchases. Leave a minimum balance to cover those. When this weekend is over, I'm going to make some other changes. For now, this is what I want to do."

Without asking any more questions, I went to the computer, accessed her accounts and after a few more questions, we transferred the very large balances into new accounts with new numbers. I wanted to breathe a deep sigh of relief but out of the corner of my eye I saw Odie striding into the bank, and without pausing, rushed into my office.

"Miss Maddie, what are you doing in here? I thought you needed to put something in your safe deposit box."

I'll give that old woman a lot of credit. She was very quick on her feet and instantly changed her pleasant expression into the disagreeable look we all knew.

"I was just giving this uppity thing a piece of my mind for blocking the entrance to our gate. Let's go, Odie."

As he preceded her from the room, she looked fleetingly and apologetically in my direction. Immediately, I heard the echo from my phone call this morning, "Nothing ever happens in Three Bridges."

# $\mathcal{T}$welve

**Vonda Sue Gunderson watched as Odie and Maddie** Wallace left Julie's office. Why had he taken up with that old woman? Money, most likely. Odie always talked about wanting more from life, but had very little interest in working to get it.

Several years ago, Odie's mother passed away, leaving him all her worldly possessions. When he returned to Three Bridges and bought The Flower Box with money inherited from his mother, Vonda began to hope anew. As the years passed and nothing changed, that hope had turned bitter.

She looked again as the odd couple passed her office door. Miss Maddie was staring at her with a strange, incomprehensible look.

When Vonda contemplated that look, which seemed somewhat apologetic, it left her with an unsettled attitude. Even though she knew he wouldn't answer, she placed a call to Odie's cell.

"Odie, I want to talk to you about something important. Will you call me so we can set a time to meet?" The question was recorded on his voice mail, but she doubted he would answer.

Maddie wasn't prepared for the sense of embarrassment that swept over her as she looked at Vonda Gunderson. From some place deep within, an image of R.J. floated into her mind, and she could see him laughing at her, reminding her that she was a silly old woman trying to steal the affection of a man almost half her age. Yes, R.J. would think she was silly indeed.

What her late husband might have thought didn't matter, but some things did and she must put them right. She'd made a start, and this afternoon, she must review the information she had given Judge. There might be one or two things that needed to be fine-tuned.

I watched as Maddie and Odie left the bank. An unlikely couple to be sure. I wondered how Maddie Wallace had fallen for Odie, and not for the first time, I wondered why Vonda had stayed in that unhealthy relationship so long.

*Put that aside, Julie, you have your own issues.*

First of all, where was my life going? Quick answer, nowhere. For some time I'd dabbled with the idea of moving away from Three Bridges, but I never got beyond the thought. Or the daydream.

Three Bridges is home now and Lafayette is but a distant and unhappy memory. My relationship with Sydney and Catherine, my siblings, was strained by distance and circumstances. When Grandmother left me such a large inheritance it had been difficult for my mother to deal with.

My mother threatened to have my inheritance revoked and Sydney always seemed to fall in line with her thinking, even when she threatened to sue to have the will set aside. Catherine is so involved in her medical career, that she has pushed everything else aside. Surely, there will be some way to mend these relationships, someday. I've got to try, they're my family.

*Grandmother, did you know this would happen when you left everything to me? Why? I never asked for anything. Now I have this family mess to contend with and I am clueless in dealing with these issues.*

*No more time for this fuss about my life. Back to work.*

I picked up the file of past due loans and smiled. There was one name that should drop off the past due list very soon.

"Hey Julie, are you going to take a lunch break? I brought a leftover casserole from home, and thought we could share if you have time."

"Great, I didn't even realize it was lunch time. Too much work. Let's go to the break room."

We settled down with homemade broccoli rice casserole, and a side salad. Cynthia was a wonderful cook, and we often shared her leftovers for lunch.

"I wanted you to know that I'm almost done with Krystal Kelly. TTC has agreed to settle for two-thirds of the balance she owes. We will pay that as an anonymous third party, and then Judge and Rev. Peppers are going to present her a check that will cover most of the loan at the bank. On your suggestion, I called Hortense, and then I will arrange to take Krystal out there before the week is over."

"Wow, you've really been working on this. That's great."

"It helps me forget that I don't have a social life. Have some casserole—there was no recipe for this. I just dumped some things in a baking pan and cooked it."

"Thanks for the food and the inside information. I won't ask what's in it."

I took a tentative bite. Sometimes, Cynthia crossed over the line into tofu when she wanted to cook healthy. "This is good, really good."

"When is that reluctant banker boss of yours coming back? Hey, doesn't that sound like a title for one of those paperbacks, 'The Reluctant Banker'. Have you heard anything else?"

"I guess that falls under the don't-ask-don't-tell category. I don't ask and they don't tell me. I did get permission to hire someone, a temp, if I can find someone."

Jessie appeared at the door, "Julie, you have a customer that needs immediate attention."

With a rather indelicate swipe of my face with a napkin, I cleared the table of my used dinner paraphernalia and returned to work. I would freshen up my makeup when my customer left.

However, I wished I had dallied a little longer in the kitchen the instant that I saw the person waiting for me. It was Odie Marshall, blustering, irate, and impatient.

"Well, did you finally decide to come back and do some work? Isn't that what the Watsons pay you to do?"

"What can I do for you, Odie? I'm here now. By the way, everyone gets a lunch break."

I took an exaggerated look at my wristwatch, and pretended to count the minutes.

"Let's see, Odie. My lunch hour lasted . . . well, about twenty-three minutes."

"Poor Julie. Look here, I came to cash a check, and Jessie says there's not enough money in the account. Miss Maddie wanted me to cash a check for seventy-five hundred dollars and Jessie wouldn't cash it. What's going on, Julie? You know I can sign on her account. I came in to get the money and I need it today. We need it today."

"Just a minute, I'll check on it, but Jessie is seldom wrong."

I turned to my computer screen to access the account in question, although I knew without looking that there was less than two thousand dollars in the account. Much more than I thought Miss Maddie should leave, but she was worried about some automatic withdrawals and wanted to make certain they would be processed.

"Looks as if Jessie was right. She always is, you know. There is some money in the account, but we also have some pending withdrawals and that leaves about thirty-seven dollars and forty-nine cents. Would you like to rewrite the check for that amount?"

I thought the man would implode, if that is humanly possible. His face turned red, then purple and finally, he began to turn white around the mouth. The look of hatred in his eyes almost made me shudder. I'd never experienced such vitriol and I watched as he struggled to gain his composure, but he didn't really succeed.

"What about the savings account? Can I make a withdrawal from that account? I know there's a lot of money in savings. Get me a withdrawal slip and I'll take the money from the savings account."

I watched from the corner of my eye, aware of the tension that sprung from this man like an unhealthy fog.

"Let me check that balance for you, Odie. No point in filling out a withdrawal slip until we check."

Again, I went through the same routine, accessing the account on the computer and at the same time gathering courage. I thought briefly of summoning Vonda or Jessie to come in but quickly decided that I would just handle this myself. I asked God for courage and wisdom.

"Odie, there is only two hundred and fifty dollars in that account."

I had no time to offer any other words. He pushed back the client chair with such force that it ricocheted off the back wall of my office, and I feared the glass would break. At the same time, I was thankful for the glass wall that gave a clear view to anyone in the bank. He strode through the door, with me following closely behind.

Blinded by anger, he narrowly averted hitting Cynthia as she left the bank. Even that didn't daunt him or slow him down. He stopped at Vonda's office, pointed a finger at her, and said, "I'll see you later tonight. Be there!"

I was glad that was over. I had known the moment that Maddie took away Odie's signing privileges that I would be the one to bear the brunt of his outrageous anger. I was right. Still trying to calm my frazzled nerves, I was immersed in paperwork when a soft knock interrupted the chaos in my mind.

"Julie, I need a minute. You know I get off at two o'clock today, and I need to talk to you about something before I leave."

"Sure, come on in and let's talk, have a seat if you have time."

I looked at Vonda, wondering if she wanted to talk about Odie and his outrageous manner a short time ago, but I decided to keep an open mind, and thankfully I did just that.

"No, can't stay. I need to get to Tyler before three-thirty. I have a doctor's appointment this afternoon and again tomorrow morning. I should be back in Three Bridges around noon. I know we're shorthanded, but I've had this appointment for weeks and if I give it up it may be months before I get another."

"Vonda, are you ill?"

I was astonished. This woman never missed work, never.

"No, this is just something I'm considering." She touched her face, gently running her fingers down the left side, then shook her head.

"This is preliminary, just looking into some possibilities. I'll make the decision later. But the other thing I wanted to ask you is this. I have a friend who recently retired from First State Bank in Tyler. We're meeting tonight for dinner and I have an idea that she might like to work part-time, at least for a while. Do I have your permission to ask if she's willing to work at Three Bridges?"

"Yes, yes! Did you ever work with her? How'd you meet?"

"We first met at Tyler Junior College. She worked in banking in Tyler, and of course I started here right after college. We kept in touch, and whenever possible, we always partnered when we went to a banking school."

I watched Vonda speak with an animation usually absent. The obvious enthusiasm for this person was spreading a degree of hope.

"Why did she retire so early? Does she have health issues?"

"No, she's fine. Her husband was very ill for a while, but he's doing great now. Anyway, I think she would like some part-time work. I'll ask if she can come out for an interview tomorrow morning if that's all right with you."

"Oh, Vonda, if she's interested, this could be an answer to prayers. What is her name, just so I'll know who's asking for an interview?"

"Her name is Leslie Phelps. I think she would fit in very well here, and she's really smart."

I jotted the name down on my daily calendar. I had way too much on my mind to try to remember names.

"Thanks, Vonda. Now, back to your medical appointments,

is there anything I should know about, as your boss?"

"Yes, I guess there is. If I decide to do this, I'll need about six weeks off work. In fact, I was going to ask for a two month leave of absence, in case something didn't go exactly right. I probably had Leslie in mind to cover for me during that time. Julie, I don't want to talk about this until I know more, and it may come to nothing. After tomorrow morning, I'll know more."

She started to leave the office and then turned around. "Julie, I made these appointments with Martha, our Dr. Martha."

She left my office with more determination and pride than I'd ever seen in her. I was overwhelmed with astonishment and a strange sense of pride. Vonda was reaching out to make some changes in her life.

She hadn't spoken the words, but the manner in which her hand tentatively ran down the left side of her face, past the drooping eyelid and the sagging ear, I felt certain that she was thinking of corrective or cosmetic surgery. Fantastic.

# $\mathcal{T}$hirteen

**About an hour before closing time another brief and intense** rainstorm interrupted the quiet of the bank, and my mind went to the festival scheduled for this weekend. If the rain continued, it was going to be one big, hot, humid, and wet mess. Again, I thanked God that this year I wouldn't be working, either at a booth or for the festival committee.

I looked at the clock, wishing the hands would move faster and I could end this week. I wasn't even close to being caught up with my work, but I was restless. I wandered between the drive-up teller window and back through the bank lobby, gazing through the locked front door of the bank and then back to my office. I was so lost in thought about Vonda, the farm, the job, especially my '*Reluctant Banker*' boss, that I didn't even hear the phones buzzing until Jessie finally got my attention.

"Julie, can you take this call?"

I wanted to say, "No, no more stuff today, I need a time out." I wanted to protest that I had not signed on to run a bank with a shoestring staff, even if my boss thought I was well qualified. I thought those things, but instead, I answered the call.

"Julie Trahan, may I help you?"

"Don't hang up on me, Julie. It's Ryan. I was rude to you the other day and I apologize for that. Julie, I really need to talk to you. I know it's been a very long time in coming, but it's imperative that I explain some things to you. There are things that I should have said years ago, but didn't have the courage. I'm not looking for anything except the chance to say what needs to be said and to explain about my life now. Could we have dinner tonight?"

I wanted to throw the phone across the room. I wanted to scream at this man that wreaked havoc on my life years ago. There were many other things that I wanted to do, but something stilled my angry spirit and I began to think.

Perhaps I should have dinner with him, hear his side of the story. I wanted to hear his explanation for leaving me only days before our wedding. I needed to know why he ran out on me without even saying goodbye.

I wanted to hear all those things, but not here, not in this town where everyone seemed to know everyone's business and gossiped about that which they did not know.

"I'll meet you in Tyler. I could be there around seven tonight. There's a small family-owned restaurant just off the loop called Mama's Italian Kitchen. I might be late. Everything depends on how long it takes to close the bank."

I didn't care if he had to wait. Ten years ago, I waited for a phone call that never came. If he wants to apologize now, he can wait.

"Sounds good, actually I'm in Tyler now. I'll find the restaurant and meet you there." The line went quiet, I was about to hang up when I heard his voice again.

"Julie, thank you. This . . . well, I guess all I need to say is thank you."

I closed the bank without thinking about the process, just trusting the skills and the habits of seven or eight years to guide me. I'm not even certain that everything balanced. No matter, that would be easier to resolve than what I was facing.

The weather cleared and left steaming puddles of water in the streets, humidity in the air, and that brilliant Texas sun shining brightly in the western sky. Summertime in East Texas and the sun is still visible above the tree line even at seven in the evening.

As I drove, I was hounded by self-doubt. Why did I agree to this? Hadn't I spent years trying to put my ex-fiancé as far from conscious thought as possible? Yes, and now here he is again, turning up like that proverbial bad penny. I had given my word and against my better judgment. I would meet him for supper.

I merged into the right lane when I reached the Tyler loop, surprised that I was here already. I must have driven on autopilot. I had no memory of the familiar landmarks that I normally passed, and I uttered prayers of thankfulness for God's protection. But now I was on the loop, and the closer I came to the restaurant where I had agreed to meet Ryan Daigle, the slower I drove.

Because of my distraction, I failed to make the left turn that I should have made. For a brief moment, I considered driving around the city and home again, but I didn't have the courage to do that. I made a promise, and even though I regretted that promise, I would double back to Mama's kitchen and connect with my past.

I entered the lobby and stopped dead in my tracks. He was there, just inside the door, pacing back and forth, but he hadn't seen me enter. Not yet, but soon he would turn and walk back in my direction. For that brief moment in time, I stared at this man that I had loved so dearly when I was young. That recurrent pain again grasped my heart in an icy grip and squeezed, but I breathed in air and hoped my lungs would work, and they did. One further step and he turned and began to walk toward me, very slowly.

I would have passed him by had I not expected to see Ryan Daigle. He is thirty-four, just one year and eight months older than I. He looked much older. Premature grey hair threaded into the dark curls that should have been a little shorter. That ever-present mischievous twinkle in the grey eyes was missing, and permanent frown lines had taken residence on his brow. I stood there, just inside the entrance, uncertain how to greet him.

He came forward, and when he motioned toward the dining

room with his right hand, I realized that he was as uncertain about the protocol as I was. After all, how should one greet the woman left at the altar so many years ago?

"Thanks, Julie, for meeting with me. I hope you don't feel too uncomfortable having dinner with me. I'm flying out of DFW very early tomorrow morning and I want to leave with some things from the past resolved. If possible, I want to see that some of issues are made right. You deserve an explanation—even if it is ten years too late."

I had no words to answer with and no desire to discuss this while standing in the lobby of a very busy restaurant, but felt I must say something, no matter how inane.

"Have you put our name on the list? The restaurant seems rather busy tonight, but then it always is."

He didn't answer, but directed me midway along the right side of this cozy restaurant. When I considered a safe place to meet with Ryan, I could only think of Mama's Kitchen, with the high back semi-private booths.

The restaurant was crowded, as I knew it would be. Tonight, there were an assortment of people around us, but my eyes failed to recognize any familiar faces. I could only hope there was no one I should have greeted.

We were seated, and still I could find no reason to speak. I waited while a faceless person placed large, faux leather menus in front of us and set a basket of garlic bread in the center of the table. We ordered robotically. Finally, I could wait no longer.

"Ryan, let's just get to the point. Why did you want to see me? Why is this so important that you had to talk to me tonight?"

"Julie, as I said earlier, I am flying out of Dallas tomorrow morning. I seldom come back to this area, but there were business issues that I had to resolve. It was a short trip and I have to leave, go back to work tomorrow."

He seemed as reluctant to talk as I was to hear his words, but finally decided to continue.

"There are so many things that I want to say to you, but this is so much more difficult than I ever thought it would be. First of all, I want to apologize for leaving all the senseless messages without my name. Even though I'm ten years older, sometimes I wonder if I'll ever be that stable mature person I'm supposed to be."

I looked at him as if to say—so what? Is this what you brought me here for—to help you wallow in self-pity?

Seeing that I wasn't going to speak, he began again. "I guess I should start by saying that I live and work in Paris, Julie."

Still, I didn't exactly feel inclined to ease his discomfort. I took a sip from my water glass and wondered if I would be able to swallow that tiny teaspoon of water that felt like a river in my throat. And I waited.

"This story starts back home in Lafayette, such a long time ago. A lifetime ago. The day before I broke our engagement, I received an offer to come to Paris, to interview for a position with one of the most prestigious law firms in international law. It was my dream job."

He took a deep breath and pulled in some courage.

"I was like a kid with a brand new toy on Christmas morning and I wanted to share it with you, but you were doing your 'girl-things'. I couldn't find you, and I was restless, at loose ends, so I called your house again and asked if I could come out even if you weren't there. I thought maybe I could use the pool to work off some energy. Your mom invited me to come on over."

He reached for his glass of ice water, took a big gulp and an even deeper breath. I watched as he placed the glass back on the table and then rearranged the silverware to his liking, lining it up with the edge of the table. All these delaying motions were playing havoc with my nerves, but finally he started speaking again.

"Julie, the day that started out with such euphoria ended up being the worst day of my life. I want you to know that I loved you with such passion and such completeness, but I messed up and sometimes things just can't be fixed."

"Ryan, why don't you just finish the story? You're making

me very nervous. What happened? Explain!"

"I have practiced this speech so many times, and I think I need to tell you just the way I rehearsed—just as I remember it."

I listened to the sound of his Cajun accent that hadn't entirely faded into the language of Paris. I listened as he told the story as if he were narrating a play.

"I parked my car next to the garage, you know, on that parking pad. I went straight to the pool house, changed into my trunks, and thought I'd just swim a few laps. Didn't happen. Your mom was waiting for me in a very brief bikini. She was sitting at a table with a tray of drinks and sandwiches for lunch. Stupid me, I sat down to eat a sandwich and had a drink, and then another drink. Finally, I made an effort to get into the pool. Dear God, this is tough."

I watched as he hung his head in shame, but he drew no sympathy from me, only confusion, and I wanted to hear the rest of the story.

"Julie, your mom jumped into the pool with me and started making advances. Things got pretty steamy, and one thing led to another. What I thought would be an innocent swim got out of control quickly, very much out of control."

My mind was spinning with a thousand questions. What was he trying to tell me? What? I don't remember speaking, but I must have asked because he finally spoke again, this time his voice was low-pitched and husky with pain.

# Fourteen

**I stared at Ryan, wondering what would be the next words** out of his mouth, but it really didn't matter what he said. I didn't want to hear anymore. This was more, much more than I should have to bear, but I didn't have the courage to get up and leave.

"Julie, your mother and I wound up in bed in the pool house—all afternoon. I must have gone to sleep for a time. Anyway, when I woke up it was late and your mom was gone. I looked at my watch and knew that I had to get out of there because you and your dad would be home soon."

"I left, but I didn't go home. I found a bar and I drank until the bar owner called a cab and sent me home. When I sobered up the next day, I told my family about the job offer in Paris, and I left. I couldn't bring myself to tell you the truth when I called from the airport. I had cheated on you with your mother, and I was so ashamed. It seemed that the only decent thing I could do was simply break the engagement and run away. It was cowardly, and you deserved so much better."

Neither of us had eaten more than a few bites. I pushed my plate away and summoned the waiter, asking for a to-go box. I didn't want the food, it was merely something to do, some action that might be normal. I think Ryan was still explaining, but I had tuned out the sound of his treacherous voice.

When the waiter returned, he must have understood from our expressions that things weren't going very well at this table. He merely placed the packaged food on the table and left quietly.

I couldn't decide if I wanted to just get up and leave, or sit there to hear more of this—this abomination. I reached for my purse and began to slide from the booth.

"One more thing, Julie, before you leave. You need to hear the rest of the story. It seems that I had told your mother all about my job offer, and even the name of the law firm. Julie, within a few days, your mother followed me to France and she stayed until the fall. I have no excuses for my behavior. I can only say that I got caught up in the snare that she set for me. I guess I liked being sought after by such a beautiful older woman, but I should have turned away."

I wanted to scream out the basic truth. *My mother. This was my mother you are talking about.* But still I said nothing, only stared at him with undisguised loathing as I struggled to bring air into my lungs.

"This went on for a time, and then she became restless and decided to return to Lafayette. She thought she could go back to your father, but apparently, this was the last straw for him. By this time he had already started divorce proceedings, as you know. I don't think she expected that. Since that time your mom has been back and forth to Paris many times."

"Two years ago, she settled more or less permanently with me and that turned out to be not exactly the best situation. I soon found out that she is far more unstable than I realized. After a while, I discovered that she was also seeing some foreign guy, some oil rich Saudi."

He paused, as if waiting for some sympathetic response. He would wait a very long time for any sympathy from me.

"Anyway, that discovery was the last straw. I couldn't live with her any longer. She'd ruined everything good in my life, but I couldn't allow her to ruin my future. Last month, although it was years late in coming, I asked her to leave and reluctantly she did. If she comes back to Paris, I won't be there. I'm going to be working from Barcelona for a while, then who knows."

For the first time, he reached out and touched me and I wanted to scream. I felt defiled by his touch. In disgust, I pulled my hand away, and edged a little further from the booth.

"Julie, I have wished a million times that I'd turned around and run from your house that day, but I didn't. One other thing, the most important thing, I want you to know that this was not your fault. You did nothing wrong and you certainly didn't deserve what I did to you. You're a beautiful and wonderful person and you deserve to have a happy, loving marriage."

I inched closer to the end of the booth. I wanted to leave but without causing a scene. But Ryan seemed impervious to my reactions, and he continued to speak as I planned my next move to leave this restaurant.

"Your mother is really bad news. Julie, she's manipulative and greedy, and I know she wants your inheritance. I can't presume that you'd accept advice from me, but I say again, your mother is toxic. Stay away from her if you can."

Like an automaton, I left the booth, and then the restaurant. Without thinking, just going on autopilot and stumbling into at least two tables before I got to the lobby where one of the hosts opened the door for me. I was focusing on putting one foot in front of the other as fast as I could, just trying to reach my car before I fell completely apart.

I hadn't known what to expect when I agreed to have dinner with Ryan Daigle tonight, but this was almost more than I could handle. My chest felt as if steel bands were tightening around my lungs, but some even stranger emotion was grabbing my mind, forcing me to think thoughts I never wanted to envision. Images, wickedly evil images flooded my mind, and I wanted nothing more than blankness. No thoughts, no visions, no feelings.

With trembling fingers, I managed to unlock my SUV and relock the door. I threw away the things I was carrying to the other side of the seat as if it were Ryan Daigle. The sobs erupted and I placed my head on the steering wheel and cried from the depths of my soul.

The recent years of peace had been removed and I was back in that time of fresh hurt. A stinging pain cut so deeply through my core that I feared for my life. Again, my heart seemed to break. I cried for all that I had lost. I cried for my innocence, my joy, now forever taken from me. I cried for my broken romance, so cruelly sabotaged by my mother. I cried for the loss of a happy family life and a future without promise and hope.

After a time I had no more energy for my sorrow. I started the car and drove to the first McDonald's to order coffee from the drive-thru window. Not once did I think of my splotchy face, my swollen and reddened eyes, and nose. For me, nothing was important except regaining enough control to drive back to Three Bridges.

Odie Marshall was standing at the back door of Vonda's house, wanting to pull the door off the hinges because she wasn't home. Where was she? He'd told her to be there. This was not his first trip to her house tonight, but the third and where was she? She was always there when he wanted her and tonight when he really needed to find some peace and quiet, she was gone. She would pay for this.

He was hungry, angry, and tired and he had no idea where to go. He had given up his apartment several months ago. The planned renovation of the residence above The Flower Box had never progressed beyond the planning stages. It seems that he mistakenly thought Maddie Wallace would finance the work, but sometimes he had slept upstairs over The Flower Box on those nights when he couldn't find a welcome bed elsewhere. He didn't want to do that tonight, especially after he'd taken the sledgehammer to the upstairs.

He needed to think, he needed to plan. Vonda was gone and there was nowhere for him to go. No place except the estate where Maddie Wallace lived. He opened his cell and called a number that was newly familiar.

"Denise, baby, what's for supper tonight? Look, sweetie, I'm hungry, tired, and I really don't want to see Maddie tonight. Can I come in the back door of your apartment? Will that be okay with you?"

❦

Denise Hougan, foolish woman that she was, hurried about, trying to find a garment that would flatter her. The prospect of spending time with Odie thrilled her beyond words, so much so, that she could barely think straight. In near panic, she searched frantically for something that would make her look young and exciting, and thirty pounds thinner.

There wasn't anything in her closet that came close except for a flowing caftan lounger. It wasn't glamorous, but it would have to do. She added a touch of recently purchased makeup, bought at the same time she splurged on some very expensive fragrance to add to her meager collection of cosmetics. Overwhelmed with expectation and breathless, she heard his knock on the back door.

Like a silly teenager on her first date, she welcomed him into her apartment. Odie looked at Denise and recognized the excitement permeating every gesture, and he couldn't resist reacting to that flattering interest.

Odie believed that he was a man of the world and as such, believed that worldly men never turned down any opportunities, especially if he were likely to receive a benefit—of any sort. Without a qualm of conscience, he opened his arms and embraced Denise with an unfelt passion. But he was very skilled at playing this game.

❦

With God's protection, I drove home without incident and without collapsing into another hysterical screaming fit. But the words kept forcing themselves through my mind.

*Mother . . . bikini . . . drinks . . . pool house . . . Paris. He slept with my mother and he lived with my mother for years. But shouldn't it be that MY MOTHER slept with my fiancé?*

I pulled into the garage at Grandmother's house and wished again that she was still here to comfort me as she was that day ten years ago when my father brought me to Three Bridges.

Dad had rearranged his busy schedule and brought me to this wonderful house, to his mother-in-law, so that I would have a chance to recover from the heartbreak of my failed romance.

Of course, I never suspected that my mother was the reason behind the broken engagement. What kind of woman would steal her daughter's fiancé? What kind of woman had given birth to me? How could this woman be my grandmother's child?

Had my father known what was at the bottom of my heartbreak? Probably.

My pain was so enveloping that I had never thought of anyone's feelings except my own. But surely my father knew and that is why they divorced only months later.

Now I realize that Ryan had probably not been the first young man that my mother had seduced—but he was my fiancé. Yes, surely, my father must have known. Those thoughts made my stomach turn in knots of despair. Instead of giving into the anger, I reached out to God.

*Thank you, heavenly Father, that you gave me an earthly father that was so wise and loving, and now, Lord, I realize that his heart must have been broken also, and probably not for the first time. Lord, look after my dad, bless his life, and Lord, please remove these hateful bitter feelings I have for my mother. Thank you, Lord. Amen.*

Clearly now for the very first time I understood my dad. I understood why he resigned from his successful medical practice and volunteered to work in the mission field. My heartache and sadness for him somehow lessened my own pain.

I was overcome with a strange and unexpected desire to reconnect with my brother and sister. I needed to know what my family felt for me, and if we could ever be a family again.

I prepared for bed while still processing the enormity of everything I heard tonight. Suddenly I was struck with a thought. My brother and sister, do they know about this? Is this why Catherine never speaks much about mother?

What about Sydney, does he know? He was only nineteen when I left home. After the divorce, Dad stayed in Lafayette until Sydney graduated from LSU. I never considered that anyone else was hurting. I must have lived in a fog or with blinders. Why had I not seen all the things that were going on around me?

# $\mathscr{F}$ifteen

**Still in an emotional fog, I entered my house and attempted** to fall into my normal nighttime routine. I checked the refrigerator for sandwich makings for tomorrow's lunch and found nothing interesting. Not a problem, I'd grab a sandwich from City Café or open a can of soup at the bank. Food was not very important tonight, until I remembered the takeout container from dinner.

Had I gotten to the car with it? I had no clue, so I backtracked and found the container of food on the floor of my car with the lid still intact. Amazing. Goldie must have honed in on the garlic-scented pasta. She was swishing her tail and whining in anticipation of the delectable food. I couldn't even remember what I'd ordered.

Still whining pitifully, Goldie hurried me to the back porch, about to jump out of her furry skin. She wanted this food that I was carrying, but I wasn't about to allow her to eat all that pasta tonight. I added more confusion to this poor dog's life when I picked up her bowl and went into the kitchen.

Goldie is very well trained and knows that the house is off limits. No exceptions, ever. She stopped just short of coming into the kitchen and waited behind the closed screen door, while I ,accompanied by the saddest cries known to dog lovers, scooped a large portion of pasta into the plastic bowl. It was lasagna. This dog was eating very well tonight, courtesy of my ex-fiancé, Ryan Daigle. I put the food and fresh water in the usual spot and said good night to my faithful companion.

I was exhausted, but I didn't go to bed. I couldn't think of sleep with all those horrible thoughts racing through my head like a locomotive running out of control. Why couldn't my thoughts crash burn and give me rest? I wasn't that lucky, it didn't happen.

*"Your mother has been living with me . . . she followed me into the pool . . . I had too much to drink . . . she was very aggressive . . . I shouldn't have done it . . . you were busy doing girl-things"* . . . and my anger hit a new level.

In fact, I didn't want to think of anything tonight. I was weary and tired to the depths of my soul. I picked up my grandmother's Bible and thumbed through the well-worn pages, looking for comfort.

I stopped thumbing the pages after I reached the book of Jeremiah. Again, I read that God had plans for me. If this was God's plan, then I surely didn't understand it, but I did trust in him. If God declared that he wanted me to prosper, to have hope and a future, then I would try to lay aside my anger and doubts. In the final analysis, I trusted God much more than I trusted my raging emotions.

&#8766;&#8766;

Maddie Wallace had trouble sleeping after such an exhausting day. Perhaps Odie had forgotten about the elaborate security system. Or perhaps he didn't care that she had access to everything that went on at Wallace Way. That was the silly name that R.J. had tacked on to this vast acreage years ago. The original gate carried the name in bold letters for a long time until a tree downed by a thunderstorm landed squarely on the center of the gate.

The replacement gate was more ornate, tall, and white with the twining roses. Maddie had said this would symbolize their relationship and he agreed. Neither reflected on the truthfulness of the symbol.

Tonight she had seen Odie when he came up the driveway and when he entered Denise's suite. And she hadn't wanted to see anything else.

Her mind was not as easy to turn off as the security system, and she slept with the shame and remorse of her recent actions.

≼ら≽

Thoughts of my grandmother surrounded me as I sat at my dressing table, putting on my makeup and getting ready for work. I remembered one of the last conversations we had before she became so very ill.

*"Julie, I have several things on my mind today, but I want to talk about you about the life you're living. You don't date, and you have very few friends your own age. I know you've made some friends in town, but they are all older than you are.*

*I don't want you to become an old woman before your time. You need to enjoy these special years of youth, because before you know it those years will be gone.*

*Possibly this is my fault. You've had too many responsibilities since you came to live with me. I think I should not have pushed you so hard. I believe that I made you forget about being young.*

*Julie, after I'm gone in a few weeks or months, after you finish grieving for me, I want you to think about being young again."*

As I looked into the mirror, I realized that my grandmother was right. I didn't know what it was like to be young and carefree, especially now. Only days ago, as I sat across the table from a very handsome and charming young man, I accepted the reality that I had forgotten how to be young. But I couldn't worry about that now. I had to open the doors of The Bank of Three Bridges.

≼ら≽

"Jessie, I need to see you before your window opens. Gloria can handle the drive-thru by herself for a while."

Gloria Wilson was our one and only part-time teller. She works only a few hours a week, mostly in the early morning or during the noon rush. She still lives at home and helps to care for her ailing handicapped mother. She was here today and needed badly.

I spent a few minutes bringing Jessie up to date about Vonda's absence from work and was not surprised at her response.

"Julie, we're hardly scraping by as it is. How are we going to manage? By the way, I overheard you and Cynthia joking about Jeff, calling him *The Reluctant Banker,* and I love it. He needs to get his rear end back here and go to work. Don't know what in the world his mother is thinking, letting him get away with this. Sorry, Julie, you know I always speak my mind when I should be silent."

I laughed. Jessie always had the knack of bringing good honest humor to any situation.

"Don't apologize, everything you said is the truth. Anyway, back to Vonda. She's sending in a friend today, a woman by the name of Leslie Phelps that recently retired from the First State Bank in Tyler. I hope she's willing to work because we can't keep on running this bank with so few employees."

Something about bank policy had been worrying me. I was the newest hire and the youngest of the staff, but I was the only employee appointed to management level. I had graciously accepted the promotion, but I was also aware that others had been passed over in my favor. To their credit, no one seemed to hold this against me and seemingly, we all enjoyed a very good working relationship.

"Jessie, when Jeff Watson returns, I'm going to tell him that you need a promotion. You do the work of a manager and I think he needs to promote you to Vice-President. This exclusion of everyone except family members and refusing to promote from within has got to stop. I really don't have a clue why Clarke promoted me."

I looked up to see Jessie vigorously shaking her head!

"I don't want a promotion. Clarke approached me but I told

him flat out that I wasn't interested. He didn't much care for Vonda so he overlooked her and went to you."

"Oh no, I never dreamed that was the case. Why did he do that?"

"I think he just never accepted Vonda's talent and her work ethic. He couldn't look beyond her background and appearance to see that she's a good worker."

"Why weren't you interested, Jessie? You're so good at your job."

"Julie, I can't deal with any pressure. I know you think I've got this cool, together personality, but inside I'm a bundle of nerves in any new situation. Besides that, I'm retiring in thirteen months and eight days and too many hours. I found one of those countdown clocks and I keep up with it every day. But thanks for the thought."

"Well, this all comes as a shock to me, but it makes me feel better that he considered you. What do you think about this woman coming in today? Do you know anything about her?"

"I think I remember Vonda mentioned her couple of times, especially when she came back from a banking school. Even though Clarke didn't like her very much, he sent Vonda to several schools and she always did well. You know, I think this Leslie person may work out. I surely hope so."

Leslie Phelps was prompt for the interview and arrived just minutes after the doors opened. She was an impressive woman: tall, a good example of the plus size figure, and a woman so completely comfortable in her own skin that she seemed to welcome the grey in her hair and the age on her face. Her smile was almost electric, brightening her eyes and her expression.

After a brief interview and looking at her resume, I had no problem offering her this position with The Bank of Three Bridges. Thankfully, she readily accepted.

"Julie, I'm so thankful for this opportunity. I made a hasty decision to retire when my husband became ill. But the surgery was successful, and he's doing great. He's back at work full-time and I'm twiddling my thumbs at home. When can I start to work?"

"How about now, at least to get familiar with our routine here? Jessie knows everything there is to know about Three Bridges, both the bank and the town. She'll take care of all your questions. Will that work?"

"I came prepared to work through the morning if you needed me. Vonda and I had a really nice dinner last night and she filled me in on the possibility that she might take a leave of absence, but I don't know the details. I'm hungry for work, so lead me to it!"

*Thank you, Lord, for sending me this remarkable woman.*

The remainder of my day was filled with a number of unremarkable people and commonplace events, just a typical Friday at the bank. Shortly before noon, as promised, Vonda returned from her medical appointments, but didn't comment on the outcome and I hadn't expected any explanations. She would give the bank notice of her plans when the time was appropriate.

I should be working, but I couldn't concentrate. After a while, I couldn't suppress thoughts of Ryan, of what he had told me, and how my life changed because of what my mother had done.

I could stand it no longer. I needed to talk to someone, my older sister Catherine. I knew she was probably still busy at the family practice clinic even on a late Friday afternoon. I couldn't call but I sent an email asking her to call me tonight. I said that I needed to talk about Mother.

The email was sent, but had I done the right thing? Bottom line was this: it really didn't matter. I did what I thought was best at that moment.

# $\mathscr{S}$ixteen

**Denise and Odie had cozied up and enjoyed the other's** companionship from Thursday evening, throughout the long night, and into Friday morning. Each entertained thoughts, briefly, of where this relationship might go, and then shelved those thoughts for the pleasure of the moment.

Denise was rather inexperienced for someone her age. This was actually the most exciting night she had known, ever. And he basked in her obvious enjoyment of his company. It boosted his ego and almost touched his heart. Almost.

It was a very thin line for her to walk and she knew it, but that sense of danger merely challenged her to proceed. She'd never had a boyfriend or even a casual romance, and now that this was happening, she wasn't going to push him away, no matter the cost.

She needed this job. She liked working for Maddie and knew that she was walking a very fine line with Odie, but like many other women, she was flattered by the attention of this man. This man who had been much more than a friend to her employer.

Miss Maddie rang for her breakfast around nine-thirty. Denise took a deep breath and focused on being professional, but she was uncomfortable in the presence of her employer. It was difficult to make eye contact when she entered the third floor master suite.

Maddie Wallace was also uncomfortable, but she had an advantage over Denise. She'd played this game before. More than once. She had often been privy to the fact that R.J. had not always honored his wedding vows, and more than once Maddie was forced to be nice to a woman who knew her husband on a more intimate basis. But, she had learned to play the game.

The marriage of Maddie and R.J. Wallace was an entanglement of rules, understandings, and business. The business part of marriage required that she ignore his wayward behavior. She felt no such allegiance to Odie Marshall at all. She did, however, feel sympathy for Denise.

The woman would never be described as beautiful, or charming, and her only skill was in the kitchen. Maddie's only skill had been financial, and like Denise, she had neither beauty nor charm as a young woman.

❧❦

For a time Odie Marshall had been able to block out everything but this liaison with Denise. Those hours allowed him to relax and forget his duties, but this was an important weekend and he couldn't hide forever. As chairman of the Blueberry Festival, he should have been in town, taking care of last-minute details.

He should have spent time taking care of those obligations, but the winds of change had recently blown into his mind like a Texas Norther and made him forget all about those pesky obligations. New ideas and other plans demanded his attention.

But, eventually, he finally powered up his cell phone, and reality reached out and grabbed him by the throat. It was time to go back to Three Bridges. Cynthia Bickers was on the warpath, and Odie was in her sights. He could feel the rage rising in his throat like last night's bad casserole as he listened to the message.

"Odie, if you're not in my office by three o'clock this

afternoon I'm going to send the sheriff after you. I know where you are. I'm not doing your job anymore, I have my own work to take care of. Work that I get paid to do."

He didn't believe that Cynthia knew where he was, but she might. He did know, very well, that she would follow through on her angry words. There was neither respect nor friendship between these two.

He had little choice. He had to check in at the festival, but he was very reluctant to leave Denise. There was an unusual sense of comfort being with her, a comfort that he wouldn't want to become accustomed to.

The night had been very satisfying on many levels but this was never going to be anything but a relationship of convenience to him. Denise didn't matter and could never matter to him. No, he wouldn't allow that to happen.

The security camera tracked Odie as he left Denise's suite, spun his tires reversing from the garage and raced toward the gates. Impatient, he sped between the partially opened gates, barely missing the expensive wrought iron creation.

Maddie Wallace watched with dichotomous emotions. Two years ago, during a particularly challenging time, she had been flattered by the unlikely interest of Odie Marshall. A few harmless dinners, a weekend trip to New York, and a wild Mardi Gras week in New Orleans had changed the companionable relationship into something that now caused her extreme emotional pain. She couldn't wait any longer to talk to Judge.

"Rosalie, this is Maddie Wallace. Tell Judge that I'm on my way into town. I'll be there in a few minutes." They had no appointment, but she had to know. Had Judge completed her will?

Odie drove into Three Bridges in a tizzy of anger and Cynthia Bickers was the target. He was driving much too fast on Main Street, but he knew no one would stop him. Cletus Stamper was much too busy doing whatever it was that Cletus did, and it was seldom the business of the town.

When he reached the edge of town, he whirled into a parking slot in front of Cynthia's office and slammed on the brakes. His truck came to a full stop when he hit the curb. Another thing to raise his anger, but he slammed out of the truck, attempting to gain control.

Three steps took him to the offices for the town of Three Bridges. Another three or four steps and he was facing Cynthia Bickers, Deputy Mayor, and Town Clerk.

On the twenty mile drive into Three Bridges, Odie had tried to cage his anger. He wanted to handle Cynthia in a cool and controlled manner, but as he neared his destination, the anger returned and the words erupted tersely through gritted teeth.

"Never again, do you hear me? Don't ever call me and tell me what to do. I don't work for you and you have no authority to order me around. Got that?"

He turned and walked from her office with the same speed and anger that propelled him through the front door. Feeling the need to reinforce his authority, Odie paused with one hand on the opened door.

"Make certain that your duties are carried out tomorrow. You have many things to take care of early in the day. Make sure that those things are done correctly. I don't have time to clean up any messes you make."

If he'd stayed near the building, Odie Marshall would have become even angrier. Instead of being intimidated by his show of authority, Cynthia Bickers was laughing. She was laughing very, very loudly.

The founders of Three Bridges used very little imagination

and even less planning as the town expanded and grew. Main Street crossed the small creek that some liked to call a river and continued northeast, connecting to the state highway that eventually connected to the interstate.

The first few blocks on the north side of Main Street had never developed, leaving a vast expanse of open land. The current residents weren't certain why, but this area was used each year for the Blueberry Festival, and in certain years when a traveling carnival came into town.

To cool his anger, Odie toured the festival grounds. He stopped beneath the blue and white banner that was strung at the grounds entrance. **Welcome to Three Bridges Annual Blueberry Festival.**

The committee members had done the work, but perhaps it would be best to be seen taking charge of things. After all, he was the festival chairman.

From one vendor booth to another, Odie made the rounds. He checked to see if all the electrical connections were done according to code. He talked to the guys unloading the portable toilets and then made them move everything fifty feet to the north. He walked from one end of the festival grounds and back again, checking vendor locations against his master list, taking care of business, just as any good festival manager would do.

Before he left the grounds, he called all the vendors together and had them gather in a circle around him as he stood on an overturned bucket. He liked the feeling of being in control, of being above everyone else. His anger subsided as his ego inflated and he spoke to the group, encouraging them to ask for whatever items they needed. "Remember, we're here to help."


Feeling as if he'd handled his civic duty with exceptional skill, Odie Marshall stepped off his improvised podium and left the area, with his mind already on another problem—The Flower Box.

⌘⌘

Judge was more than a little put out with Maddie Wallace. She was rushing him. The will was almost done, but he needed to review it once more.

"Rosalie, when Maddie gets here, I want you to keep her occupied, do whatever it takes. I need to go over this document one more time before I can show it to her. It has to be right. Make the woman some tea and get her talking about Europe. That should take a few hours."

He closed his study door firmly and immersed his well-seasoned legal brain in the task at hand. He read, revised, and researched until he was completely satisfied that he had done the very best with the information he had been given.

He silently prayed as he walked to the door and yelled toward the kitchen. *Dear Lord, let this be a thorough and sound document.*

"Rosalie, bring Maddie in here and let's go over this will. And bring me a cup of coffee, I won't get any sleep tonight anyway."

Two hours later, Maddie Wallace left, satisfied that Judge had drawn a will that would meet all her requirements.

Instead of turning left to go back to her home, Maddie took a right and drove toward the river and toward the festival grounds. The banner was cheerful and welcoming, and people were milling around tending to last-minute details. She drove on past the grounds, crossed the bridge, and turned around, carefully. She retraced her path and was planning to go straight home.

Her Mercedes was nearing the entrance, when suddenly a black pickup sped out of the entrance. Just in time she brought the car to a screeching stop. As the truck pulled into her lane, she could see that a car in the other lane was forced into the ditch to avoid hitting the truck.

Odie Marshall had driven onto Main Street between two oncoming cars, and had almost caused an accident. How could he drive away as if nothing had happened? He could have killed someone.

❦❦

"What just happened? Where did those cars come from? Straight out of the blue?" He took a quick look in the rearview mirror and shook his head. He took another look in the rear view mirror and felt anger rise again.

"What's that old fool doing out here? Is she looking for me? Well, she almost found me." Odie hit the steering wheel with his right hand and laughed. The sound was strange, almost maniacal, even to his ears, but still he raged.

"Crazy old coot. Just wait until I go back out there. I'll give that old bag of bones a piece of my mind. Dang fool almost got me killed."

❦❦

Maddie was too nervous to drive much further, so she made a second impulsive decision. She steered her Mercedes into the parking lot of City Café and went inside. She ordered supper but was oblivious to the people around her. Her mind was flitting from one thought to another. One thing she knew for certain, she wasn't ready to go home and face Denise. And another thing—this chicken fried steak was delicious.

❦❦

Jessie and I closed the bank without incident, and I went home as fast as my car could take me. I was tired from the happenings of the week and wanted to relax. I made very quick work of scrounging up some dog food for Goldie and giving her fresh water before I locked the back door and headed for my bedroom.

I stepped out of my shoes as I went down the hall and continued to shed my clothing as I walked. In the closet, I either rehung my clothes or tossed them into the clothes hamper, then

107

grabbed a robe. I headed for the bathroom and a long hot shower. As the water coursed over me, I imagined that the cares and burdens of the last twenty-four hours were washing down the drain.

Dressed in shorts and a well-worn tee shirt, with a towel around my damp hair, I was scrounging for food in the kitchen. Some fruit and Ritz crackers was good enough supper. After the third bite of apple I finally realized that I had missed the all-you-can-eat catfish at the City Cafe. Well, another day.

# $\mathcal{S}$eventeen

**Since I'd missed eating supper with my friends, I puttered** around the house, watering the ferns hanging along the deep porch. I ventured out to the flower beds that surrounded the porch, plucking a few courageous weeds fighting for growing space between the petunias, marigolds, and begonias planted in huge pots beside the entrance to the porch. Then I pushed up to the third step and sat down, thinking.

My thoughts were running a race with my anxiety. Maybe I shouldn't have called Catherine. Maybe I won't tell her what Ryan said, maybe this, maybe that. I finally decided that if I were going to be beaten to death by words, that word would definitely be bolder than that wimpy word *maybe*.

I came inside as the light began to fade, thinking of going to bed early tonight. Didn't happen. About nine o'clock, the sound of footsteps hitting the wooden steps leading to the kitchen was accented by cries of "Julie, open up, Julie."

Odie drove away from the scene of the near collisions, still ranting about Maddie Wallace. She was getting paranoid. Was she actually following him? Another thing to take care of and he would, very soon.

The short distance from the festival grounds to The Flower

Box didn't normally allow a driver to speed, but Odie accomplished that without a problem. Without checking oncoming traffic or the rear view mirror, he made a wild left turn into a parking space near his business. No screeching brakes this time.

It was nearly six o'clock and The Flower Box was still open. What was that woman up to? He tried to control his agitation as he fairly burst through the front door.

"Ms. Rushing, why are you still here? You should have closed the store by now. Just leave everything until later. I have some work to do and don't want to be disturbed."

"Mr. Marshall, since you're here, I need to ask about my paycheck. You missed last week, and I like to get paid."

"I'll leave it for you on the desk. I have other things that need to be done first. Now, please go home and come back next week. Good night."

The woman looked at him with unasked questions, but only picked up her purse and left the store.

He sat at the desk and allowed ideas to form in his mind, but everything was filtered through a dark cloud of confused thoughts and strange emotions. He needed to do something. He needed to get his life under control, but how?

In a corner of the store was a steel safe containing his meager financial records and a few files from his past. Anger grew as he registered the bleakness of his financial state. There was no money. Only this store, his truck, and the clothes on his back. Not much to show for forty-five years of fighting to survive. Things should have been different. Things were supposed to be different by now. Maybe it was time for a change.

He worked for a while, making lists and jotting down ideas, trying to plan his future, but couldn't put his thoughts down on paper. Frustrated, he called Maddie Wallace.

"Hey there, Maddie honey. Haven't seen you in several days. In fact, I haven't seen you since last week. What's going on? Are you okay? Are you avoiding me?"

"I haven't been avoiding you at all, Odie, not until this

afternoon when you pulled out of the festival grounds in front of my car. You could have caused a serious accident. The car in the other lane had to take to the ditch. Where was your mind?"

"Oh Maddie, I had plenty of room. I didn't cause an accident. You old people probably shouldn't be driving."

"You're most likely right. Odie, if you're calling to say that you're coming out, you should make other plans. I'm not feeling very well, and in fact, I'm certain that Denise is feeling the effects of that same bug. I'll talk to you tomorrow after the festival, Odie. Hope everything goes well for you."

*What was going on with Maddie? She must have known that I've been hanging out with Denise. Of course, I shouldn't have expected to put anything past her. She keeps a close watch on that house, like a mother hen with her chicks. That house has always been her first love. No time for me tonight, but you'll see me tomorrow. Yes indeed, Miss Maddie Wallace, you will see me tomorrow.*

It was late, and only a few minutes before City Café closed for the evening, and he was hungry. He walked down to the café and just as he opened the café door, those silly women spilled out onto the sidewalk, pushing him aside and ignoring him. He stood back and watched and listened as they giggled towards the car park, but there were only three. Julie Trahan was missing from the group. He went inside and ordered dinner.

My friends, the ladies of the Three Bridges Social Club, placed the assorted desserts on the kitchen table and I began to set out plates, forks, and offering drinks.

"Julie, you should have gone to supper with us. It was a very interesting evening."

"Why, what happened?"

"First of all, Maddie Wallace was eating an early supper, sitting in the first booth all by herself. No Odie for a change. Something wasn't right about the way she looked. Didn't you think so, Dr. Martha?"

"I don't want to make a professional opinion, but as a casual observation, Maddie didn't look well. She seemed very nervous, and oblivious to everyone, and it's hard to ignore us. I even spoke to her and she didn't hear me. It was strange."

"Yeah, Martha, she looked nervous and rattled to me also. Even an interior designer can figure out that something was going on with her. Poor thing."

We laughed at Marlene, not the situation, but the laughing started a round of silly chatter until suddenly Cynthia remembered something else.

"Julie, the other strange thing was this. As we were leaving the café, Odie was going in. He's another one that doesn't show up there on Friday night, and certainly not alone. If he saw us, he didn't speak."

Finally, Cynthia couldn't resist asking what was on everyone's mind.

"Julie, we've been very polite and haven't probed, but I want to know why you didn't come to City Café tonight?"

Throughout the evening, I had tried to steer the conversational flow away from myself. I didn't want to talk about Ryan. I only wanted to bask in the normalcy of our friendships. Silly me, did I really think that could happen?

"Like everyone says, *where do I begin?* Cynthia, didn't I tell you about those strange calls for Juliana Elizabeth Trahan? Yesterday, I found out who was calling. After all these years, ten years, I got a phone call from Ryan Daigle. He asked me to dinner. He wanted to talk and I guess I wanted some answers, but what he told me was very hard to hear."

I paused and shook my head. This would be a very hard thing to do, to tell my friends what happened so long ago, but I needed to say this just once.

"The truth is, I didn't come to supper because I wouldn't have been good company. Probably like Maddie Wallace, I'd be lost in my own world. You see, I found out that my mother had enticed Ryan Daigle to sleep with her the day before he left Lafayette. As horrible as that is, there is more."

I had to tell the story, I had to say those awful words at least

112

once, and then start the process of healing. I told them as briefly and succinctly as possible because they were my true friends, and they cared.

Even Marlene was crying with me when I finished. And everyone was saying the same thing. "She was your mother. How could she do that to you?"

"He was your fiancé. How could he do that to you?"

When my friends left, I locked up the house, feeling as if I could move on with my life and put Ryan Daigle back into the past where he belonged. Telling the story to my friends had been very therapeutic, but exhausting. I was also tired from a long workday and a sleepless night on Thursday. A most welcomed sleep captured me only moments after I went to bed.

❦❧

Vonda couldn't go to sleep even though it was well past her normal bedtime. All evening she'd thought about her future. She wondered how she would look after the cosmetic surgery. She wondered how looking different would change her life. And she wondered something else. Did she have the nerve, the courage to do it, or would she spend the rest of her life blaming the past?

Dr. Martha said the procedure would be somewhat simple, and when healed, Vonda would have a beautifully symmetrical appearance, and look younger. Although that wasn't her prime objective, erasing the years from her face might give her a chance for a future. If she could finally come to terms with her past.

A shameful teenage pregnancy had condemned her mother to a life of hard work in the family business, even after the father of the child took the baby to be raised as his own. The shame never left, even though Vonda was born later after a marriage to a poor and unfortunate young man who died much too soon. Throughout all these trials, Vonda's mother never turned bitter.

Instead, she turned to God's Word, but she walled herself away from everyone.

*Oh, Mother, how did you live in this town after all you went through? Where did you get your strength? Why didn't you remarry after Dad died? I remember that you were still very pretty even though you were worn down with work and worry.*

She reached over and picked up her mother's Bible. She began to read and understand and she continued to read—and read until she found the solace she desired.

The verse was simple and easy to understand, and it was all Vonda needed to see.

*Come unto me . . . and I will give you rest.*

"Jesus, can you give me rest? My heart is so weary. How can I take your yoke? What does that mean? Yes, Jesus, I do want to learn of you. Maybe I won't feel so alone if I learn of you. My mother knew you, and I want to know you also."

# &ighteen

**My eyes opened slowly and I did that mental calendar** checklist thing, with my sleep befuddled brain attempting to sort out if this was a workday or the weekend. Finally, I concluded that this is Saturday, the second Saturday in July.

The Annual Blueberry Festival has been held on the second Saturday in July since its beginning, and today I can breathe a sigh of relief and enjoy the day. I've always participated at the festival and worked at whatever chores Odie Marshall assigned me, but not today. This year I will have no responsibilities at the festival, other than a personal one as I wander through the throngs of people at the festival and look for a special piece of pottery. I'm not a collector, exactly, but close. I have a few hand-thrown ceramic pieces, and usually I look for something unique in color, shape, and size. Sometimes I find it, and sometimes I don't.

I turned over for a few more minutes of sleep, but my mind kicked in gear and pushed me from the bed—my mind filled with questions. I checked my cell phone for messages. I also checked the landline phone, and other than a series of hang-ups with no messages at all, there was nothing. Could that have been Ryan trying to apologize again?

I shoved those unwelcome thoughts aside and went to the

study and logged on to my email account. Finally, I found a response from my sister.

*"Hey sis, sorry, but I won't be able to call until next week sometime. I've taken a few days off and am traveling with friends. Should be back in town by Wednesday. Give you a call then. Just so you don't get any ideas, I'm with a group of young doctors, their wives, and a few nurses on a camping trip. Perhaps I've lost my mind. This isn't what I would normally do for fun, but when the opportunity came up, I grabbed at it. Camping in the backwoods gives one plenty of thinking time. Call you next week."*

⤙⤚

"Rev. Peppers, this is Vonda Sue Gunderson. You don't know me, I don't go to church, but I really need to talk to someone today—I need a minister. Last night I read my mother's Bible, and I read about Jesus, and how he could give me rest. Rev. Peppers, I want to understand what that means. Could I see you this morning?"

"Absolutely, Vonda, I'll be at the church for a while this morning. Can you come over now? And Vonda, I do know you from the bank, but the important thing is this. God already knows and loves you."

She wasted no time, but dressed hurriedly and drove the short distance to the church. The sign in front of the church caught her eye.

### Community Baptist Church, Rev. Roger C. Peppers, Pastor

The white plywood sign was secured between squarely made red brick posts and topped with weathered brass coach lanterns. It was fresh looking, as if newly painted. Under the pastor's name, a succinct directory of church services was displayed in clear lettering.

She read the words and felt a tremor of anticipation. This was a big step, if she followed through, her life would be different. Was she ready for this change? Yes, she wanted to put her past sins to rest. She parked and entered a door that said, *Welcome, Church Office.*

"Hi Millie, I didn't know you worked on Saturdays. I called and asked to speak to Rev. Peppers, is he in?"

"He'll be right with you, Vonda. He stepped over to talk to the worship leader and asked me to offer you a cup of coffee, so how about having one with me?"

Vonda didn't really want coffee, but she was nervous, and maybe having a cup of coffee to hold in her hand would even out her nervous anxiety. She reached out and took the offered cup.

"You're right, I don't normally work on Saturday, but we are trying to get ready for Bible school next week. It's a little later this year, and we're running behind. I'll be here most of the day, getting everything organized."

"I don't want to be a problem. Maybe I should come back another time."

"Vonda, Roger Peppers is the best pastor I've ever known, but he's still a man. He would rather be talking than working any day, but don't repeat those words. Go on into his office, he'll be right in. Take your coffee with you and y'all have a great visit. If you keep him busy long enough I might get out of here before lunch."

Laughing at her own humor, Millie motioned Vonda towards the pastor's office just as Roger Peppers came down the hall.

"Vonda, good morning, I see you've got a good mug of coffee."

She looked up as the man entered the room, and really looked at him for the first time. She'd seen him around town and in the bank. In fact, she'd waited on him several times through the years, but had really never *seen* him.

He was probably mid-fifties, and his curling red hair was showing a little grey around the temples, giving a dignified maturity to a face that could claim openness and honesty instead of handsome features.

"Thank you for seeing me this morning, Rev. Peppers. Probably, I should have waited until another time, but last night when I read the Bible, in Matthew, those words about peace called out to me. I don't know that I've ever known peace. But I've done such horrible things in my life that I doubt God has a place for me."

"Vonda, God has a place for everyone, and he welcomes everyone who will ask to be forgiven of their sins. Jesus gave his life to pay for all our sins."

Roger Peppers paused long enough for her to allow those words to permeate into her mind and heart before he spoke again.

"Vonda, I have nothing to do for about two hours, and I would like to hear your story. Then I will tell you how Jesus can and will give you peace."

Neither watched the clock as she talked and he listened. Her heart had been hidden from the world as surely as her mother had escaped from the world behind the wall of trees and shrubs that surrounded her little house. Telling the story was slow and arduous at first, but soon nothing was held back. Nothing at all. Every remembered sin and shame was laid on the table, and before she stopped talking, she even told about visiting Dr. Martha to discuss having reconstructive facial surgery.

"Vonda, that's a very brave step toward a good future. But think about this: Dr. Martha can give you a new face, but God can give you a new heart, transformed by his love into a pure and beautiful thing. Will you pray with me that God will forgive your sins?"

Without being asked, she fell to her knees before his desk. He left his chair to kneel beside her. He led her through the sinner's prayer and welcomed her into God's family when she asked forgiveness of her sins.

He helped her stand, and they both sank into their chairs, emotionally drained. This woman had touched his heart as a pastor, but also on a very human level. He had not been this aware of another's pain in many years. He walked with her to the office door, and smiled at her as she gathered her oversized purse.

"Vonda, I am thrilled that you gave me the pleasure of

telling you about God's love, and I welcome you as my sister in Christ. I hope to see you in service tomorrow morning. Have a wonderful afternoon."

Vonda walked out of the church with a smile and a small handful of Sunday school books and devotionals that would reinforce the things discussed this morning. The transformation that started during the long night of Bible reading, soul searching, and praying had ended in inexplicable joy this morning when she asked Jesus into her heart.

*A new person in Christ.* What a beautiful thought. It was joyful but a little frightening to become a new person, but she would do as Rev. Peppers asked. She would read and study the Bible and take God's Word into the depths of her heart and then measure the world against those words.

One thing was certain, she needed to make some serious changes in her life, and most of these changes involved Odie Marshall and their off again-on again relationship. She'd always known that this relationship was wrong—incredibly wrong on every level. And now by the grace of God, she had the emotional strength and courage to end it.

Sooner or later, Odie would most likely stop by her house. He always did. With that in mind, it was easy to leave this matter until the festival was over. When his duties at the Blueberry Festival were finished, she would have his full attention.

Two blocks west of The Bank of Three Bridges, the undeveloped parcel of land was designated as the festival grounds. The land was separated into parking and festival space. I found a spot near the back of the lot and trudged up the graveled lane to the colorful venders' area. I walked from booth to booth, looking at the wares, closely examining several pieces that vied for my attention, but nothing spoke to me. Nothing said, *"Take me home,"* so I kept looking.

"Hi, Julie. Hey, Julie. Hey, Miss Trahan." Those words of

greetings reached out to me as I walked. Even though I met many people, bank customers, church friends, and casual acquaintances, I didn't run into my co-workers or my close friends. Must have been bad timing on my part, but a good time to shop.

As always, the last place you look is where you find *it*. I found my newest treasure at one of the new and smaller booths displaying a collection of handmade pottery. From the top shelf, a simply styled pitcher was calling to me. The pitcher was glazed in shades of blues and browns with just a hint of burgundy blended through the glaze. It was beautifully crafted and larger than any in my collection. Of course, it was also very expensive.

I thought of all the hours I worked just last week, and what I knew would be facing me next week. I decided that honest work deserved a commensurate reward. My newly purchased pitcher and I went home to cool off, rest, and scrounge for something to eat.

⭜⭝

Odie was very, very busy glad-handing at the festival, making his presence known and at the same time, plotting his strategy for a break with this town. The details were still fuzzy in his mind. How was he going to leave without Maddie Wallace? What to do about Vonda?

He was also having second thoughts about his business. Was he certain that he was ready to shut it down? Could he just lock it up and walk away? What was left for him at The Flower Box? Nothing but silly women wanting his time and talent for the cheapest dollar. Yes, he was tired of The Flower Box, Vonda Gunderson, and Three Bridges. If he thought about it, he was probably tired of Maddie Wallace. It was time to move on.

With a smiling face, he visited from booth to booth, greeting those he knew and meeting new people. He was passing time, pretending to be a part of the Blueberry Festival, but all the while, his mind was formulating his plan of action.

# 𝒩ineteen

**Maddie had spent the most of the night thinking about** Odie, but nothing was solved. No plan came to her mind and when daybreak came, the problem was still with her. What should she do? She had never been afraid of Odie, but these past few weeks, something had changed. He acted differently; his actions were strange and unreasonable. More than once, his temper had flared over unimportant things.

She would find a way of dealing with that later, but before she tackled that problem, there was something she neglected to do yesterday.

"Good morning, Judge. How are you today?"

"I'm fine, Maddie. How are you? Do you have any questions about that will you rushed me to complete? Did you find any errors? If you did, it's because you pushed me like a mad bull to get it finished."

"No, Judge, you didn't make any errors. None at all that I could see. I'm calling because I didn't thank you properly, and I didn't even offer to pay you for writing the will. Do you want me to stop by today and pay you?"

"No, Maddie, that's fine. If anything happens to you before you send me a check, I'll just take out my fee before I start dispersing your assets. But that won't happen. Have a good weekend and stop by sometime on Wednesday and we can have a cup of tea and settle the account."

She smiled at Judge's brash attempt at humor, but also thought that sharing a pot of tea would be a very pleasant experience. Perhaps they could do just that, next week.

There was another thorny problem that must be handled now, before anything else happened. Denise had fallen under Odie's spell as so many other women had done. This had not escaped Maddie and now, there was only one course for her to take.

"Denise, would you come to the library, please?"

❦❧

From time to time during the festival, Odie stopped to call Denise on the direct line to her suite of rooms and each call was sent directly to voice mail. His anger was escalating and by the third call, he was also a little concerned. He knew women, and Denise was wrapped around his little finger. She would never ignore a call from him. She was supposed to be there, they had made plans. Or rather, she had agreed to the plans he'd made.

After the next unanswered phone call, he was filled with raging anger. Anger at Denise, Maddie Wallace, and most of all, Vonda Sue Gunderson. Since the beginning, his association with Vonda had been a love-hate relationship on his part.

They were just out of high school when they first started dating, and he was never proud to be seen with her. She was smart, and charming, but far from pretty. In his mind, it would be charitable to call her plain. But for the most part, it was a relationship that worked if he didn't think too much about it. And if she didn't try to turn the situation into something more permanent.

That had happened more than once through the years, especially after he returned to Three Bridges. Vonda wanted much more from the relationship than he was willing to give. Memories kept gnawing at him, and he decided that those strange love-hate feelings for her had gone on long enough. It was time to take action—time to do something about Vonda.

Up one aisle of vendors and back through another, Odie

walked through the festival grounds, pretending to be the man in charge, but only thinking about his personal life. He continued to greet people as he walked the grounds. A few more backs were slapped and a few more ladies were kissed on the cheek and then, he was on the edge of the festival grounds.

The weather was hot, he was uncomfortable and glad to leave the festival grounds. Sweat was pouring down his back, being absorbed by the black cotton tee shirt that was part of his everyday uniform. He wiped the perspiration from his face as he neared his truck.

The sun-baked metal burned his fingers when he unlocked the truck door and sat cautiously on the hot black leather seats. He started the engine. One hand reached out to redirect the A/C vent and the other wiped the sweat from his forehead. He headed out, but doubted that the vehicle would cool very much before he reached his destination.

The truck was still uncomfortably hot when he parked a few blocks over in the rear of that little house on Honey Grove Street. Vonda Sue Gunderson was going to get what was coming to her.

To stoke up that anger burning inside his head, he deliberately replayed conversations from years past in his mind. *"Let's get married, Odie, I don't want to live like this anymore. Why can't we get married? You stay here most of the time, anyway. Why can't we get married?"*

Didn't that stupid, moronic woman know that Odie Marshall would never marry anyone without money and a pretty face?

Boiling anger filtered through his blood as he strode the distance to the house in only a few steps. Each advancing step was fueled by pent-up rage and frustration that had consumed him ever since Maddie Wallace closed down the money pipeline. He opened the kitchen door knowing that finally the rampant anger would find release.

She was on her knees in front of the refrigerator, cleaning out the crisper when she heard the back door open. Before she could even get to her feet, Odie Marshall was behind her, dragging her to her feet. He was more than angry, he looked possessed.

"What are you doing down on your knees, scrabbling around in that pathetic refrigerator. Get up when I come in. Don't you have any manners? Get up!"

She tried to pull away from him as he yanked her upright and pushed her against the kitchen counter. She had witnessed his anger before, but it had never been aimed at her. He was still holding her upper arms in a tight grip and his facial expression seemed to become more enraged with every second of time that passed.

"Odie, maybe you should just leave. You're angry, and I really don't like being with you when you're so angry. Maybe you can come back later and we can talk then. There is something I have to say to you, but not now."

For the first time ever, he slapped her across the face. The blow landed squarely on her right cheek and her jaw ached. Surely the teeth were jarred loose. She reached up to put her hand to the bruise but he grabbed her arm again and pushed her into the cabinets on the opposite side of the kitchen.

"You don't want to talk now? I thought you wanted to talk, Vonda. Isn't that what you want? Well, this is how I am going to talk today."

Again, he hit her. Uncontrolled fury directed hands and feet as he slapped and kicked and then drew back with a fisted hand that connected with her stomach. She dropped to the floor, barely conscious.

Vonda had fought as well as she could against him and he was winded from this physical onslaught. He took great gasping breaths and walked around the room. Curses gushed from his mouth but it did little to ease his rage.

Odie Marshall hadn't planned exactly how he was going to "deal" with Vonda, but for days, the pounding in his head followed the tempo of his angry thoughts. When he saw Vonda on her knees, doing the same work his mother had done for so many other women, anger and frustration found its target, but did little to erase the shame his mother had brought to his overly prideful young mind. He took one final unfeeling look at Vonda, still unmoving on the kitchen floor in an ever-expanding pool of blood.

She was badly hurt, but still alive. Her chest was moving with shallow breaths. That might be a problem but he couldn't be concerned about that now. For now, he needed to get out to Maddie Wallace's place because there were other things to take care of there.

He raised a booted foot that landed with a thud and pushed Vonda across the room. He left the cottage without fear of being seen. The neglected overgrown shrubbery was the perfect privacy screen.

Tearfully, Denise Hougan cleared out her personal belongings, not really packing but stuffing her accumulation of personal effects into plastic grocery bags, trash bags, anything that would hold them.

She'd been fired before, not often, but once or twice. It was difficult to find a job as a personal chef, and this had been the best she could ever hope for. Miss Maddie was eccentric, even weird at times, with the elaborate details and rigid timetables one had to follow. She had learned to accept the rules because the pay was excellent, the work easy, and the secluded location satisfied her.

She tugged the bags of clothes out to her car and was stashing them in the car trunk so lost in her thoughts that she didn't hear him arrive. Why was he here? Surely he couldn't really care anything about her. After all, she was older, rather plump, and definitely plain. But he had been interested, their time together had been special, and she welcomed his advances and passionately returned his attentions.

Odie jumped out of his truck and hurried forward with a frown on his face.

"What's going on, Denise? Are you leaving? What's happened?"

She took one look at the questioning expression and mistook it as concern for her personal welfare and the floodgates of tears opened once more.

"Miss Maddie fired me, Odie. She fired me because you and I have *formed an unhealthy relationship*'. Not only did she fire me, she unplugged the phones in my quarters and locked me out of the rest of the house. I'm supposed to leave here before three o'clock this afternoon."

One glance at her watch had her shaking her head. "Didn't make that deadline. Wonder if she'll fire me again?"

Odie reached out and hugged Denise, holding her close and giving her at least a sense of support, a feeling that someone cared.

"Come on back in, Denise. We need to work out what you're going to do, what you and I are going to do."

She followed him back into her former quarters, and waited for him to tell her how she was going to manage this disappointment.

"Denise, I've got big plans, but there are two or three things I have to take care of today. I'll need to go back to Three Bridges and see about the festival, but after that, you and I are going to leave this miserable place and go west. Didn't you tell me that you have a cottage in New Mexico?"

"Yes, it belonged to my family, but Dad gave it to me a few years ago. Sometimes I rent it out, but it's empty now."

"Great, maybe we can spend a few cozy weeks getting better acquainted, okay? I understand why Maddie fired you; she's jealous. We'll go away together, but we'll need to leave in separate cars. You go on to Tyler, get a hotel room, and I'll be in late tonight. Will you do a few errands for me?"

He gave a long and detailed list of things she should do, things that popped into his head as he talked. Nothing had been preplanned except to get away, and he wanted Denise out of the way for a few hours. He thought of one last thing for her to do, something that would surely keep her busy for a while.

"Next, I want you to go to Macy's or Dillard's and buy a new wardrobe, everything from the skin out. Here's my credit card, use this. When you finish shopping, go back to the hotel, and give me a call around nine or so."

He stood up, pulled her to her feet, and wrapped his arms around her. She wasn't the sort of woman that had attracted him in the past, and he was surprised by his feelings. For whatever reason, Denise held some strange appeal. Perhaps it was her trust in him that gave him an unknown sense of comfort.

"Gotta go, hon. I've got things to wind up at the festival and some things to take care of here. When I hear from you we'll put the final touches on our plans."

# $\mathcal{T}$wenty

**"Hello, Odie, I've been expecting you. What took you so** long to get out here? Come into the living room, you and I need to talk." Maddie sounded very welcoming, the perfect hostess, sure and in control of things. This wasn't what he had expected, but no problem. He could always handle Maddie Wallace. Always.

"I'm here now, Maddie. What's up?"

"Odie, I have behaved foolishly lately and done several things that I shouldn't have done. Even so, you have behaved much worse. You used a hurting old woman to satisfy your greed. You took my affections and walked all over me. But that's over. You will not manipulate me any longer and you will no longer have free range at this house."

She had been sitting in a very expensive wingback chair near the fireplace. He knew it was expensive; he had chosen it carefully for this room. He knew to the penny how much the chair had cost and how much profit he had made from selling it to her. He shoved those thoughts away and began to analyze Maddie and the words she had spoken.

He had never seen her so . . . so firm and commanding. Unable to think of any answers to her words, he watched as she pushed herself out of the chair and walked to where he was standing just inside the living room door.

"I know about all the money you have taken from my

accounts, and I've put a stop to that as I'm certain you know by now. I've also fired Denise and told her to leave. She was a good and innocent woman and deserves better than you can give. You shouldn't go around using women like you've done all your life. It's time for you to grow up and become the man your mother thought you could be."

Those words worked swiftly and surely to stoke the anger that had taken residence in his soul. He took a step toward her, but she raised her hand as if to ward him off.

"I don't know if you have any personal possessions in my house, but next week, I'll have the housekeeper sort through everything and package up whatever belongs to you. I want you to leave and not come back."

He took a deep breath and tried to calm his nerves. He didn't want to give her control over this situation—he wasn't ready to end things just yet.

"Now, now Maddie, don't get all riled up. We've been a good team for almost three years. Why spoil a good thing?" He walked toward her, arms extended, and tried to embrace her, but she pushed him away.

That was it, the final straw. Hysterical rage exploded in his core, bringing memories of endless days of catering to this old woman. For the last few years, he'd had no real life to call his own. He'd been at her continuous beck and call, whenever she wanted an escort for a special event or only someone to occupy her time.

He remembered the affectionate pats that she loved to bestow on him, placing her hands on any part of his body, and always demanding some show of affection from him, particularly if they were in public. He thought of these things and evil wrath filled the air he breathed.

Still, he walked toward her, arms extended and a phony smile frozen in place; his face felt strange from the effort. He reached her, and instead of a hug, he struck out in a rage, hitting her, once, twice, and then again. Her head took the brunt of his last strike, and he heard a snapping sound as she fell to the floor.

For a moment, he watched her crumple to the floor and then he lowered to a squatting position beside her. He tentatively reached toward Miss Maddie Wallace, touched her arm, and then shook her gently as he called to her.

"Miss Maddie, wake up."

He shook her again and watched in fear as her head rolled to the side. Her sightless eyes stared vacantly toward the ceiling. In an instant he knew she was dead. He must have killed her with that last hit. Had he broken her neck? He fell to his knees with his face in his hands and began to wail silently, like someone in the throes of extreme grief, or extreme panic.

He couldn't stop shaking, his throat constricted, and he was gasping for air. He had never even seen a dead body up close, at least one that was not already in a casket, prepared for burial. Miss Maddie was dead and he had killed her.

He only wanted to get even, he hadn't meant to kill her. What was he going to do? He had to get out of here, away from that dead woman lying in Maddie's house. He needed to think. He had to figure out a way to fix this mess.

He ran through the house and into the garage. Denise must have left, because Maddie's expensive car was the only one in the garage. He jumped into his truck and left the estate as fast as he could.

When he got to the intersection 470 and the highway, he turned to the right instead of turning left to go into town, and drove a few miles up the road to a small roadside café. He went in and ordered coffee and a burger, but the twangy sounds of country music played havoc with his nerves and the cutesy waitress didn't get his attention, either.

"Hey, honey bunch, don't like our coffee? Need anything else? I might can find something that would interest you, if you know what I mean?"

"Not today, sweet thing, not today. I've got something to take care of, something that won't wait."

⧉⧉

He went back to Miss Maddie's house, but avoided the living room. He didn't want to see that old woman lying still and lifeless on her prized oriental rug. He had to do something. He walked around, picking up accessories they had purchased in the day trips around the area. She was old and never pretty, but she had been so rich that he could overlook a lot.

And then things changed. Why had he become so unhinged? He didn't mean it to happen but it did. He had to do something and he couldn't put it off any longer. Like it or not, he had to go back to the living room. A sound—half giggle, half sob— escaped from Odie as the thought of *"returning to the scene of the crime"* flashed through his brain.

Well, he couldn't just leave her here. What could he do with her? Nervously he walked around the room, straightening pieces of furniture that had fallen or been shoved askew during the brief altercation, and then stopped. What could he do with Maddie? Should he just leave her here? No, that wouldn't work. There must be some place.

The storm shelter—he could put Maddie in the storm shelter and no one would ever find her. Yes, that would work.

He grabbed the key that hung by the back door—close at hand in case a tornado was reported—and walked swiftly to the shelter, only a few short steps past that monstrous structure—a fake oil derrick that R.J. put up just the year before he died.

He walked slowly and deliberately, searching in every direction as he moved toward the storm shelter. No one should be about, but who could tell. Miss Maddie's farm was some distance out of town, on a narrow, lightly traveled road. The house was barely visible by a passing car, but you could never tell when someone might trespass. He couldn't make any mistakes now, he had to be careful.

The slanted door rose only a few feet from the ground, and he had to kneel down to open the hasp lock. It was rusty and the key was hard to turn, especially with shaking fingers. A few jiggles more and the key turned. He removed the lock from the hasp, but years of weather must have rusted the metal together as effectively as a weld.

This wouldn't do. Somehow he had to open this lock. He ran back to the garage, into a room that had at one time been R.J.'s tool room. One drawer and then another was pulled out, some of the contents dumped and some not until finally he found a large screwdriver with a long steel blade.

In short order, the hasp was pried open and the door screeched open. He shivered and almost gagged at the damp smell of decay. It was very dark down there, maybe he should get a flashlight.

He walked back into the house and found a set of sheets. He fumbled with still shaking hands until he found the flat sheet, and threw the others aside. At first he thought that he couldn't touch her dead body, but he had to. To save his own life he had to do this, and he wrapped Miss Maddie's body tightly in a fine Egyptian cotton sheet that was not designed to be a shroud.

Once the body was securely wrapped, he took off his belt, wrapped it firmly around her feet and began to pull the body through the house, through the rear door of the kitchen, and finally through the grass covered ground that separated the house from the storm shelter. This time he had remembered to get a flashlight from the kitchen cabinet. Even though the light was meager, it was bright enough to guide his steps into the underground room.

His nerve was leaving him. He wanted to scream, to cry in horror of what had happened, and he wanted to be on his way out of town. He picked up her body, smaller and lighter than he expected and hurled it into the anonymous darkness. Maybe she should have a more respectful resting place, but he no longer cared about anything.

He turned to walk back into the house but stopped. A voice was yelling at him, *Check it out, check it out. Make certain that she is hidden.* So he went into the vile smelling storm shelter and walked to the far corner of this damp and smelly room.

Like so many others scattered about the county, it was built years ago as a refuge from the frequent storms. Well, Hurricane Odie had hit tonight and Maddie was his victim.

She had landed almost in the corner of the small space, and he pulled two wooden boxes that contained heaven knows what in front of her body. He would be safe, she would never be found.

He began to inch backward out of this despicable place. With any luck, he would never have to open this door again. One more glance to where Maddie Wallace lay, and then he climbed the short set of steps to the entrance of the storm shelter.

In the dim light filtering from the garage, he could see marks in the grass where he had drug her body. That wouldn't do. He found a leaf rake in the garage and began to lightly rake the ground in opposite directions, obliterating the path Miss Maddie's body had made.

There was nothing to do now but wait. Yes, he would plan his moves and wait. Not much time had passed before he realized that he had unfinished business in Three Bridges. He left his truck in Maddie's garage and borrowed her Mercedes. It might be a good idea if the car was seen about town.

Denise had driven to Tyler, checked into the Hilton, and tackled the long list of errands Odie had given her to do. Throughout her life, she had always been told that she wasn't overly bright, and believed it. She never spoke openly about things, but still she thought and pondered many things. Now, doubts about Odie were at the top of the list.

Well, she would follow through and take care of the list. She would get the cell phone, stock up on water and snacks and everything on the list. She was afraid not to. Odie had been very stressed lately, and he seemed to be always lost in thought. Thoughts that made him frown.

# $\mathcal{T}$wenty-One

**Consciousness returned. Confused thoughts wandered** through Vonda's mind like white lab rats caught in a maze. From some fog-like state, she realized that she was on the floor of her kitchen, looking up at the stained ceiling as breath-zapping pain coursed through her body.

*Why am I lying on the floor of my kitchen? Is this blood around me? Am I lying in a sticky pool of blood? Why?*

Then she remembered. Odie had been here. He'd charged into the kitchen in a crazy rage. She remembered the kicks from his booted feet and his fists landing in her stomach. She remembered but wished she couldn't.

*I'm hurt, I need to get to a hospital. How can I get out of here? Everything hurts, but I have to try. I have to get out of here.*

She was a bloody mess. Carefully, she touched her face and could feel the blood flowing from her head. She tried to push her hair back and wipe away the blood from her eyes. Odie must have kicked her in the face. Her eye was swelling, but she could still see.

*Odie did this to me. He must have kicked me with his boots, everywhere. Dear God, help me. I've got to get out of here, I've got to go to a hospital. Where's my purse? There, on the cabinet by the back door.*

Determined grunts accompanied each struggle, but she was able to inch forward, toward her purse. Slowly, painfully, she crawled crab-like across the kitchen, at times using every chair, table or wall within her reach.

*I've got to rest a few more minutes, then please, Lord, help me get out of here. What if Odie comes back? Got to reach my purse, find my keys, and get out of here. Odie might come back here and I need to get away—get some help.*

She struggled to an upright position, sitting with her back against the counter. She needed to reach the purse, but that wouldn't work. Her brain was slow, working at half speed, and finally she realized that she could place her left side against the counter and reach over with her right hand and get the purse.

She could have run a marathon and used less energy, but at last the purse was in her lap.

*Keys, should I look for my keys? No, what if I drop them before I get to the car? But at least I can put the purse over my shoulder. I can carry it that way.*

Each simple movement exhausted her and sent her arms and legs raging with pain. Even her lower stomach ached—Odie must have kicked her there also.

She rested, trying to catch her breath and wait for the pain to subside. She waited with unusual calm, waiting until she could inch her way to the car.

She didn't know how much time passed, but it seemed a long while. She couldn't tick off the minutes, but she knew that she was using almost every ounce of her energy. Her lungs labored as each breath was sucked in.

She had to do this, she had to push against the cabinet and brace against a chair pulled from the kitchen table, and finally she could stand. One more step, if she leaned against the wall, she could open the door and get to the car—but the door was kicked open, and she met her attacker face to face.

What was going on? He had expected to find Vonda where he left her, and he expected her to be as dead as Maddie Wallace.

"Vonda, where do you think you're going? Got a heavy

date?"

The sound he made was a cruel imitation of laughter. He released his hold on to the kitchen door and drew back a fisted hand. The blow never connected because she fainted and fell to the floor. But that didn't stop him from landing another kick to her head, hoping to put an end to her life.

"Vonda, you are a bloody mess. If you could see your ugly face, it would make you cringe in disgust. You disgust me. I don't want to touch you, you're such a disgusting bloody mess. Well, Miss Maddie won't mind how you look when you come calling tonight. She won't even see what you look like."

The maniacal laughter continued as he left the room, looking for something—anything—that he could use to cover the blood soaked body. He had to get her out of the house, and he couldn't pick her up with all that blood.

In the bedroom, he vented more anger, trashing and breaking anything he could reach until the rage passed. Then, he yanked a sheet from the bed and returned to the kitchen.

He gritted his teeth in disgust but wrapped her up just as he had Maddie. It took a while, and finally she was stashed away in the trunk of the car. Very soon she would be hidden away to rot alongside Maddie Wallace. What a pair they would make.

He laughed again at the thought of the two women in his life. Hidden from the world and rotting away in a storm shelter would be fitting justice for both of them. Then maybe everything would be all right.

Vonda was aware of movement, jolts and jars to her aching body. She struggled against her restraints with very little success. Fear enveloped her very being, fear so intense that she felt it permeate her core, chilling and intense. That very fear gave her courage to push harder against her restraints, to twist her body as much as she could in the limited space around her. Where was she? Had he thrown her into a closet? No, no, that couldn't be because she was feeling some sort of vibration, and a sound. It sounded like a car motor. It sounded the same way as her car did when she drove at high speed on the highway. Was she in a car? Odie must have put her in the trunk of a car.

*Oh, God, don't let me die in here. Don't let me suffocate. Help me, Lord. Rev. Peppers, I hope you're praying for me. You said you would pray.*

She rested for a brief moment then was at last able to loosen—only slightly—whatever was wrapped around her body. She tried, but she still couldn't get free. She was too tired to struggle anymore, maybe later.

But that chance never happened. The car slowed, and she was thrown against the car frame. They must be turning. Where were they? He was going much slower, and finally the movement of the car stopped and it was quiet.

Was this her final destination? Odie would come for her soon and then what? She would wait. He would open the trunk soon, wouldn't he? He couldn't just leave her in this car trunk, could he?

*God in heaven, protect me, keep me safe.*

Clunk. What was that? Odie must be opening the trunk.

*I have to be ready, I have to try to get free somehow. Oh God, give me strength.*

She endured the pain of being pulled from the vehicle, felt his struggle with the weight of her body, and felt the awful bone-jarring pain as he merely dropped her to the ground. Once again she felt a blow. He must have kicked her in the face.

Her head was spinning but she was still alert, aware of the sounds around her. She heard him walking away and the rustling sounds confirmed what her body already knew. She was lying on a graveled path somewhere. Suddenly, she was again picked up and being carried a short distance.

*This may be my only chance. I've got to try to get away.*

Despite the pain that ravaged her body, Vonda began to struggle and kick and she felt one shoe slide from her foot. She continued kicking her feet with every ounce of energy she had left, trying with all her might to free herself from his grasp.

It didn't work. The more she struggled, the angrier Odie

became, and the stronger his grip. She was being lifted up and then released. She was free of his grasp and falling.

Falling, she was falling, falling, but where? Where had he thrown her? Was she ever going to land? The answer came when her already battered body made contact with the ground. She had only a moment to form a rational thought before she passed out.

*Where am I? Where is this place?*

<hr>

My perfect pottery piece that I bought this afternoon was giving me a bit of trouble. I couldn't decide where to put it. So far, my new pitcher had been in almost every room of the house, and now was back in the kitchen, sitting in the center of my grandmother's oak table. It looked terrific and would look better with some flowers in it. Maybe some roses. Tomorrow morning, maybe I could cut some roses.

My thoughts were interrupted by the telephone.

"Hello."

"Julie, Miss Trahan?"

"Yes, this is Julie Trahan."

"This is Deputy Troy Humble. How are you tonight? Look, Julie, this isn't police business, it's personal. I enjoyed the dinner we had a while back and wondered if you were free one evening next week? Maybe we could see a movie?"

"I'm sorry, Troy, next week is not going to work for me. I'll be working from eight until after six every day, and I wouldn't be very good company. Thanks for asking, anyway. Have a great week."

*What is wrong with me?* I turned down a date with a very handsome man, and I shut the door on another offer. *What is wrong with me?* Thoughts came at me from every direction, most of them were the same thoughts that God and I had discussed so many times.

I really don't like living alone. I want a life shared with a husband and children. Until this week, I assumed that there must be something about me, something lacking in my personality, my appearance, or something. Some solid reason why Ryan walked out on me.

Learning the truth—well, that didn't automatically erase those feelings—it just shoved them over into another category. One that would take a while to process. But Troy Humble would not likely be part of the solution.

I was restless, and Deputy Troy Humble was responsible for most of my apprehension. He wasn't my type, there was no connection, or however you want to say it. I knew there wasn't going to be any future there. It saddened and depressed me that there was no one in my life.

*I want a future, I want to find some godly man that can be my life partner. I want to marry and have children. I want a life.*

I paced, and fussed, and thought, and came to a possible solution. A two-part solution.

I hadn't been to the farm in days, but not being there seemed right. Perhaps it was time to sell Anderson Farms. I thought back to those days before my grandmother died and remembered a conversation that led my life into yet another direction.

*"Julie, when I'm gone, you are going to grieve. No doubt, you'll feel lost and alone. You probably can't count on your mother for comfort, that's just not her way. Don't look for her to see you through this loss.*

*Julie, I think that you're going to need this farm, you're going to need the responsibility and pressure of work. There is little time for grief when faced with the day to day busyness that something like this provides. This farm will be a direct connection to me and through it you will know how much I love and admire you.*

*There is one important thing you must remember. Whatever I leave here in Three Bridges is for you alone. You've given me more love and joy than I ever thought I could know."*

❧❧

Anderson Farms was part one of my two-part solution. The Bank of Three Bridges was part two. This bank had become a great source of worry and stress in my thirty-two-year-old life. When Clarke Watson died, everything changed. Jeff Watson truly was the reluctant banker, and he had foisted his duties off on me. This wasn't working, and I needed to make some changes.

I sat up tall and straightened my shoulders, and then I prayed.

*Dear Father, I know we humans can be impulsive and dumb with our choices, and Lord, I want your wisdom. Lord, what do you think about Julie Trahan resigning as Executive Vice-President of The Bank of Three Bridges?*

With much trepidation, I began to put my plan in place.

❧❧

"Jeff, this is Julie Trahan. I need to speak to you."

"Julie, it's Saturday night. Couldn't this wait until Monday morning? I'm a little busy right now."

"Sorry to interrupt your date night, but this is very important. Jeff, I can't continue to run this bank by myself. There are so many issues that I cannot handle, things that require a higher level of authority than I possess. Unless you can assure me that things will change very quickly, I am offering my resignation tonight."

# $\mathscr{T}$wenty-Two

**The sound of a ringing telephone at half past the crack of** dawn changed my Sunday plans. Who could be calling so early? Must be trouble. No one calls with good news this early. Especially on a Sunday morning.

"Hello."

"Julie, this is Olivia Watson. Jeff called me last night around midnight and told me you wanted to resign from the bank. I know you've been overloaded with work, but will you come to lunch today so that we can talk about this?"

"Lunch, today?"

My brain must still be asleep because this wasn't making sense to me. I thought for a while longer, then tried to be polite. Olivia was not my enemy.

"Thanks for the invitation, but shouldn't I be talking to Jeff? Or will you be assuming a management role at the bank?"

"Julie, I'm ever so hopeful that my banking days are long over. Yes, you should and will be talking to Jeff. In fact, you and I will be talking to Jeff. This has gone on too long. Come to lunch and let's see what we can accomplish."

"Thanks, Olivia. I was planning to go to church, so it'll be around one o'clock before I can get to Tyler."

"Jeff is flying to Tyler-Pounds Airport, and should be here about that time also. Come on in and come hungry. I always cook too much when I have a problem. As you know, Jeff has been a problem for a while now."

᪥

"Good Morning, church. Isn't this a beautiful morning to serve our Lord and Savior?"

Roger Peppers stood at the podium, filled with God's love and more than a tad of curiosity. He'd been looking for Vonda Gunderson all morning. He hadn't seen her in Sunday school, but he was certain that she would be at the regular worship service. He continued to greet the congregation but allowed his eyes to roam over each pew, and she wasn't there.

A praise chorus rang out through the sanctuary and the congregants were mingling and greeting each other, a typical Sunday morning at Community Baptist Church. Roger Peppers left the podium, walked into the congregation, and shook a few hands.

"Morning, Rosalie, where is Judge today?"

"He went to the hill country to have a barbeque lunch with some of his lawyer buddies. I hope that old man has enough sense to eat right and not get his blood sugar out of whack."

"I think he'll watch his diet. After all, he knows you'll be after him when he gets home. When is he coming back?"

"He should be home sometime tonight."

He shook a few more hands, greeted as many of the widowed ladies as possible, and spoke to some of the teens. From the podium, he began to bring the lesson that was on his heart.

"How wonderful is our Savior's love. Today, right here in Three Bridges, hearts are being changed and people are finding a new life in Christ. Do you know him?"

At the close of the sermon, even as he gave the invitation, he still hoped to see Vonda. Where was she? He was so certain that she would be in church today. That uncertainty left him feeling disappointed and confused.

*Dear Father, watch over your child. Keep her in your loving arms. Amen.*

᪥

I pulled my car into the third slot of the garage of Olivia Watson's home. The house that she and Clarke had built when their three kids were young and growing so quickly they needed more space and more bathrooms. It was a lovely home and much too large for just Olivia, but it was home. I knew all this because she had told me when I visited after Clarkes' death.

I walked around the parked car in the next space and recognized the car. Jeff Watson, *The Reluctant Banker*, must have returned. Did I really want to be at the Watson home for lunch? Probably not, but I had accepted the invitation, so I must also accept whatever comes along.

The meal was wonderful, and the table was dressed to perfection with flowers from the backyard. She had undeniably cooked too much. Salads—two pasta salads, shrimp salad, chicken salad, an exotic fruit salad—and hot rolls. I was afraid to look at the sideboard, but from the corner of my eye, I could see at least two cakes and several pies. Olivia must have been very upset indeed.

"Mom, is the football team from UT-Tyler sharing our meal?"

"Cooking is my therapy. I'll find a way to use the leftovers, probably call some friends for supper or something. Julie, ignore my son and sit down. After we eat, you two go into the library and talk."

Olivia is the kind of woman most of us would chose to emulate—if we had the choice. Beautiful, charming, and capable, most of the things that I am not. Plus, she was a fabulous cook. I tried at least a small amount of every salad, and went back for seconds on some. Was I stonewalling?

If so, then Jeff was also because he must have gone back three or four times, until finally Olivia said, "Jeff, save some for tonight."

I wanted to laugh. This thirty-five-year-old architect and reluctant bank president was still his mother's little boy, and fell back into that behavior pattern whenever he sat down at her table. Then I thought of all the problems he had caused me in the weeks since Clarke died, and I forgot about laughing.

❦❦

"Okay Julie, let's see if we can talk this out, and find an alternate solution. I don't want you to resign. You're too important to the bank and to the customers. First, will you tell me what is going on at the bank that you can't handle?"

I told him, briefly and firmly, about the past due loans. I related the details of cars that should be repossessed and two businesses so delinquent that foreclosure proceedings should begin. All these issues were beyond my authority. The other issues I had were less pressing, but later, I would tell him that Vonda might be on medical leave for two months. Now, I wanted to see how he would respond.

"I apologize. I didn't know things were so bad, and I didn't intend to abandon ship and leave you with so much to handle. Truthfully, I don't much care for banking, and if Dad had lived, I would still be in Santa Fe, trying to be the best architect in town."

"Frankly, Jeff, those are your personal issues. This bank needs a strong hand at the helm, and it can't be me. I'm sorry that you don't like banking, but something has got to change and I can't take your place. "

For a time, we just sat and waited for the other to speak, uncertain how to take the next step. After a few minutes, I knew I would have to move this conversation forward.

"Jeff, we really don't know each other on a personal level, so perhaps I should tell you a little about Julie Trahan, the person, not the bank employee."

He looked at me with a strange expression, as if he'd rather not hear anything that would make me more real than the anonymous person left to handle the bank. But I was determined.

"Lately, I've had to deal with several difficult personal issues. That process has led me to believe that the time has come to sell the property that I inherited from my grandmother. Because we have so few people on staff at the bank, I can't take any personal leave time to deal with this. I'm tired of working ten hours a day and trying to take care of things that are beyond my responsibility."

I paused, but as expected, got no response, so I forged ahead.

"Selling Anderson Farms would give me the freedom to start over somewhere else if I wasn't tied to The Bank of Three Bridges. I think you should come back so I can get on with my life."

For a while, he didn't say anything, but looked at me with open assessment. If I were a blueprint, he would be able to read and understand, but I had grave doubts that he could understand me as a woman. After a moment he stood up and reached out his hand in some sort of conciliatory motion.

"I need to think about how to work this out and I always think better when I walk. Could we drive over to the walking trail and work out some of these cobwebs in my brain?"

I was wearing sandals and a dress, but actually the prospect of some exercise was appealing. I wasn't very comfortable having this discussion in his mother's house. There was another reason that a walk was appealing. I had eaten too much lunch.

We walked along landscaped and shady paths and Jeff asked questions about banking practices and I supplied the answer as I knew them. Clarke Watson had made all the banking decisions. I merely did as told, but I knew more than Jeff did. We walked and talked, and occasionally sat on a convenient bench to talk more.

"Julie, will you at least give me the rest of the summer? I can't run this bank without you. There's no one else to fill that slot. I'll raise your salary, see that you have a little more time off, whatever it takes. Please stay, I'd like to work with you. My dad thought you were terrific and he was seldom wrong. I'd like for us to know each other better. Will you stay through the summer?"

Was this what I really wanted? I could stay for a while and help get Jeff on a firmer footing. I owed the Watson family at least another few weeks to help get the bank back on track. After that?

❧☙

I didn't go home. Instead, I headed out to the farm. At least I would have plenty of time to think on my journey through this wide-open county. Elbamarle County can lay claim to lots of roads, lots of open farmland, and I had plenty of thoughts to occupy my mind as I drove.

Had I done the right thing by agreeing to stay through the summer? It seemed to be the best solution for now. Moving away from Three Bridges would be difficult, but my life was feeling so stagnant now, with few opportunities to meet Mr. Right. Perhaps that would never be in my future, and if God didn't have someone special for me, I could accept that.

I had made a commitment to stay at the bank until things were straightened out and I would honor that commitment.

I left the state highway a few miles out of Three Bridges and turned onto a narrow blacktop road that leads to my farm and to the estate of Miss Maddie Wallace. I had driven only a few miles down this narrow and potholed road when suddenly I was forced to move over—almost into the ditch because of a fast approaching car.

Was that Odie Marshall driving Miss Maddie's car? I recognized Odie, but the car passed so swiftly it was difficult to identify the passenger. I assumed it was Miss Maddie—who else would it be?

Two more miles and I was at the entrance to her farm, but the roadway was partially blocked by a semi and flatbed trailer, loaded down with a big red tractor. The driver was trying to

146

negotiate through the decorative gate and narrow entryway and facing a real challenge. However, two very large dump trucks loaded down with good old East Texas red dirt were parked inside the gate. George Camp must have brought his entire crew out to do some work, and on Sunday at that.

"Sounds like a lot of overtime to me, but why isn't Maddie here to supervise? That's not like her at all. Give it up, Julie, file that under 'not your problem', and get on with your own stuff."

# Twenty-Three

**I drove through the gates at Anderson Farms** with such somber feelings that I might have been going to a funeral. Then I reminded myself that I shouldn't be sad. Selling Anderson Farms was nothing more than turning the page or taking a step toward my future.

Was it really time to sell? Would Hortense want to buy the property? We had never discussed this and it was most probably wrong to assume anything.

If Hortense and her children didn't want to purchase the farm, I would have to list it with a realtor, and it might take a very long time to sell. Running a successful farm—of any sort— was a full-time job.

Grandmother left me this farm, but she always knew that someday I would be ready to take that hard step and move forward with my life. My plans to leave the bank immediately hadn't worked out, but I felt that the offer to sell Anderson Farms to the Salazars would be accepted and a good step for me. It was time to let go of the past.

Hortense greeted me with an affectionate hug and invited me into her kitchen. I eagerly took the glass of sweet tea and sat at the table while she continued to work. She was testing a new recipe for blueberry cream cheese pound cake, and my mouth watered from the enticing smells of vanilla, butter, and blueberries, but I reigned in my taste buds and jumped in with both feet with my plans.

"Hortense, we need to talk. Can you sit with me a while? I have something important to discuss with you."

"I always have time for you Little Julie—but what's wrong. I thought everything with Rudi had been settled. What has happened?"

"No, nothing is wrong. This is something else."

Now that I had her attention, I wasn't certain how to begin, so I just jumped into the middle of it and started talking.

"Hortense, I think you know that Grandmother left me this farm, hoping that the hard work would help to ease the loss of her death. Three years have passed and I still miss her, but I think it's time to move on with my life."

We sat at the kitchen table, each with a tall glass of iced tea. I took a deep drink; my mouth was dry from the anxiety, but finally I was able to proceed.

"For a while now, I have been feeling as if I'm swimming upstream. When Jeff left me in charge of the bank, I had no time or energy to come out here every day. It's only been a week or so, and I realize that Anderson Farms works very well without me. I appreciate not having to get up so early every morning. Perhaps I wasn't meant to be a berry farmer."

Hortense merely nodded in agreement, and her face showed a quizzical concern, but she waited for me to finish my thoughts.

"I've been toying with this idea for a while, but never really considered how to do this. Recently, I sort of put all my cards on the table and made some hard choices. I've prayed about this and God has given me the courage to do this. Hortense, I believe it's time for me to sell Anderson Farms."

Oh, Miss Julie, this is a shock. Are you certain you want to do this?"

"Yes, I'm certain and I would like very much if you would consider buying this farm. That seems the natural thing for me to do, and I believe it would have pleased grandmother, knowing you would still run everything. Hortense, do you want to buy this farm?"

She didn't answer at first, and I sensed that she was trying to find the right words. Did she need to be persuaded? If so, I could do that.

"You don't need me out here. The amount of actual work I do is very small. You've run this business for a long time—you and your children. If you buy Anderson Farms, you can run this business like the Salazar's want."

I hadn't known what answer to expect but not tears, ever. Indeed, tears filled her eyes and turned into deep sobs, but only for a moment. She fought back the tears, wiped her eyes with a napkin, and looked at me.

"Miss Julie, I love you as if you were one of my own, and your grandmother was more than my employer, she was my dear friend. Thank you. My family and I would be honored to purchase this fine business, but we will continue with the same business plan and the same business ethics that Elizabeth taught us."

We sat in the kitchen and visited for a while longer, talking about how to work out the details of the sale. Both of us felt very comfortable asking Judge to handle the legal aspects. Thinking of legalities brought Rudi Salazar to mind.

"Hortense, how is Rudi, what's going on with him?"

"Rudi is very repentant right now. I'm sorry to say that I watch him closely to see if he has actions of remorse to back up his words. So far, he hasn't disappointed me. Growing older brings emotional scars and callouses, and those that result from the grandchildren are very painful."

It had been a long day and now I needed to go home. I was pleased and satisfied with the agreements reached today. I drove home with my mind more on the future than what was around me.

❧❦

George Camp wasn't a cursing man, but today he came mighty close. The road into Maddie Wallace's farm was narrow, and his rig was big. Not a good combination, and he hoped he could get through those fancy gates and unload his tractor without any major happenings.

Inch by inch he moved forward, and wondered for the umpteenth time why he had agreed to do this job when Odie called.

He disliked Odie Marshall, and he distrusted the man. He always had. With a scowl on his face and frustration in his mind, he moved the rig that carried the big tractor onto the grounds and began to size up the operation. The dump truck drivers were impatient to get back home, but he had to look over the ground and search for any possible soft spots. Nobody wanted to get stuck on Sunday afternoon. Overtime was good, but these guys would rather be home and he couldn't blame them.

He walked the grounds where Odie told him to dump the dirt. He walked first in one direction and then in another to see if the rains of the past week had left the ground too soft to bear the weight of his equipment. He circled the area around the old storm shelter twice and muttered to himself with each step.

"Seems mighty strange to cover up this storm shelter. Maddie may think that those slanting doors that served as the entrance to the underground shelter are unsightly, but if a big storm comes up, she might need to use this place. But Maddie Wallace don't care none about what I think. I'm just hired to do a job."

So he walked around again, covering a slightly wider path and abruptly stopped dead in his tracks.

"How in tarnation did I miss this? I've walked every step of this area, but must have overlooked it. It's been so dry and even with the rains, the grass is about dead, so maybe it blended into the grass. Or maybe it was too close to that dead limb on the ground, but why would this shoe be out here?"

George Camp picked up the sandal and looked at it for a time before sliding it into a back pocket of his denim overalls. Well, right now, this was not his problem. Right now he had dirt to spread. He turned and gave the orders for the men to unload the tractor, then pointed out where he wanted the dirt unloaded.

There was work to be done.

⤟⤠

Hortense and I had made a schedule and a plan to proceed on selling the farm. As I left, she said something that tugged at my heart and made me want to tear up.

"Julie, you worked beside us in the fields when you first came here as a child and then when you moved here. As long as I'm here, you will always be part of Anderson Farms."

I could speak no words so I gave her a hug and fought back the tears. Hortense had been like a second grandmother to me and I loved her.

Back in Three Bridges, I pulled out a stack of folders concerning Anderson Farms and worked through the files as Sunday quickly slipped from afternoon into evening. As usual, I sorted into three stacks. *Keep, Shred,* and *Decide Later.* As the process continued, I moved some of the *Decide Later* files into a stack for Hortense.

The deeds to the property were of course in a lockbox at the bank, and I could get those whenever they were needed. I had sorted two drawers from the three-drawer oak file and decided that I needed a break. Good timing, because the telephone was ringing. I really should get caller ID. I hate answering unexpected phone calls.

"Julie, this is Jeff. Did I get you at a bad time?"

"Actually, I needed a break. I was sorting through some very old files about the farm. What's up?"

"After you left, Mom sat me down and read me the riot act. For a while I thought I was back in junior high, but she made her point. Julie, I owe you more of an apology than I delivered today. I took advantage of you by asking you to take on a job that I didn't want to do and I didn't give you enough backup. Mom convinced me that I need to fix things with you."

"Jeff, I thought we had already sorted everything out. You apologized and I accepted, and if you stay and work, that's all we need. Things will run much smoother at the bank if you're there."

"Well, I've done the best I can for the moment. I've talked to some of my associates in Santa Fe and have everything arranged for a few weeks at least. After that, we may have to do this one day at a time. Now, I called with an offer that I think you should consider. Interested?"

"I never say yes to anything unless I know all the details. What's your offer?"

"I am certain, Miss Trahan, that this is too good for you to turn down, even sight unseen. How about if you take tomorrow off, and enjoy a little down time. Mom told me how tired Dad was after a long week at the bank, and you've had several difficult weeks. Enjoy tomorrow and I'll see you Tuesday."

I thanked him and started to hang up, when I heard my name again.

"Julie I think you and I got off on the wrong foot—for whatever reason and after our long talk and the walk this afternoon, you have sparked my interest—on a personal level. Have a nice Monday away from the bank and I will definitely look forward to seeing you again."

What was that? Was Jeff Watson coming on to me? Hmm!

I poured tea from the refrigerator into a glass of crushed ice, picked up a small blueberry muffin and went to the porch. Even though it was Texas in July, the evening was surprisingly pleasant. I sat in one of the rocking chairs on the porch and watched as little winged luminaries flitted about. I followed the path of the lightning bugs until I caught sight of a familiar figure approaching.

"Hey, Cynthia, it's a little late for walking. What's up?"

"Oh, you know, just those same old demons that never give me any rest. Did you have a good day? I looked for you after church but you were gone."

I went to the kitchen and returned with another glass of tea and then brought her up to date on everything—Jeff, the bank, and selling the blueberry farm. Finally, I sat back and took a long and unladylike swig of tea.

To the sound of laughter.

Cynthia was laughing—at me?

"What? What's up with you? Why are you laughing at me."

"I can't wait to tell the others. I never thought I would live to see this day. I think our Julie has a beau, and I think she likes it."

Inside, beneath a veneer of maturity, our teenage personalities were alive and well. An internal switch was turned on and Cynthia and I giggled and laughed and silly-talked as we set our teenage spirits free for a while. Maturity returned when we realized that it was getting very late and heat lightning was flashing low across the distant sky.

I was tired and it was late, but not too late to thank God for all my blessings.

# $\mathcal{T}$wenty-Four

**It was late Sunday evening and George Camp was very** angry. Nothing had gone right. His entire Sunday had been ruined when Odie called and demanded that he bring two loads of dirt and a tractor to spread the soil.

Well, that sounded just like Maddie Wallace, always wanting something done now, immediately—or sooner—and after a few months she would probably want it all done differently. Well, money was running short, so he'd skipped church and promised to take care of the job today. He'd heard the sermon about the ox in the ditch, so he called his crew and went to Maddie's.

Nothing went as planned, but at least Odie and Maddie hadn't stayed around to watch. Not too long after he got the tractor unloaded, they left in rather a big hurry and he was more than happy to wave goodbye to the pair of them. He didn't want or need any interference from either of them. He was glad to see them go, but not long after that, everything fell apart.

Vonda woke to overwhelming, all-encompassing pain. Her head hurt, everything hurt, but some of the pain was worse than others. Her left leg was incredibly painful. She would have to push aside the thoughts of pain and think. But she hurt so badly, she couldn't.

She tried to move, but her arms and legs wouldn't cooperate. The pain was fierce, so much pain that it almost took her breath away. She didn't give up. Her only chance to save herself was to move, in spite of the pain. Again, she tried to move, and finally she was able to move one leg a little, then a little more.

She must have landed on her back on some lumpy uneven surface. Whatever she was lying on was damp and smelled bad. So bad that it was difficult to breath and her back was hurting from the uncomfortable position. Maybe if she could turn onto her side for a little while, maybe she could ease some of the pain.

*Come on, push with that other leg just a little more.*

Finally, she twisted her lower body a few inches and with right arm she reached out for something, anything to grab on to so that she could move just a little more. She reached and reached and then something warm touched her hand and she screamed. But no one heard the scream. No one knew that Vonda had fainted. When she woke up something warm and alive was sitting next to her, mewing and nudging her face.

*What is this, a cat? It must be a cat. Where in the world am I? I've never liked cats but maybe now is a good time to start. If there is a cat here with me, maybe I will be okay, maybe I can find a way out of this place.*

She wondered where she was. It was dark and damp and close and she remembered falling. Odie had dropped her—into a hole? *Dear God, where am I?*

There was no way for her to gauge the passage of time as she slipped in and out of awareness. She was aware of waking, then nothing for a time, then awake and thinking the same thoughts again.

*Thirsty, so very thirsty. First things first, keep moving, maybe I can get myself braced enough to get up. Push, shove, push, shove and finally, that's it, I think I can push myself up.*

*Sitting position, head swimming—not good. Rest, rest, maybe the spinning will stop, maybe it will stop. Head still hurting . . .* and finally she dozed off to sleep. This time it was just a natural sleep due to exhaustion.

Minutes, hours, days? How could she know how much time

had passed since Odie attacked her? But she remembered that. And the waking and sleeping and waking and questioning were repeated.

She tried to open her eyes, but the lids were puffy and swollen. She could barely raise one arm and those fingers gently traced her face and forehead, and the throbbing lump on the side of her head. *Blood, dried blood. That explains the pain.* The thoughts were unspoken, judging the intense pain in her face, she doubted if she could speak.

But she could still moan and at the sound of her voice, the cat approached and jumped onto her chest. Her intense groan of pain sent the cat scampering away, later to return to her side with anxious purrs. Was he trapped in here also? Wherever they were, either the cat needed some attention or he wanted to console her.

Warily she searched around her body, feeling cautiously. Dirt, she was feeling dirt. The questions replayed in her mind? Where was she? She remembered falling, and now, she knew she was lying on dirt. Where was she?

*Don't think about it. Don't think about where you are. You can breathe and you are still alive. Don't give up!*

She allowed the fingers of her good hand to move across the dirt-caked floor, reaching only a few inches at a time, until she felt something pushing against her side and it was not the cat. It was soft and leathery feeling!

*Oh dear God, my purse! I am still holding my purse. Thank you, Lord, thank you.*

෴

George Camp was berating himself for sending everyone home. He should have kept at least one of the other drivers on the job. Now he was out here with a broken tractor and no help. Not that either of those boys would have known how to help without being told, but sometimes George liked to have someone to yell at.

This job had felt wrongheaded from the beginning, but he was trying to do as Miss Maddie directed—through her right-hand man, Odie Marshall. He had two loads of top soil to spread and so far he'd moved only a few bucket loads to the back side of the storm shelter. Everything was working great until he tried to raise the bucket after dumping the dirt. Nothing happened, the bucket wouldn't move in any direction.

After George had done all the tinkering he knew how and nothing helped, the only thing left to do was reload the rig and start over tomorrow. One ruined Sunday. Never again would he be tempted by overtime. No siree, next Sunday George Camp would be in church where he belonged.

∽᳁᳁᳁᳁᳁᳁᳁᳁᳁᳁᳁᳁᳁᳁᳁᳁᳁᳁᳁᳁᳁᳁᳁᳁᳁᳁᳁᳁᳁᳁᳁᳁᳁᳁᳁᳁᳁᳁᳁᳁᳁᳁᳁᳁᳁᳁᳁᳁᳁᳁᳁᳁᳁᳁᳁᳁᳁᳁᳁᳁᳁᳁᳁᳁

*Where am I?* The question came each time she opened her eyes. *How long have I been in this smelly place?* That was the second question and there was no answer for either.

Moving with guarded movements to avoid as much pain as possible, Vonda raised her right arm high enough to grasp the strap on her shoulder, and with a gentle tug, positioned the purse so that she could open it. Concentrating on the process shoved the knowledge of her pain into the background.

The magnetic closure on the big sack-like purse opened easily. She searched the contents knowing that treasures were hiding inside and waiting to be found. If she ever got out of here, she would tell all those people that made fun of her suitcase-size purse that she was right. This proved it. She needed every single article inside this purse—it was her life support system.

Water. She had found the water, but did she have enough strength to open it? She rested for a time, waiting for the waves of pain to lessen and then she tackled the job of opening the water bottle. With her right hand, she placed the bottle between her aching ribs and her swollen left arm and pressed it to the floor while turning the cap. The bottle had been opened before and took only a few turns to get the lid to open, but the process used most of her energy. She rested briefly and then managed to dribble a small amount of water into her mouth, swallow, and repeat the process. Such small actions had tired her beyond measure and she slept.

Before seven o'clock on Monday, George pulled his rig through the gates of Carlton's Tractor Repair. After several cups of really bad coffee—it was free—and a huge amount of tall tales shared with other guys waiting for their rigs, Carlton returned with a diagnosis that George didn't want to hear but was expecting—a broken hydraulic hose. The hose would have to be fabricated locally, but at the end of the day, the tractor would be working again.

George called Sadie, his wife and asked her to pick him up. No sense moving the big truck, and Carlton had plenty of parking space. There were other things that he needed to take care of. When the tractor was repaired, he'd take the rig back out to Maddie's and work a while if he had any daylight left.

I felt like a heathen when I woke at nine-thirty Monday morning. A day off from The Bank of Three Bridges and no plans, but that would change soon. I savored a second and then a rare third cup of coffee as the wheels spun in my head.

My decision was made. Today I would buy a new car.

I drove around the loop in Tyler, twice. I drove past every car dealership I could find and looked at the cars parked next to the highway while I irritated the drivers behind me. I should get off the loop and onto one of those car lots with giant American flags, balloons, and inviting signage. But which one?

An overly irritated driver honked and I pulled into the next auto dealership I came to. As quickly as flies attracted by newly tossed out rotting fruit, I was soon accosted by a charming smile and a warm handshake. Anticipation gleamed from the salesperson's eyes and my own were filled with skepticism as we played the game of car shopping.

Five car lots later, I was exhausted beyond measure, but I drove away in a new white Mustang convertible with a complimentary bottle of water from the salesman. The sizeable check I had written for the car should have warranted a free steak dinner—for twelve—but the water was welcomed.

Around two o'clock, George sat down in his recliner and settled back for a nap. Something was digging into his back. He twisted a gnarled hand around and into his back pocket and pulled out the shoe he had picked up from the ground near the storm shelter yesterday. For a time he looked at the shoe, turning it one way and then another as if answers were written in the leather.

Why was that shoe out there on the ground? Had it been tossed aside, like yesterday's newspaper, or had the shoe been lost by the wearer? Not likely—no woman would walk off and leave a good shoe behind—not if she could help it. The questions continued without answers but he came to one conclusion. He knew the owner of this shoe.

Maybe he should go back to town and see if he could find her. He felt certain that he knew how to find the person that owned the shoe, or maybe he just needed to think on it a while longer.

Finding the shoe in such an unlikely place bothered him and he didn't know why. Maybe he could figure it out if he kept thinking about it. He thought until the telephone roused him from a snoring sleep. It would be noon tomorrow before the tractor was ready, the part had just been delivered.

Vonda woke and sipped a little more water. She must try to drink as much water as she could, but even those two sips tired her tremendously. A new resolve entered her mind, she couldn't give up. She wouldn't—not yet.

She wished she owned a cell phone. But who would she call? How could she ask someone to find her if she had no idea where she was? No cell phone and no real friends. Odie Marshall had been the one person who could claim that title—and he was responsible for her being in this place, hidden from the world.

A peace overtook her and a thought like sunshine on a stormy day filled her soul. She had a friend, she had someone to trust, and someone who cared for her so much that his Son died for her. She knew God, and she would trust him to provide for her rescue. She prayed and as sleep claimed her again, this phrase ran through an internal loop in her mind. It was there when she woke again.

*Don't give up, keep fighting, don't give up, God will save you, but don't give up, keep fighting.* Encouraged, she searched for her keys, and found them clipped inside the purse. She fingered her way through the lot of them, fumbling and starting over, until she found the small flashlight attached to the key chain.

Sleep came, but for how long? Calmness had been replaced by panic and the fear of being trapped, but she fought to find that bright ray of hope and trust. Her trust in God was in a war with fear, and for a while the doubts and questions seemed to be winning.

*Where am I? Does anyone know I'm missing? What day is it? I know it was Saturday when Odie came to my house and hit me, but how much time has passed after that? Lord, please don't let me die down here, give me a chance to be a better person. Lord, I'm so afraid.*

# $\mathcal{T}$wenty-Five

**Odie Marshall was driving west. West to New Mexico and** a cabin hidden in the woods, according to Denise. The destination was now uncertain, and west was only a direction, but he was still driving.

He and Denise were traveling separately, but had agreed to meet Monday evening at six o'clock. It was seven thirty. Something must have happened, because she hadn't showed up. He would call again in a few minutes to see where that fool woman was, but all he could do now was stay on the move. Every mile he drove took him further from Three Bridges, but not from the memory of dealing with that infernal old man.

George Camp had always been a pain to deal with. He always had to back talk and question, and never did what Odie told him. The old man thought he could only work for Maddie, and that was part of the problem Sunday afternoon. He wished he could go back and stuff that old man in the ground between Vonda and Maddie Wallace. It'd serve him right for causing so much trouble.

☙☙

Saturday night had been the worst nightmare he could imagine, and Sunday was no better. When George parked his truck on the street and walked the one-quarter mile up to the house, Odie knew two things. Trouble was brewing and George Camp was set for an argument.

"Is Miss Maddie here, Odie? You said she wanted some work done. I need to talk to her."

"George, you know dang well that I handle Miss Maddie's business affairs. Why did you stop out on the road? That dirt won't do any good out there. Look, George, see that old storm cellar? Miss Maddie wants it completely covered up. We want you to dump all that dirt over the doors, and spread it out a little bit. Just leave it like a flattened out hill. We want to plant some spring bulbs, a few azaleas. Got that?"

When he was certain that George Camp was indeed going to follow through on the orders, Odie sped from the garage with a vengeance and left the estate, heading west with a fierce determination to carry out his hastily arranged plans.

Even though the body of Maddie Wallace was now swathed in very fine bed linen, and stored below ground as if already interred, it must appear that she was riding beside him in the passenger seat. It must have worked because George Camp waved a rude farewell to what he assumed was Maddie Wallace. No other person would have such a close look at the figure in the car. He would make certain of that.

Mrs. Marshall's youngest boy may not have been the smartest of the bunch, but he had always been the craftiest and the most cunning. Late Saturday night Odie had rummaged around Maddie's sewing room until he found a pair of sharp scissors. Then he returned to the master bedroom and pulled several overstuffed down pillows from the bed. He opened these pillows, took the contents, and stuffed it into a pair of the dead woman's very expensive panty hose.

When these were full enough to duplicate the size of Maddie Wallace, Odie repeated the process with modifications to duplicate the arms. The pillow stuffed panty hose were then placed in one of the dead woman's pantsuits. He carried this "mannequin" filled with pillow entrails to the Mercedes and secured it with the shoulder harness.

The "body" was completed with one of Maddie's wig stands stuffed into the neck of the pantsuit and the unreliable connection was hidden by a scarf. A bouffant and brilliant auburn wig and large felt hat completed the look. Yes, Odie knew the hat was not appropriate for the season, but it was the largest she owned, and frankly, no one else would notice the style. The casual and unquestioned wave given by George Camp let him know that the hastily contrived and stuffed pantsuit had passed the test.

He sped through the white, wrought iron gates, anxious to be out of here, and his nerves were jangling like a panic alarm. He was driving much too fast as he rounded a slight curve in the road and veered across the faded yellow line in his lane toward an oncoming vehicle. He jerked the wheel to the right, barely missing the car. Another bad sign. Julie Trahan had been driving the oncoming car.

On a normal day, there was very little traffic on this road—mostly the farm workers at Anderson Farms, and of course, Julie. There was no surprise when he recognized her car. He only hoped that she probably wouldn't put much importance on seeing him driving Maddie's car.

He had taken an alternate route toward Dallas, driving county roads and state highways until he was miles away from Three Bridges. Whenever he spotted a roadside garbage can or dumpster, he left parts of his *passenger*, scattered one piece at a time from Three Bridges to Dallas.

❧❧

Denise had been traveling west also, but her pace was much slower than that set by Odie Marshall. Every mile she drove was driven with reluctance, questioning why she so eagerly agreed to a trip with a man that she didn't know very well despite the several nights they had spent together.

Something was holding her back, and she was confused. Enthusiasm for a relationship with Odie was lessening by the moment. From the beginning, this man had captured her emotions like a thunderbolt striking a pine tree in a summer rainstorm.

But now there was something in Odie's eyes that frightened her. She usually saw this strange, angry look when he was thinking about something, and not connecting with her in conversation. She couldn't always describe what she saw. Sometimes it was only the briefest glimmer of hardness. At other times, the look from his eyes was a fierce, burning hatred or something equally sinister.

Those invading negative thoughts about Odie and his quirky personality were paramount, but not her only concerns. The other problem was her back. Sitting behind the wheel of her car, remaining in a seated position for long hours, was wreaking havoc on her back.

A injury several years ago frequently came back to haunt her, and those twinges she was now feeling were beginning to worry her. She was okay most of the time, if she was careful and didn't stress her back, but driving for hours without stopping wasn't working out. The very idea of this trip was stressful and confusing.

She hadn't seen Odie since he left the hotel room in Tyler on Sunday morning. She had gone back to sleep after telling him goodbye, and slept until the housekeeping staff knocked on her door at noon. She checked out of the hotel and found a diner that served breakfast all day. With no regrets, Denise enjoyed several cups of freshly brewed coffee and a leisurely and unhurried meal.

From time to time, her newly purchased cell phone rang, but after talking to Odie about six o'clock on Sunday evening, she ignored the ringing phone. From Tyler, she drove with caution but decided to stop outside of Ft. Worth. It was getting late, but on the western edge of that city, she found a motel and checked in for the night.

Again, she slept late. When she woke, it was a struggle to get it all together and out of the motel by the noontime checkout. Sleep had been impossible until the small hours of the morning as thoughts kept running through her head. Perhaps the most persistent was Miss Maddie's voice—

*"Denise, you should watch out for that Odie Marshall. Lately, there is something strange about that man. He prefers older women, especially older women of means. The younger women, once they've served his purposes, he tosses them aside. Even though he's been with me for a while, he's always looking around to find another weak and wanting woman. I've watched him and seen it coming. Something is going on with Odie Marshall. Denise, don't sell yourself short. You can do better."*

Now Monday was almost gone and she couldn't stop thinking that she was making a huge mistake. At the core of her being, she had this overwhelming urge to turn her car around and go back to Three Bridges. Should she retrace her steps to Maddie's estate and beg for her old job? Could she do that?

Maddie Wallace had usually been fair. Not always nice, but usually fair. Denise Hougan straightened her chubby shoulders, fastened her seat belt, and exited the fast food restaurant with a right turn, heading east. Her firm determination was immediately threatened by the persistent ring of her newly acquired cell phone. Only Odie had this number. As soon as she could, she left the roadway and stopped in a parking lot, opened her purse and picked up the phone.

❧☙

By now he had been driving for hours. Hours of anxiety, apprehension, concern and confusion. He was tired, and the hours behind the wheel had blurred his mind after only snatches of sleep last night.

It was time to refuel, past time to eat and once more, he would try to get in touch with Denise. Why didn't that stupid woman answer the phone?

Still Denise didn't answer when he called and he knew he had programmed the number correctly. Hadn't she answered Sunday evening and planned to meet him today? What was the crazy woman up to? He slammed on the brakes and made a U-turn, unaware of the blaring horn of an eastward-bound eighteen-wheeler forced to brake for Odie's illegal U-turn. He crossed the median and headed back to the east. By now, he should have been near New Mexico instead of heading back into trouble.

Once again, the game had changed, but he could handle it even though he was angry, very angry. He raised a fist and shook it as he yelled aloud—to himself or to God?

"Never again will I let some stupid woman dictate what I should do, where I should go or anything else. Never again—got that?"

✧✧

I know it was very silly. At least I certainly felt silly, but I had a new car and I wanted to show it off. If I hurried, I could be in Three Bridges before Cynthia ate supper.

I drove into her driveway with the horn blaring. She ran from the kitchen with the telephone in one hand and the other holding a gun. Sometimes I forget that my friend is a woman well connected at Town Hall.

Thank goodness, she put the gun and the telephone down on a table on the porch and stood with hands on her hips, shaking her head.

"I guess you know, you scared me out of my wits. What's going on, and whose car did you borrow? Is this your car? Julie, did you buy a new car?"

She hopped barefooted down the steps and tiptoed across the sticker infested grass and hopped into the passenger seat.

"Lord have mercy, I can't believe you did this. I heard that you and Jeff had a meeting of the minds and he gave you the day off work—now look at you. Girlfriend, let's take this thing out on the road and try it out."

I backed out onto the street and then reversed into her driveway, stopping at her back porch. "Cynthia, get your purse, lock your house, and put on some shoes. We're going somewhere to eat supper. My treat."

# $\mathcal{T}$wenty-Six

**Tuesday morning, I went to work with a tad of** apprehension. Had I imagined that Jeff might be interested in me as a woman? Was I feeling any interest in him as a guy? Way too soon on both counts. We hardly know each other. With my track record, I need to take this very slow—slower than the snail.

I shouldn't have been concerned. When I opened the door to the bank, Jeff was already at his desk, going through a stack of papers. I said a brief, "Good morning," and went to my desk to find an equally thick stack of folders placed front and center on my desk. Ugh! I would need coffee to get through this, so I grabbed a cup and dug in.

"One day off and she's right back at work without even saying good morning."

I smiled in spite of myself.

"Hey, Jessie, how're things? Sorry for ignoring you, but I've got a lot of work to catch up on. I guess that's what happens when you take a day off. Need something?"

"Yes, two things. Julie, there was a new convertible parked in your spot. Is that what you did yesterday? Did you buy a new car?"

I couldn't control the smile that sprung from my soul. I had indeed ventured into the world of new car salesman and came away undamaged—except financially. "Yep, I bought a new car. What do you think about it?"

"All I can say is that it's about time. And if I were twenty years younger, I'd want one just like it! I'm proud of you Julie!"

I couldn't help myself—I grinned from ear to ear, proud as a kid with a new toy. "Yes, I spent yesterday buying a new car. They didn't actually laugh when I turned over the keys to my old clunker, but mentioned something about donating it to a charity. What was the other thing?"

"It's Vonda. She didn't come in yesterday, and she's not here today. I called her house a few times yesterday, but I figured she had another doctor's appointment and that you had scheduled a day off for her."

"No, she asked for time off last week, but other than that she never mentioned needing extra time. You know she's practically a workaholic. If she was going to be out of town, I know she would have said something. Have you called today, did she answer?"

"I've called several times this morning and no answer. This isn't like Vonda. Look, sometimes I know that I jump to conclusions, but I wonder if something is wrong, if she's ill or anything. Oh gosh, look at the people standing at the teller window. I'll get back with you in a bit."

I put my head in my hands, wondering just what was going to happen next. Then I gave myself a mental jerk, logged off my computer and went to the other side of the bank. At least I could take deposits and hand out cash. Once more, the voice of my mentor and grandmother sounded in my ears.

*"When life hands you a plateful of things to deal with, there's probably not a dessert among them. Just attack each issue as it comes, resolve that problem and go on to the next. Sometimes we just have to provide our own dessert."*

For the next three hours, we cashed more checks, took more loan payments, and accepted more deposits than we usually do in two days' time. In addition to those teller duties, I also sat in the banker's chair, dealing with loan payoffs and applications for loans. The most cheerful task was opening checking and savings accounts for a new family moving into

Three Bridges. All of this before lunch—what would the afternoon bring?

I took my lunch break, put my feet up, and just existed for a time. There was only one thought running through my mind.

*"I'm much too young to be feeling this old and over the hill. Did I make a mistake by letting Jeff talk me into staying at the bank?"*

∽⟨♦⟩∾

Just before two o'clock, George Camp entered the lobby of The Bank of Three Bridges, and walked in the direction of the teller windows with as much speed and agility as his seventy-plus-year-old body could manage. He was looking for Vonda. She wasn't anywhere to be seen so he headed over to Jessie Baker. They had known each other for years. In fact, George was married to Jessie's aunt.

"Uncle George, what can I do for you?"

"I'm looking for Vonda Sue, Jessie. Have you seen her? Is she at work today?"

"No, she's not here and she wasn't here yesterday. What did you want to see her about, George? Is there anything I can help you with?"

"Oh, I just had a question for her. She'd asked me to give her a price on clearing out around her house a while back, and I never got back to her. Thought maybe she was ready to do some work. I'll check back later. Do you think she's at home?"

"Julie and I have been calling whenever we have a chance and can't get an answer. We've been so busy today that we haven't had a chance to go check out the house. I plan to do that when I get off work. We are so shorthanded and Julie is just swamped, so she can't go. Sorry, but that's the best I can offer you on that front."

"That'll do. Thanks, Jessie, I'll see you later."

That settled it. He may be an old fuddy-duddy in some folks' minds, but he could add two and two and get four. He was worried about Vonda, and he was going straight to Judge to get it sorted out. No use stopping at the police station. He didn't have much use for the chief because the man didn't have enough sense to tie his shoelaces. *Guess that's why he always wears boots. How in the world did he ever get elected to office?*

❧❧

"Judge, I know Rosalie told me to come by at three o'clock, and I'm a few minutes early, but I really need to talk to you about something—something really important."

"George, what's going on? What's got you in a mess? You look as nervy as a bag full of worms going to the fishing hole."

"I've got something on my mind, Judge. I think we got a real problem, but I know you can figure it out."

George Camp strode into the room and made short work of shaking Judge's hand, hardly missing a beat in the storytelling.

"Here's the deal, Judge. I found this shoe—just one shoe— out at Miss Maddie's place on Sunday afternoon. Odie Marshall called me out there to cover up that ol' storm shelter. Said Miss Maddie was tired of looking at it. Well, you know how Maddie is. When she gets a bee in her bonnet she wants action. So I took my rig out to the place and while I was waiting for the two loads of topsoil to be dumped, I was sorta walking around, checking the spot over."

George paused in his storytelling to hand the shoe across the antique desk so that Judge could look at his evidence. He backed up to the client chair and sat down before taking up the story again.

"On the north side of the storm shelter next to a fallen limb, I found this shoe, just one shoe. You can tell that it's a good shoe, not worn out or nothing. The other thing you can tell is this shoe probably belongs to Vonda Sue Gunderson. She is the only one I've ever seen wearing anything like this, winter and summer alike. I guess the reason I always noticed her shoes is they remind me of the hippie generation, and you know I can't stand hippies."

Judge didn't attempt an answer, but it would have done no

good anyway—George barely paused in telling his story.

"Now, before I came over here I just stopped at the bank to talk to Vonda and guess what! She hasn't been at work today and she wasn't there yesterday, either. They can't get in touch with her, and I think that now they're beginning to get a little concerned. I would've gone to the chief with this but, well, you know the two of us don't exactly see eye to eye."

"Can't say I blame you too much for that, George. He's not exactly the sharpest knife in the drawer. So, what are you thinking here? You found a shoe that you think belongs to Vonda, and she's not at work. You say she wasn't at work yesterday either?"

"That's what I asked Jessie, and she said Vonda was not at work yesterday and they can't get her to answer the phone. And you know Jessie is always on top of things."

"Okay, let's look at the facts again. A shoe found where it shouldn't be, Vonda isn't where she should be, and nobody can get her to answer the phone. George, are you—do you think Vonda has come to some harm or has been victim of some foul play? Spell it out man—what exactly are you thinking?"

"I don't know, Judge. Everybody in town says Vonda is crazy in love with that Odie Marshall and he don't really give her the time of day. All I know about that is that Odie Marshall and Miss Maddie took off for Vegas Sunday afternoon. I saw them leave while I was out there working. Maddie was wearing a big hat and was sitting beside Odie looking straight ahead—like she does when she has a bee in her bonnet. I don't know what all this means, but one thing for sure, Vonda Sue Gunderson *did not* leave this shoe out there on purpose, or my name ain't George Camp."

"Okay, George, let me get Rosalie to bring you some coffee. I need to think on this thing a while."

"Sorry, Judge, I really can't stay. Need to get back to my rig. On top of everything else, a dang hose broke on me and I had to haul that dude back up to Carlton's. He got the part in late yesterday, and it's finally fixed. I need to get out to Maddie's place. I'm way behind."

George took a few steps toward the door, but turned around and looked at Judge with a frown on his work-worn face.

"Judge, I've never been a superstitious man, but seems to me somebody put a hex on me for doing that job. I stayed away from church just to make a few extra dollars, and I ain't had nothing but trouble since. On top of that, I think Vonda has come to some harm, or something. Why on earth would her shoe be out at Maddie's house? You think on this, I trust you to come up with something."

Judge thought about everything that George told him, then turned the facts around in his mind, and thought a while longer, but couldn't come up with an answer. After about half an hour, he reached for the phone and called Rev. Roger Peppers.

"Roger, I need to see you. I've been presented with a problem that I can't solve and I think I need another person's point of view. If you can come on over now, I'll have Rosalie put on a pot of decaf coffee and slice that coconut pie."

After thinking a while longer and waiting for the good preacher to arrive, Judge decided he might as well call Julie and see if she knew anything about Vonda. No sense in getting in a tailspin if the woman had been located. There could be other explanations for the shoe, but this was a conundrum. There was one thing he could do before calling Julie. He could pray.

*"Father, I come to you praying for Vonda Sue Gunderson. Father, some of us are concerned for her safety, and we ask you to guard her with a band of angels, keep her safe and return her to us."*

# Twenty-Seven

**Time was a seamless continuum with no definition** between night and day. All she knew was pain and darkness. In the few moments of lucidness, she felt the cold and smelled the horrible odor of something indescribable to her senses.

She felt the cat nudging at her again, pushing his head against her face, trying to get some attention. Why was a cat in here with her, and why was he so interested in her? But at least she had something positive to focus on. If a cat was here with her, maybe there was a chance to be rescued.

*How can I possibly hurt more than I did the last time I was awake? But I do and I don't know if I can move.* Vonda kept a running thought commentary in her mind, though words were never spoken.

She tried to move, one inch at a time. The pain was almost unbearable but she was determined to try. Each tiny advance was fueled by her self-talk. *Got to move, have to beat this. Where am I?*

Random thoughts flashed through her mind. She remembered Odie bursting into her kitchen, and remembered trying to ward off the blows. She remembered fighting for her life, and she remembered praying.

*"Dear Heavenly Father, protect me. Lord, I seek refuge in you. Heavenly Father, protect me."*

She felt for her purse and found the bottle of water. It was difficult, but she had to do it, she had to drink. At last, her mind and spirit seemed to focus on survival. With a great effort, she began to test her muscles, urging her body to respond.

Slowly, gradually she was able to move one leg. The pain was so intense it was beyond description. She tried to shift her body, but when she tried to move her left leg, she couldn't endure the pain.

She rested for a moment until she felt stronger or at least more determined. By the exertion of sheer willpower, she pushed her body until she was almost in an upright position, and then rested again. The pain was still intense and the room seemed out of focus, fuzzy, her head was spinning, but that soon lessened. Random thoughts buzzed through her awareness.

*Got to stay focused. Think! Where could I be? Whose cat is this? It is so quiet down here, wherever here is.*

Sitting with her shoulders braced against the rough wall, she reached into the handbag and pulled out the flashlight. Tentatively, she searched the area surrounding her. She looked for the cat but didn't find him.

*Where did he go? This is really a very small space that looks as if it might be a storm shelter. There is a cot, a camp chair, and other camping equipment. Wonder what was in those boxes?*

*If this is a storm shelter, then I am underground. Did Odie want to bury me down here? Where am I?*

For more than a fleeting moment she was overwhelmed with fear and panic. Odie had thrown her into an underground storm shelter. Lost, locked away from help. Was there no help for her? Then, her mind recalled phrases from the book of Psalms that she'd read so very recently: *"Into Your hand I entrust my spirit; You redeem me, Lord, God of truth. Be strong and courageous, all you who put your hope in the Lord."* Yes, strong and courageous, I must be strong.

Odie was fuming, ranting, pounding the steering wheel of Maddie Wallace's car while railing against all women—Miss Maddie, and Vonda—but most of his anger was directed to Denise Hougan.

"Denise, if I could get my hands around that fat white neck, I'd leave you in the same shape as Miss Maddie and Vonda Sue Gunderson."

He yelled loudly, although there was no one to hear. While driving, shouting was the only release for his anger. Why didn't she answer the cell? How could she ignore the ringing? He must have called a dozen times.

"Just answer the phone, Denise. Even a moron knows how to answer the phone."

Every woman he'd ever known, from his weak and backward mother, right on through every woman he ever met— had been trouble. Pure and simple, they were trouble. Especially these young and smart things that think they know everything.

"I'm talking about you, Julie Trahan. Your poor old grandmother fell for your pity line hook, line, and sinker. She took you in and gave you everything she had. Nobody ever did anything like that for me."

Odie rounded a sharp curve and the car crossed the double yellow line. The blaring of the oncoming vehicle got his attention and he yanked the wheel hard to the right. The wheels hit loose dirt and he began to slip into the ditch. At the last second, he was able to correct the skid and right the car, but he was exhausted. He pulled the Mercedes off at the next opportunity and sat back, trying to regain some composure.

He sat still and quiet. The raging anger eased out of him but was replaced by a deadly calm directed at Julie Trahan.

"Well, little Miss Julie, you just better watch out. I may have to come back for you yet. That old storm shelter has been covered up by now, but I'll find another place for you. After I lay low for a while, I think I'll just do that. Julie Trahan, watch your step, and that goes for those silly friends of yours also. I wish I could just rid the world of all useless women."

⚜

Denise Hougan opened her eyes and looked around, confused and frightened. She was in a very strange place, yet a familiar place. She had been in a room like this before—it must be a hospital. Couldn't be anything else. She must be in a hospital emergency room. What happened? Why was she here?

She frowned and searched her mind, trying to recall what had happened and finally remembered that she was supposed to be driving to meet Odie. Then she remembered the cell phone that rang incessantly. Why had he kept calling, calling every few minutes? Couldn't he figure out that she didn't want to talk to him?

She remembered driving in circles, trying to figure out what to do, and then the phone rang again. Everything came back in a crystal clear memory. There was a small shopping center just ahead with a large parking lot and only a few stores. She entered the parking lot and stopped her car next to a vacant lot, overgrown and neglected. Without much thought, she grabbed the annoying cell phone and even the charger, walked over to the grassy area and threw the new cell phone as far as she could. She felt pain—immediately. Now she was here in some hospital.

"What day is this? It must have been Tuesday morning when I threw the cell phone away. Where am I? Why am I here?"

She tried to move and the pain grabbed her and she wanted to scream. Perhaps she had screamed, because a nurse was at once by her side.

"Miss Hougan, are you awake? Denise, are you back with us? We need you to answer some questions if you can. You're in the emergency room. You passed out on a parking lot in front of a small store. Someone called 911 and we brought you here. As soon as you give us some information, we can probably take the edge off your pain."

The only words that registered in her brain was the promised relief from the intense pain. Denise would do anything to accomplish that. She would tell all, answer any question and confess to any crime.

If they could ease her pain, she would even admit to shooting President Kennedy and Abraham Lincoln.

❧❧

I looked around the office, out into the bank lobby and back to my cleared desktop. I'd done a masterful job of filing, rearranging, and in some cases even hiding the stacks of papers that had cluttered my desk. Not very much had actually been accomplished, but at least I wouldn't have to stare at past due loan folders and loan application files. I reminded myself that Jeff Watson was back now, and surely this could be handed back to him. Soon we would need to figure out a new arrangement for sharing the work.

With a clear desk and a hesitant spirit, I picked up the phone and called Judge. He was one of my favorite people. He'd been my grandmother's attorney, longtime friend, and he'd been my comfort on so many occasions. I was surprised when he picked up the telephone on the first ring.

"McGrath here, who's calling?"

"Judge, this is Julie. I need to make an appointment with you. I've decided to sell Anderson Farms and I don't even know where to start. Could you fit me in anytime soon?"

"Julie, I'm glad you called, but we need to put that on hold for a while, maybe until next week. In fact, I was just about to call you. Have you heard from Vonda Gunderson today? Did she come in to work?"

I know this is a small town, but I just didn't see that Vonda's absence should raise a hue and cry from anyone, especially Judge. Those thoughts made the back of my scalp crawl and I got a very weird feeling.

"No, Judge, we can't get in touch with her. I'm planning to go by her house as soon as I leave here. For some reason this has been a very busy day. We're shorthanded and everybody in town needs something from the bank."

"Well, Julie, that might be a subheading under the law of unintended consequences—in other words, those inexplicable happenings. Look, Julie, can you leave the bank right now and run by Vonda's house, then come on over here and talk to me for a minute? I promise to let you get back to the bank in time to close."

"Okay, Judge, I'll be over in just a few minutes. I need to tell Jeff what's going on, and Jessie also."

"I'm glad to know that Jeff is back in town. Running that bank and the blueberry farm is too much for you. Later, maybe some time next week, you and I will sit down and work on selling Anderson Farms. Julie, I'm proud that you made that decision. It's time for you to let go of that place and start living *your* life. Elizabeth must be up there smiling from ear to ear. Go check on Vonda, and see what you can find out and then come on over as soon as you can."

❧☙

I grabbed my purse and searched for my brand new set of keys and headed for Jeff's office, but I turned and motioned for Jessie to join us. She was behind me in a flash. Jeff looked up and offered me a weak smile.

"Hey, Julie, been a crazy week, and it's only Tuesday. Is it always like this? I was hoping to have time for us to talk about things."

He saw Jessie follow me into the office and looked from her to me. "What's going on? Am I being ambushed?"

"No, Jeff, it's Vonda. You know she wasn't at work yesterday, and didn't come in today. Jessie has been trying to find her, but no one knows where she is. I'm really worried, and I just got off the phone with Judge. He thinks something has happened to Vonda, and wants me to check out her house and then stop by to let him know what I find out. Just wanted you to know where I'm going."

He jumped up from his chair and walked around toward me, but looked at Jessie instead.

"Did I drop the ball on this? I thought she had scheduled a day off yesterday, and frankly, today I haven't even checked to see who was at work. What can I do?"

Jessie answered. "Don't beat yourself up, Jeff, I didn't actually tell you what was going on. I thought I should handle it. I should have followed up yesterday."

"Look, you two, we can worry about blame later, but right now I'm worried. Judge never gets involved with things like this, and if he's concerned, then something is going on. I'll be back as soon as I can."

"Hold up, Julie, do you think I should go with you? Can you handle this alone?"

"I'm just going to knock on her door, Jeff. If she's there, I'll find out why she didn't come to work. If she doesn't answer the door, I go on over to Judge's house and find out what he knows. I can handle this, and Jessie needs your help here."

"Guess you're right, but be careful. I'll help Jessie close, just keep us posted."

He looked around the bank and saw no customers waiting then followed me to the door. "Let me walk you to your car, Julie."

I didn't answer, but I was very aware of him walking beside me, and even more aware when he reached out and took the keys from my hand.

"What's this, Miss Trahan? A new car? Will you take me for a ride when we find Vonda?"

I looked up at his mischievous eyes and for a very brief moment, Vonda Gunderson and Judge McGrath were wiped from my memory.

# $\mathscr{T}$wenty-Eight

An unexpected telephone call delayed Roger Peppers, but he finally arrived at Judge's house, hoping that the coffee was still hot and the pie waiting.

"What's going on, Judge? What's happened?"

"Come on in, Roger, and I'll bring you up to date on everything I know. Rosalie will bring the coffee and pie in here. I asked for regular coffee. I've got a feeling this is going to be a long day and I most likely won't sleep tonight anyway."

They settled in comfortable chairs as Judge told about George Camp finding the shoe at Maddie's house, and then the fact that Vonda hadn't come in to work either Monday or today. Those words sent a chill of apprehension through Rev. Peppers and he quickly shared what he knew about Vonda.

"Judge, Vonda called me Saturday morning and said she had some questions that needed to be answered by a minister. She came to the church and we talked. I explained God's plan of salvation and Vonda gave her heart to Jesus right there in my office. It was a moving experience for both of us. Sunday morning, I was certain she would be in church, but she wasn't. Judge, what do you think happened?

Less than four minutes after leaving the bank, I was pulling in to the rear of Vonda's house. It was the only entrance

181

available since the entire front yard was completely overgrown with shrubs, vines, and who knew what.

Her car was under the lean-to style carport to the left of the house, and I sat for a moment looking around before I'd worked up my courage enough to get out of the car.

*Dear Lord, I'm scared and concerned about Vonda. I pray that everything is all right and this is just some crazy mixed-up lack of communication.*

I couldn't delay any longer, so I got out and followed a well-worn path to the back door and knocked. Only quiet came from the little cottage. No shuffling feet or answering words—there was nothing but still silence. I knocked again.

This time, I must have really banged on the door, because it moved about two inches and stayed open. I stood there with chills running down my spine, but I had to do this. After a mini-pep talk to myself, I toughened up and stuck my face in the crack of the opened door.

"Vonda, it's Julie, are you there? Vonda, can you hear me? I'm coming in."

Perhaps I've watched too many spooky television shows in the wee hours on sleepless nights, but I was worried about Vonda. Something about the stillness of this house didn't feel right.

Still, I didn't enter right away, but knocked again and the door pushed open a little wider. After nothing else happened, I put my left hand on the door and pushed it fully open and looked into the room.

I felt my mouth drop open. I could see into the kitchen and the sight was something unreal. Everywhere I looked I saw chaos and disarray. Broken dishes were on the floor, the refrigerator door stood open, one drawer was pulled out, and the kitchen table was pushed against the wall at a crazy angle. Chairs were helter-skelter about the room.

And then I looked at the floor. I grabbed the doorjamb to keep from falling, and took one tentative step inside the kitchen before I realized that I shouldn't go in there. Something dark red—almost brown—covered most of the floor, and I could only assume that it was blood.

If this was blood, there was a lot between the back door and the refrigerator. There was actually a pool of the dried substance in front of the open refrigerator. I kept looking and saw smears of this stuff everywhere. No, not everywhere, there seemed to be a smeared path toward this door—and then nothing but a smaller pool of—dried blood. Something horrible happened here—but what? Where was Vonda?

I wanted to leave, to get away from the awful mess in Vonda's house, but I had to try once more to see if she would answer me.

"Vonda, can you hear me?"

Nothing but eerie silence. I ran as fast as I could and jumped into my car. With shaking hands I reversed out of the graveled drive and drove with the speed of that proverbial bat. Within minutes I was running up the steps to Judge's house and I didn't wait for anyone to open the door. I ran into the living room, calling his name.

When the cat awakened her this time, Vonda was overcome with fear.

*"Dear God in heaven, where am I? I really am trying to be strong and courageous, but Lord, I don't know what to do. I put my trust in you, Lord. Keep me safe."*

Her body still hurt, her headache was only less intense than before, but now she knew she must do something or she would die.

*"Lord, if it is your will that I should die down here in some pit, then I will go quietly, but I feel that you want me to try to get out of this horrible place. Help me, Lord."*

She could hear the cat. It was a low mewling sound and close by, but where? She turned the flashlight a little to her right and near the floor of the place where she lay. She saw the cat force himself through a four-inch wide separation in the wall. He walked into the room, looked around for a second, and then turned around, leaving through the same small opening in the wall.

*So that is how you get in and out. I know that I can't get though that small hole, but maybe I can see what's on the other side.*

Normally, one or two small steps would have covered the space—if she could walk. Instead, she had to scoot and push her aching body, but she was finally in reach of the opening. Holding the flashlight firmly, she peered through the opening and couldn't believe her eyes.

✥✥

"Judge, Judge. Help, Judge, something terrible has happened at Vonda's. The kitchen has been wrecked and there is this dried dark brown stuff everywhere. I've never seen anything like it, but Judge that has to be blood—there's blood all over the kitchen floor."

I was hysterical with fear, and my cries brought a quick response. Roger Peppers followed Judge into the room—I must have frightened them with my screams for help.

"Julie, calm down. What are you talking about? Roger, make her sit down and get Rosalie to bring her some coffee. She's as pale as a ghost. Let's see if we can figure out what's going on. Now, Julie, just tell me slowly and coherently. Where did you see blood?"

I sank into the nearest available chair, took a deep breath and tried to focus on what I saw at Vonda's house. In spite of myself, my willingness to be mature and in control, I seemed to fall apart. My deep relaxing breath suddenly and unexpectedly turned into tears. I don't know if it was fear, potential grief, or just a combination of all the emotional stress that had been hounding me lately, but I couldn't stop crying.

I cried until a cup of coffee was held out to me and I gained enough control to take one sip and then another before I placed the cup on the table next to a freshly opened box of Kleenex. I grabbed a couple and tried to speak.

"I went to Vonda's house and I knocked on the door to the kitchen. Then I knocked again, harder, and the door opened. I looked inside and the kitchen floor was covered with blood. It scared me so I just ran away. I don't know if Vonda is lying dead somewhere or if she's there and badly hurt or what. I ran out and came over here. Judge, what should we do?"

"Well, I need to think for a minute, but I think our only choice is to call Cletus. This would fall under his jurisdiction. Roger, you pray, Julie, drink your coffee, and I'll be back in a minute.

᪷᪷

Vonda could see a small corridor and the cat. He was looking back at her as if to say, "Come on, come on in." Where was this place? Who did it belong to?

Perplexed and tired, she turned off the small flashlight and rested, trying to plan what to do next. It seemed to her that she had two options and both required patience.

Perhaps someone would find her. Surely by now the bank would know that something was wrong. She never missed work, and maybe they were already looking for her. Julie has probably called the police and reported me missing—at least she hoped.

Perhaps she should follow the cat and maybe she'd find a way out on her own, but she didn't have much strength. She would rest for a while and then she would try to follow the cat.

She needed something to take away the pain, something. She always kept a bottle of Advil in that capacious purse, but she was exhausted when she located the bottle. She swallowed four pills and then lay quietly, silently praying.

After a brief rest, she became more determined to find a way out of this tomb. She raised her hand and pressed against the wall opening with as much strength as she could muster. It was just enough to push against the panel until it opened.

"Thank you, Lord. You've opened the door, but where am I? I am still trapped somewhere."

❦

Judge leaned back in his desk chair and thought. And prayed. He was not only a contemplative man, but he was one who prayed. He prayed that God would assist this man elected to protect the small town and then he prayed for renewed wisdom for Cletus Stamper. Judge especially knew just how dumb this man could be.

He dialed 911, gave the operator his name and address, and made the appropriate request—police needed at scene of crime. Next, he dialed another familiar number.

"Jeff Watson, please, Jessie. This is Judge."

Jessie wanted to ask what was going on. She wanted to know if Vonda had been found, but she put those questions on hold and transferred the call to Jeff.

"Jeff Watson, can I help you?"

"Jeff, this is Judge. Julie just came back from Vonda's house and she's a little upset. It seems that something terrible has happened over there. Julie said there was a lot of blood in the kitchen, and then she kinda fell apart when she came back here, and that's not like Julie. She usually can handle anything. Could you or Jessie come over and check on her? Roger and I are going to Vonda's house to see what happened. Just come on in when you get here."

Judge went to the doorway for another look at Julie, and answered Rev. Peppers unasked question.

"Roger, I need to make one more phone call. When I get that taken care of, you and I need to check this situation out for ourselves, if you don't mind driving me."

The local police had been notified, but it would be much better if the Elbamarle County Sheriff was brought into this now instead of after Cletus had a chance to mess things up. When the call was completed, he walked back into the living room. He wanted to reassure Julie that everything would be okay—even if it wasn't, but he had to speak the truth.

"Julie, I talked to Jeff, and told him we were going to Vonda's house. I think he or Jessie will be over here in a moment. I believe that what you saw should be considered a crime scene. I think Vonda has come to serious harm or worse."

He started toward the door, but stopped. "Rosalie, come on in here and sit with Julie until someone from the bank gets here. Do not let her leave. Roger and I have something to do."

# Twenty-Nine

**Jeff walked to Jessie's window, his hand jangling his car** keys and the anxiety clearly drawn on his face.

"Julie is at Judge's house and they think something terrible happened at Vonda's place. He didn't explain and I didn't push him for more information, but he said Julie is very upset. Someone needs to check on her while Judge and Roger Peppers go over to Vonda's house."

He waited for an answer but his mind was already set. He was going to check on Julie. They had gotten off on the wrong foot, but she got his attention last Saturday night when she wanted to resign from the bank. Spending time with her on Sunday had only increased that interest.

"Jeff, I can close the bank without you. I've done it before—no problem, go on over and check on Julie. I'll try to stop by for a moment when I close the bank."

He was out the door before Jessie finished speaking.

❧❦

"Dear God in heaven! Judge, look at this mess. This is terrible. I thought the chief was on his way. How did we get here first?"

"Roger, you've only been here a few years and I've lived here all my life. I've known Cletus Stamper since he was a

188

teenager. He was trouble then and he's still trouble, only now he's wearing a uniform." Judge seemed to be thinking hard about something, but he finally continued.

"Cletus was probably at that diner out of town drinking coffee, or maybe he was gone on one of his beer runs. A dry county only increases the distance a drinker has to go to purchase his beverage of choice. Our chief has been sucking on beer cans all of his life. Can't wait until we can get rid of his useless and incompetent hide."

Suddenly the scene before them seemed to grab his attention, shaking him to the core. "Roger, what in the world happened here? Do you think she's still here? Look, there seems to be a trail through some of that blood, it looks as if—as if she crawled or was drug through this room. Let's back up and see if we can see how far this trail goes—but watch where you step. We don't want to disturb the evidence."

They left the kitchen to sounds of reverberating thunder as a flash of lightning followed almost immediately. In only seconds, the heavens opened up with rain that met the ground with a vengeance. Their only choice was to make a mad dash for the preacher's car, and both men were soaked before they got into the car.

Even though it was mid-July and very hot, Rev. Peppers started the motor and turned on the heat, trying to send some warm drying air to Judge's rain-dampened clothing. After a time, he adjusted the temperature to a more moderate setting as they waited for the chief of police.

Jeff ran to the rear of the bank and jumped into his truck, with both heart and mind racing. His heart was anxious for Julie, and his mind wondered if his dad had ever dealt with things like this. He couldn't remember hearing any stories about this sort of thing.

It was only a few short blocks to Judge's house and about

the same distance to Vonda's place. He was tempted to stop off at Vonda's first, but his heart was pulling him toward Julie. Two minutes later, he was running up the steps at Judge's house and Julie was sitting in a rocking chair on the porch.

"Julie, what happened, honey? Judge said you were upset. What happened at Vonda's?"

She couldn't speak, she just shook her head as the tears started again. What in the world had happened to her? She was not a crybaby, but what she saw—Vonda's kitchen with blood everywhere—had destroyed her composure.

In a heartbeat, Jeff was on his knees in front of the old, weathered rocking chair and was hugging her—and she was crying on his shoulder.

Rosalie came out of the back door and walked up to where Julie and Jeff were sitting. "Julie honey, why don't you and Jeff come to the kitchen and have some tea or coffee. You're making yourself sick with all this crying."

It was all Julie needed to calm down and get in control. That plus the thought that she was being hugged by Jeff Watson—and hugging back.

⋙⋘

The rain stopped finally. Roger Peppers and Judge got out of the small car and walked over to the kitchen door, waiting impatiently for the chief of police to answer the 911 call. They could hear the sirens in the distance, and then screeching tires as Cletus Stamper turned off Honey Grove Street and whirled into the driveway. The police car slid to a stop only inches behind Rev. Peppers' PT Cruiser, and slinging gravel in every direction, causing the good preacher to send up an urgent prayer for safety—from the police department.

The chief must have had a little trouble unbuckling his seat belt, but finally pushed himself out of the car and tried to walk toward the house. The overgrown shrubs gave little room for a man of his girth, and when he tried to walk between the police car and the PT Cruiser, that didn't work either. He was forced to retrace his steps to the rear of the police car to approach the cottage. Impatiently, he raised his voice, uttered a few choice expletives, and began asking questions.

"What's going on, Judge? Why'd you call me over here to Vonda's? What was that you said about blood?"

Then, as he finally maneuvered around the vehicles, the man let out a raucous sound that was intended to be laughter.

"She probably hit that no good Odie Marshall over the head and bloodied him up a little bit. That's probably what's going on. Now let's see what we got."

Judge motioned for Roger Peppers to step back, to stand clear for the chief to enter the kitchen. They waited outside for the man to make an observation of the crime scene. Instead, Cletus Stamper took one look at the bloody mess left behind on the floor and bolted clear of the room, over to some bushes at the side of the house and promptly lost his lunch. He fell to the ground writhing as if in pain, only to heave again.

"Roger, let's go back to the house. This idiot needs to get himself together. I've got to convince Jim Bolton to get on out here."

There was only one problem, the police car was almost bumper to bumper with his car, but Roger Peppers cut the wheel sharply to the right and drove through the now muddy backyard, across the shallow ditch, and back on to the side road before turning back onto Honey Grove Street.

"My goodness, Judge, if Cletus Stamper runs the police department the same way he drives that car, we may be in a spot of trouble."

"Roger, that's a fine way to put it, but from what I saw, Vonda's the one in trouble. We need to pray, this doesn't look good."

The two men hurried onto the porch of Judge's house, feeling powerless and confused.

Jessie Baker stopped by to check on Julie and to let Jeff know that she had closed the bank with no problem. Her only problem was her husband.

"Donald wants his supper. Sorry, Julie, but I guess I have to go. Call me when you hear something, anything at all."

Jeff and I watched her leave, just as Roger Peppers was driving up. I was praying desperately for some good news, but in my heart I really didn't hold out much hope. I could tell from the frustrated look on Judge's face that there was no good news.

"Jeff, glad you came over. Come on in the house with us. We need to sit down and have something to eat. I can't let my sugar get out of control. Julie, do you know if Jim Bolton called back?"

"No, I haven't heard anything. Jeff and I've been out here waiting for you to get back. Did you find out anything? What did the chief say?"

Both men just merely shook their heads. Judge went to his study but he stopped in the living room, and Rev. Peppers told us of the strange reaction our local chief of police had at the crime scene.

Judge was on the phone with Jim Bolton. We could hear the sound of his voice elevated in anger as he relayed in detail what he saw at Vonda's house and Cletus Stamper's reaction. After another minute he returned to the living room and invited us to join him for supper.

The meal was finished and we were drinking coffee when Sheriff Jim Bolton knocked on the back door. Rosalie opened the door and offered dinner, dessert or coffee, or all of the above. The sheriff just asked for a glass of water.

We stayed at the table and each of us told our story, and Sheriff Bolton took notes of every answer. When he could think of no other questions, he pocketed the small notebook and began to shake his head.

"Here's the deal. I stopped at the address you gave me and went in the back door. No doubt about it, something really bad happened in that house. As dumb as your chief of police appears to be, he has handled this pretty well, but only because he hasn't done anything yet. We're posting a guard on the house tonight and I'll be sending some lab guys out as soon as they can get here."

"Now, this is the way I see it. One, we know there was a crime. Two, we assume we know the identity of the victim. Three, we don't know where the victim is now, and until we get some other information on that, or some hint as to where to look, we're pretty much dead in the water."

"Anyway, the sheriff's department is on it and we'll do everything in our power to find this lady. Now, why don't you folks go home, get some rest, and leave this for us to handle? If I hear anything tonight, Judge, I'll get in touch with you. I hope y'all have a blessed night."

# $\mathscr{T}$hirty

**George Camp was angry and snorting about like a mad** bull. He started this job on Sunday afternoon—first mistake—and here it is Tuesday evening and he still wasn't close to being finished. What had he let himself in for, letting Odie Marshall order him around like he was nothing but a school boy? He and Maddie must be having a whopping good time, because neither of them had called to check on the progress of the job, and that was a very good thing indeed.

Nothing about this job had gone as planned, just as he told Judge earlier this afternoon. Now it was nearly dark and he still hadn't done any work, and from the look of things, he'd have to wait until tomorrow and start again.

He'd come on out here after talking to Judge, and then the bottom fell out. One thing he had always known—it's best to steer clear of bad weather. And the weather got bad—and quickly, so he and Lucky took cover in the cab of the semi. Wind and rain buffeted the big truck that he used to transport his equipment, and rain pounded the cab with such vehemence that even thinking was difficult. It was a noisy, windy, and typical summer storm that would soon pass on through.

Lucky had been content to stay close to George during the turbulence, but the storm was winding down and he was tired of being cooped up in this truck. The big black lab was peeking out every window, and whining, begging to be set free. When a squirrel looking for food braved the wet grass, Lucky was no longer content to whine and beg, he started barking, and George agreed. It was time to get out of the truck and take a look at things.

George was ready to see what shape the ground was in. Sometimes these storms brought so much water that it took a while for the earth to absorb it all, but today, well, he just couldn't tell yet. He opened the driver's door to step out and was almost knocked over as Lucky shot out before him, chasing the squirrel around and about and finally up a tree.

After sniffing around a few bushes, trees, and other landmarks, Lucky discovered something of even greater interest. His tail straightened and his ears plucked up as he investigated, scouted, and sniffed a path from the garage of Maddie's house to the old storm shelter, the one that George was supposed to cover up. Lucky had latched on to something of interest and he was determined to find the source. He scratched and whined, and then whined and scratched around even more. He was trying to communicate that something wasn't right down there, and George took notice. Whatever scent Lucky had picked up was not washed away by the rain, perhaps because of the sheltering branches of the ancient live oak trees.

George and Lucky scouted the grounds around the storm shelter and all the way back around behind the garage, but Lucky kept going back to the door of the old storm shelter to sniff, scratch, and whine. By now it was getting dark, and George didn't see too well driving at night so he hurried Lucky into the truck cab and went home.

Whatever Lucky got agitated about would be there tomorrow. He only hoped the rain would be gone by then.

The weather came in waves as so often happens in the summer with one band of storms following another. The weather radio in Rosalie's kitchen kept repeating the ominous warnings—severe thunderstorms until three o'clock tomorrow morning.

Jeff was still with us, so we all stood up and held hands while Rev. Peppers prayed for Vonda's safety. We said goodbye and Jeff held a borrowed umbrella over my head as I rushed out to my car and waited patiently for the two behind me to exit so I could get home. It was no surprise that he followed me home.

I ran to the back porch and waited for Jeff to follow, and then I fed Goldie. I was uncertain whether to invite Jeff in, and he seemed equally unsure. He took my hand and pulled me over to the old wooden porch swing, tucked way back away from the rain. Nevertheless, he pulled a handkerchief from his pocket and wiped the swing and we sat down, still holding hands.

It had been far too long since there was someone to comfort me and I readily accepted his embrace. We sat for a while in quiet, then as it sometimes happens, we both spoke at the same time.

"Jeff" . . . "Julie" . . . And we laughed and began again.

"Julie, I guess you're wondering where this is going between us. I know I am. All I know is that I like you, and I want to get to know you better. I don't want this to be about work, or Vonda, or the past. I want to see if there is something between Jeff and Julie. How do you feel about this?"

"Right now, I'm pretty leery of any relationship. I don't feel up to telling you all the details, but just a few days ago, I had dinner with my ex-fiancé. It has been ten years since he walked out on me, only a few days before the wedding. Anyway, he came back with explanations that were hard to hear. Whatever happens between us needs to be slow and certain. I never want to go through another broken romance. I obviously have some sort of feelings for you, too, Jeff. Can we just take it slow and see what happens?"

He pulled me close and kissed me—warm and tenderly— and I felt my head spin. This was not what I called slow.

He kissed me again, on the forehead, and reluctantly said goodnight. I went inside and called my friends to ask them to pray for Vonda, pray for her safety. With a fearful but prayerful heart, I went to bed.

❧❧

Vonda felt so weak and knew from the pain in her leg that she would never be able to stand, but with great determination, she scooted through the opening into a small corridor—and into another world. It was a world of light and heat, and probably offered safety if she could only move into it. She was still for a minute, trying to take in everything and visually examining the space.

"This is weird, surreal. Where am I?"

The well-lighted corridor was narrow in width, and covered only a short distance. The cat was waiting at the end of the corridor, sitting in what appeared to be some sort of opening in the wall. Was that a doorway? She watched as the cat raised his head as if to say, "Come on." She would try.

Through pain that was more excruciating with every effort, she crawled, scooted and pushed her way forward, inching slowly toward the cat. When she got closer to where she thought he was, the cat was gone, disappeared.

"Where did he go? I was watching him and he just vanished."

*Lord, I know it is by your will that I have gotten this far. Please help me get out of this place. Help me find that cat.*

She moved forward another foot, and thought about "Mr. Wonderful." The cat had appeared out of nowhere, and had helped her keep her sanity. The cat had shown her how to escape from that smelly underground dungeon, and now she needed to find him again.

Mr. Wonderful. She didn't know when she had given the cat that name, but it seemed to fit. Then she had another thought, was he for real?

*Are there angel cats? Maybe Mr. Wonderful is really an angel cat. Vonda, you're losing it, you've got to keep focused so that you can get out of here.*

Another few inches and—what is this place?

*Am I in paradise? Where am I? This is nice, but it can't be paradise, but compared to the dark, cramped, and smelly place I was just in, this surely is the next best thing. Is this real, or am I hallucinating?*

She reached out and touched every surface she could reach. This must be a real place. Her fingers traced the floor, and felt the rough texture of carpet. It was softer and much warmer than where she had been. She must have been lying on a dirt floor somewhere, but where—and where was she now?

From her swollen eyes, she could tell that the room was paneled in a dark wood, maybe oak or cherry, and it was beautiful. Not very large, but big enough for a leather sofa, TV, a huge recliner. *This must be a man's room, wherever it is. I hope whoever owns this place will find me. Maybe Mr. Wonderful belongs to the owner of this room.*

She was tired and lay quiet for a time, silently thanking God for getting her to a better place. *Only a few days ago, I trusted God for my eternal salvation. Even if I never get out of this place, I'm thankful for that.*

Sleep was coming on fast, but still she listened, trying to figure out where she was. There were no sounds, no movements from anywhere. Wherever she was, she was still alone, but the room was warm and comfortable. There was some sort of light filtering in from far above her—a sky light? Probably. She thought she could make out a tree branch that was swaying in the wind.

Then she looked around the room and burst into tears when she saw the bathroom tucked away in one corner. *If only I could crawl into that shower and wash off some of this dirt. But I'm just so tired...*

⋙⋘

I didn't sleep very well. I wanted to go to bed and pretend that nothing had happened between Jeff Watson and me, but that wasn't possible. I tossed and turned for hours, telling myself the same thing. *This is happening much too fast. I don't really know Jeff. He doesn't really know me. This is probably just because of the emotions of the day, confusing everything.*

And then I remembered how I felt when he kissed me.

I woke to the sounds of thunder rumbling far off in the distance and realized that I had slept much too late. The morning routine of preparing myself for work became a marathon event, but at three minutes before eight I unlocked those antique doors, relocked them and then unlocked the secure, almost fortress-like doors to the bank lobby. I worked as if by rote, unlocking the vault and preparing for the day. Shortly I was joined by Jessie and then Jeff.

The same question—"Have you heard anything?" was asked by both and I answered with a negative shake of my head. We put aside our concern and put on our *banker* hats.


The banking routine was always the same, customers came and went, questions were asked and answered. Checks were cashed and money deposited, but all of this was accompanied by a very somber air that touched our customers as well as the small staff. Everyone in Three Bridges knew by now that Vonda Gunderson was missing and each customer offered some expression of concern for her safety. My mind and my prayers never left Vonda.

The one thing I wanted more than anything was to see Vonda Sue Gunderson walk through those doors, treading boldly in Birkenstocks, long flowing dress and with that huge hobo-style bag thrown casually over her shoulder. If I could just see her once more, I would never be critical of her clothing style, her bland appearance, or anything, and I would fall on my knees thanking God for her return.

Jessie asked only once for news of Vonda and when I shook my head, she continued about her business. We were of like mind on that score. Talking never changed much, prayer could change many things.

# Thirty-One

**George started toward Maddie's place with a nagging** memory that he simply couldn't get his hands around. Something wasn't right. Something that he'd seen in the last two days had come back to haunt him but he couldn't pull the memory back into focus.

He pulled his truck between the unlocked gates and drove over to the storm shelter. It took only one close look at the hasp lock for the memory to jolt into his brain. Scratch marks, fresh scratch on the rusty old metal.

～ ～

"Judge, this is George Camp. I came on out here this morning to Miss Maddie's to finish my job like I told you I would, and I accidentally pulled the storm shelter door off the frame." He didn't try to continue because he knew there would be an explosion from Judge.

"Just what do you mean, you *accidentally* pulled the storm door off. George Camp, you can drive that tractor blindfolded in the dark. How in tarnation did you *accidentally* pull the door off? What's going on out there, George?"

"Judge, I said it was an accident—told you nothing had gone right on this job from the beginning. You don't think I do something stupid like pulling the door off on purpose, do you?"

"Anyway, whether it was an accident or on purpose, you'd

better call the sheriff. When I knocked the door off, I got down and took a look inside. Judge, something is dead down there and it stinks to high heaven. Call the sheriff. I think this is way too big for the chief."

He started to end the call but remembered one important detail.

"And another thing, Judge, the weatherman said we had another round of storms coming through and it looks like we're going to have a gully-washer any time now. Probably need someone to bring out some tarps to cover this up until the sheriff can get here. I 'preciate it, Judge. I'll be right here."

He didn't intend to change his story and he didn't wait for Judge to ask any questions. After all, when working with heavy equipment, any fellow could make a mistake and put the blade of his tractor down in the wrong spot. Accidents happened every day, and this could have been just as he said. Heaven knows his eyesight wasn't what it used to be.

But he had spent too many hours last night thinking about how Lucky hit on that scent coming from a storm shelter. He'd turned the problem over six ways to Sunday and the answers all came back the same. Vonda Sue Gunderson was missing and something or someone was buried in that storm shelter. And then when he saw those fresh scratch marks, he didn't need anyone's permission, he went to work.

George Camp had his philosophy about life and it was quite simple. He believed that if you waited for "procedures" and "protocol", things could take forever to be resolved. He couldn't wait around for those things to be worked out. Sometimes, it was up to him to make something happen.

He went back to the open hole in the ground and stared into the darkness. It wasn't a big place, and had indeed been a storm shelter. His old flashlight sent out a feeble beam, but an assortment of unidentifiable objects could be seen, and when he looked further into the darkened room, he thought he could just make out the form of a body in one corner.

He had done everything he could do and now he had to wait

for the officials.

જાજ

"Roger, I hate to interrupt your morning, but George has a problem out at Maddie Wallace's place, and I need to get out there. I'd appreciate it if you could drive me. He's discovered something important, and he wants me out there. I'm afraid he has found a body—at least he thinks so. If you can, I would appreciate it if you would take me out there."

"Judge, I only need a few minutes and then I'll be at your back door. The most important thing for us to do now is pray. Whatever is going on at Maddie's place, God is still in control. I'll be at your house shortly."

Judge replaced the telephone receiver into the cradle and thought about the situation. If George thinks he has found a body, then he is probably right. That man could try the patience of any saint, but through the years, he had learned that when George told you something as unmitigated truth, it was all of that and more.

Now, he had to make the call that should have been made before he called Roger Peppers—he had to call Sheriff Jim Bolton.

"Jim, this is Judge. We need you out at Maddie Wallace's place. It seems as if George Camp accidently knocked off the doors to an old storm shelter, and it looks as if there's a body down there—I'm afraid that we may have found Vonda Sue Gunderson."

The next phone call was to Cletus Stamper. Using his most forceful and authoritative voice, he relayed the instructions from Sheriff Bolton to bring tarps, tents, and other materials to the farm. Hopefully, Stamper wouldn't mess this up.

જાજ

Waiting for the law enforcement personnel to arrive, George Camp cranked up his tractor and began to move some of the dirt away. The rain had made a muddy mess and he wanted to

*202*

give the workers more space to work. It was difficult and muddy work and in truth, he didn't accomplish very much except to fill the empty gap of time until the police arrived.

Soon the cars began to gather, and not surprisingly, Roger Peppers and Judge were among the first, followed by a deputy sheriff, and finally Cletus Stamper and his boys.

◈◈

Slowly Vonda opened her eyes. The room was brighter than last night, and she could see what looked like grey skies, and something else—some sort of metal structure over the skylight. Another day but the hurting was still as bad as before and she was so weak. *God, is this the day I die?*

A sound interrupted her thoughts—what was that noise? It was the first sound she had heard since Odie threw her down into that pit. Was she only imagining that she heard something?

No, somewhere from a distance, she could hear a noise, a muffled roaring sound that seemed to be coming from somewhere overhead. Something else was happening. What was that? A shaking from somewhere, a slight vibration of the floor—yes. The noise came and went in waves, and with the rising sound, she could feel a slight but steady pulsation of the floor beneath her. What in the world was happening? Then the vibration and the noise stopped and silence returned.

Hope had been revived and questions were running through her mind. If that was some sort of equipment making the noise and vibrations, there must be workers also. Could they find her? She dozed again with the quiet, but a few minutes later the sound started again and finally, faded away.

*"Dear God in heaven, please let them find me, let someone come to rescue me."*

Just as she finished her brief prayer, she was joined by Mr. Wonderful, who came to offer his friendship. He placed his furry body close to her and nudged her with his head as if to say, "Come on, we have work to do," and she tried to respond.

With her good hand, she reached out, tried to leverage into a sitting position, but she just couldn't make her body move. Unwilling to give up, she tried to turn over, but a jolt of pain rushed through her leg, and Vonda's world spun into darkness.

≪≫

Roger and Judge remained standing against his small car that was parked over to the side and away from the storm shelter, and watched the various officials arrive on the scene. Before long, the place was filled with vehicles from the local police departments, the county marshal, a deputy sheriff, and even the local volunteer fire department. But the investigation couldn't begin until Jim Bolton arrived. He had insisted on that.

Tarps had been placed around the storm shelter, trying to cover up the rain soaked dirt that had quickly turned to mud. A tent was being erected over the opening, portable lighting had been set up close to the opening, and everyone was waiting for the sheriff to arrive before entering the ground.

Roger Peppers hadn't stopped praying for Vonda, praying that the men were wrong in their speculation that she had been killed and left to the consequences of nature. Until she called last Saturday, she had been just a teller at the bank and one of the people he saw around town. He was ashamed that he had never made an effort to know the real person.

Saturday, he had gotten to know a little about Vonda Gunderson, the person, not Vonda the bank teller. Never had he known anyone so eager to accept God's forgiving love. For some reason, he felt a bond with this woman who was probably dead in that hole. His heart gladdened at remembering how she embraced God's salvation. If she was dead, she would be with her heavenly Father. Everyone seemed certain that a decaying body was in that shelter. If it wasn't Vonda, who could it be?

He paused from his prayers to look at Judge, and was shocked to see the man pale and shaking. This wasn't good. Judge needed a place to sit down. In the distance, he spotted some lawn chairs. "Young man, you over there. Get those lawn chairs and bring them over here quickly. Judge needs to sit down."

The youthful policeman made very short work of returning with the two chairs, but instead of taking them to where they stood, he placed them in a tent that had just been erected a short distance away from the storm shelter, and motioned for them to have a seat away from the expected rain.

∽᭜᜶

Eventually, the county sheriff, an ambulance, and several other emergency vehicles could be seen entering the road to the farm. With practiced efficiency they pulled to a stop and began exiting their vehicles. The sheriff and his deputies approached the tents, walking quickly to escape as much of the downpour that had erupted from the heavens only moments before. With hand extended, the sheriff greeted everyone under the tent.

"Judge, Rev. Peppers, I've been the sheriff for almost ten years and on days like today, I wonder why I stay. Pray for all of us, Preacher, this ain't good and the weather is going to make things worse"

With trained efficiency, the response team set about doing their job. They brought pry bars and finished pulling the door off and in only a matter of minutes, two EMT's entered the old storm shelter and then reappeared. They motioned for the sheriff to come down and view the remains of a body.

Sheriff Jim Bolton had been expecting the worst so he donned a small mask and descended the steps into the storm shelter. After only a few minutes, he came out and looked around for the medical examiner. Finally, he spotted the car, just pulling in from the driveway to the farm. As he waited for the ME to reach him, he gestured for the EMT's to bring in the body bag.

"Give the ME plenty of room and let me know what he has to say."

Then he walked slowly back to the tent as Judge and Rev.

Peppers waited for the bad news to be made official.

"We definitely have a body, but I doubt that it's the woman you say is missing. Even in that underground shelter, this extreme heat and humidity has probably hastened the amount of decay. In my experience, the body has been down there a few days, but what I can determine is this appears to be an older woman, with bright auburn hair. Does that sound like your missing lady?"

Roger Peppers and Judge answered in tandem. "No, praise God."

"No, that definitely is not Vonda Sue Gunderson."

Roger Peppers took a deep breath and then continued. "That's not Vonda, but it could well be Miss Maddie Wallace."

# $\mathcal{T}$hirty-Two

**Judge seemed to weaken when he heard those words. He** tried to sit in the lawn chair, but his legs gave away and he dropped into the chair, covering his face with his hands. He prayed for Maddie—prayed that she was resting in peace. His relationship with R.J. and Maddie Wallace had spanned many years. They'd been casual friends, and occasionally been involved in a professional relationship.

Only a few days ago, Maddie had called and apologized for not offering to pay him for writing her will. He remembered his flippant response—"Don't worry. I'll just take out my fee before I start dispersing your assets." He never imagined this would be a necessary action.

Time passed slowly as the medical examiner and police continued to do whatever it is they do in a crime scene, making notes on the evidence and taking pictures from every angle around the exterior of the shelter.

Rev. Peppers and Judge continued to sit, wait, and pray—for Maddie and for Vonda. She was still missing. Everyone thought Maddie Wallace had been in the car with Odie Marshall. Was that really Vonda sitting beside him as he sped away?

No, that just couldn't be. Something terrible had happened in Vonda's kitchen. If she wasn't buried in that storm shelter—where was she?

I didn't know if I could remain cooped up in this bank with all that was going on outside the town at Miss Maddie's farm. I knew there was nothing I could do, but I wanted to be there to see for myself how things were going. I paced my office and roamed the bank lobby, and remembered how badly I had treated Vonda through the years.

I was the newest hire of the three of us. Jessie Baker was hired first, then Vonda, and finally I was. Even then, it seemed to me that no one placed any importance on Vonda Sue Gunderson. She was hardly more than any office fixture. Like a calculator or printer, she had been expected to do her job and then forgotten until needed for the next task. Sadly, I had followed in that path.

This morning it seemed as if I were viewing my past sins, and that Vonda had been the one person most sinned against. Perhaps *sin* is the wrong word—perhaps wronged would be a more fitting adjective—but aren't those words one and the same? I think so.

I think Grandmother knew how Vonda was treated, and how I played the same game of ignoring the woman and even judging her for her lifestyle, her attitude, and the clothes she wore to work. Grandmother's words of caution came back to me—"Be careful how you treat each person. Those people may be sent from God to test you. Remember God wants us to love everyone."

At first, I could blame my youthful ignorance and arrogance, but I've had many years to develop a better relationship with Vonda, and little has changed. Now, looking back, I realize that she was a better person than I am, because she'd never been rude or indifferent to me even though I was in a position at the bank that probably should have been hers.

I walked back into the vault looking for a quiet place to pray.

*"Father, I have sinned against one of your children and I beg forgiveness. Through all these years that I've worked at the bank, I have never tried to be Vonda's friend, and now it looks as if I may never have that chance. Forgive me, Lord. Amen."*

☙❧

George Camp came over and sat on his haunches next to

Judge. "Judge, did you know that ol' R.J. Wallace had a second underground shelter built down there?"

"What do you mean, another shelter built down there—down where? What in the Sam Hill are you talking about, George?"

"Well, it was a while back. Maybe seven-eight years ago I think it was. R.J sent Maddie on a trip to Europe, and while she was gone, we built another shelter down there—oh, just about here."

George pointed to a spot on the ground about ten feet to the left of the open shelter, closer to the house. He was pointing to an area that contained a replica of an oil derrick. The derrick was elevated and dramatically landscaped with the centerpiece being a huge Lone Star symbol.

"It's a doozie too. Nothing plain about that room. There's even a bathroom built in down there with special plumbing that pumps everything back up and into its own waste system. Heated and cooled, with TV and all the comforts of home. Ole R.J. wanted a place where he could go to smoke a good stogie and have a drink—pardon me, Reverend. Anyway, we finished it about a week afore old Maddie came back home. That's it under that fake oil derrick. That thing was put up to disguise what was built under it."

"What are you getting at, George, rambling on about underground toilets with special plumbing? Man, if you are trying to tell us something, get on with it!"

"Judge, all I know is that I built another underground room down there. You can get to it three different ways, from this old storm shelter, from the house, and there is a door hidden in that fake oil derrick over there."

"Well, we'll have to wait until the sheriff can get free enough to talk to us, then you tell him your story and maybe he'll send someone down there."

"Okay, Judge, we'll do things your way."

But George walked away with other thoughts in his mind, talking to himself.

"I found that shoe, just one shoe all by its lonesome, the one that I think belongs to Vonda. I *accidently* opened the storm shelter and found a body that wasn't Vonda. Nobody knows where she is. If she wasn't in that old storm shelter, she has to be somewhere. I can't imagine how she would get there, but I think we should look for her in that new shelter. I think she may be in that other room down there."

❧☙

While the police and the medical examiner teams were assessing the crime scene, taking pictures and measurements, marking spots where clues were found and examining the area, Mr. Wonderful decided to take things into his own hands, or rather his paws. With silent steps he entered the area unseen, and went up to one of the sheriff's deputies, and in characteristic cat-like manner, greeted him. At the sound of a cat meowing, the officer became so rattled that he ran out of the storm shelter, with the other members of the team right behind him.

"What in tarnation are you guys running from? Did you see a ghost?"

"There's a cat down there, and he wasn't there when we went in. Came up behind me and scared the stew out of me!" replied one officer.

"Now where would a cat come from? Are you sure you didn't imagine it?"

There was no need for the men to answer. Mr. Wonderful stood on the first step of the storm shelter, and greeted the crowd with a very loud and angry "meow." He then turned and ran back inside the shelter.

A look from the sheriff quickly sent the deputies back down to look for the cat, but he couldn't be found. A very nervous group of professionals, skilled in their individual jobs, returned to the scene of the crime. They worked with one eye always looking for a cat.

❧☙

I left the vault and went back to the pretense of working. I was still trying to avoid Jeff. Whatever had happened between us last night could not become part of our work routine. As long as I avoided looking into his office, I didn't have a problem thinking of him as my boss instead of a potential boyfriend.

Apparently, he felt the same way because he had also avoided making eye contact with me the two or three times we'd spoken today. Jessie Baker had given us strange looks as if wondering if we'd had an argument.

No. We definitely hadn't been arguing last night, but today we struggled to find an easy work routine. I didn't have time to worry about a Jeff and Julie relationship; finding Vonda was far more important. I could do nothing but pray.

I looked up the see Cynthia running into the bank, dripping wet and without an umbrella. "Julie, I just heard the report on the police scanner—Miss Maddie has been found in a storm shelter. She was dead. Oh, Julie, who killed that woman?"

Everyone in the bank came running to my office as Cynthia told me the news. Jeff darted from his office and both Jessie Baker and her customer followed quickly. The entire town of Three Bridges knew Miss Maddie. We all wanted to know the details, but there really was nothing else that Cynthia could tell us.

She left as quickly as she came in, and Jessie and her customer returned to finish whatever business they were involved in. Jeff and I were left staring at each other in disbelief.

He closed my office door, but we were very aware of the glass that created the office walls. I sat back in my chair, shaking my head in disbelief, and he sat in one of the client chairs.

"You all right, Julie? You look a little pale."

"I'm okay. You know, Jeff, through the years, and especially lately after she became so involved with Odie Marshall, Maddie Wallace was a terror to deal with. Nothing I did could please her. She was—well, everyone has seen that side of her. But the other day, not many days ago when she came in here to take Odie's name off her accounts, I saw a different Maddie Wallace."

"What do you mean, honey, how was she different? I certainly only saw the rude and abrasive, uppity side of her. What did you see differently?"

"Well, she was almost nice, soft-spoken and just different. Then Odie came back in to the bank and she quickly reverted to the person we all knew. Which personality was the real Maddie Wallace?"

He didn't answer for a while, then spoke very softly. "I think that may be a life lesson for all of us. No one knows when we'll draw our last breath, or under what sort of circumstances. From now on, I hope to be a better person. Julie, I need to apologize to you again. I really took advantage of you because I was running away from my responsibilities."

I could think of no appropriate response, and I just shrugged my shoulders. Jeff then said what I was only thinking. "This isn't the time or place to discuss personal matters, but soon, very soon, we need to find out what this is between us. We need to see if this is real. Could we have dinner Friday evening? How about me bringing takeout to your house so we can talk without interruptions?"

I smiled. My heart smiled, but I could think of only one silly thing to say.

"Sounds like a plan to me."

I tried to concentrate on my job, but I quickly lost the battle to anxiety and concern. I didn't want to be cooped up in this bank. I wanted to be out at Maddie Wallace's place. I wanted to find Vonda.

"Jeff, I need to leave, I need to go Maddie's place. Can you cover for me again? I really need to be out there to find out what I can about Vonda."

# Thirty-Three

**The first few miles from the bank to Maddie Wallace's farm** were driven on autopilot. The way was so very familiar—I've probably driven this road hundreds of times. Maddie's farm was just a few miles from Anderson Farms.

Funny how my mind had completely shut out everything about Grandmother's farm. These terrible events that were unfolding before our eyes had made me forget that only a few days ago—last Sunday afternoon—I'd asked Hortense Salazar to buy Anderson Farms. Fear for Vonda's safety and then learning that Maddie Wallace was a murder victim had driven all other worries from my mind.

The miles between the town and Miss Maddie's farm were driven much too fast, but I reached my destination without landing in the ditch, or anything worse. I said a prayer of thankfulness as I pulled through those distinctive wrought iron gates where I had taken refuge from the storm not many days ago.

The sight before me was amazing and sobering. Official vehicles were everywhere, reinforcing the fact that a crime had most likely been committed at this estate. I drove my new car through the muddy yard and parked near a tent, but I was quickly challenged by an angry looking policeman.

"Ma'am, visitors are not allowed—this is a crime scene. What's your business out here? May I see some identification?"

The words were barked at me as if I were the criminal, but I was saved from answering by Judge McGrath.

"Steve, let up. Miss Trahan is out here to see me. Come on over, Julie. Make yourself useful, young man, and find another chair for the lady and then you can find someone else to bully."

I swallowed the response I wanted to make to that upstart young man and asked the obvious question, "Is it true? Did they find Miss Maddie?"

Rev. Peppers and Judge both nodded in agreement and the angry young patrolman returned with another very wet lawn chair. I brushed off most of the water with one hand and sat down, not overly concerned with the state of my clothing. I looked at the men in front of me and could only read sorrow on their faces.

Rev. Peppers pointed to the group of men under the other tent.

"Julie, the body of Miss Maddie Wallace was found in that storm shelter. We don't know the nature of her death, but someone wrapped her body in a bed sheet, and placed or threw her into that storm shelter. Since Odie was the person that ordered the shelter to be covered up, we're assuming he would also be responsible for her death."

"What about Vonda? Is there any news of her? Are you certain she wasn't down there with Miss Maddie?"

"No, that's all we know. We can only pray for her safety."

✧✦

I sat with Judge and Rev. Peppers beneath the tent and watched the events unfold around us. Men were hustling about, some with cameras, one or two with clipboards, making notes of some sort, probably detailing the operation. I gazed at the black bag that obviously contained the body of Maddie Wallace and was overwhelmed with sorrow. I hadn't liked this woman very much, but no person should die at the hands of another and be so heartlessly abandoned.

Men continued to walk back and forth, doing whatever

things they were supposed to do, but it looked disorganized and the pace seemed so slow.

But then I remembered—Miss Maddie was dead—speed wouldn't change that fact. In only moments, the gurney that carried the black body bag was loaded into a waiting vehicle and Miss Maddie Wallace left this elaborate estate for the last time.

Several official vehicles—one of them the medical examiner—drove in a slow convoy, taking her body to endure one more indignity before she could rest.

⁂

George Camp watched with growing impatience. Judge McGrath had been his friend for more years than he wanted to count and he always tried to do as Judge advised. But not today, at least not right now. He was tired of waiting for the sheriff.

He knew the room was down there—he had helped with the construction. For three weeks, he and R.J. Wallace had worked frantically to get the hidden room finished before Maddie returned and they had succeeded.

Common sense had gotten him farther in life than education, because he had much more practical experience than lessons learned in a classroom. His instincts, everything he knew, told him that Vonda may very well have been hidden down there. Whether she was alive or dead, he didn't know, but this place needed to be investigated. He also knew that he could sit here quietly and wait for the sheriff to hear him out, but as usual, he decided to take action on his own.

He sauntered casually over to the replicated oil derrick, and walked around to the rear of the structure. While out of sight of other people on the property, he searched until he found the hidden key and opened a door concealed in the base of the oil derrick.

He descended—slowly and with trepidation—down into the private sanctuary of R.J. Wallace. After only a few minutes, he reappeared, crawled back onto the oil derrick, and shouted as loudly as he could.

"Hey, Judge! I've found Vonda Sue Gunderson. Hurry up, Sheriff, she's alive, but you better get down there fast. She don't look too good."

Rev. Peppers, Judge, and I jumped to our feet when we heard the words spoken by George Camp and started to follow the crowd, but once again we were confronted by the angry patrolman, barking orders to us.

"Folks, just go on back under the tent and let the professionals take care of this." So we backtracked and resumed our wait, but we waited with ever growing impatience.

The EMT's rushed into a door pointed out by George Camp and then back out. One man reported to the sheriff while one ran to the ambulance and back again, apparently gathering needed supplies. Moments later, another EMT rushed to the driver's seat of the ambulance, reversed, and then made a wide swing to the rear of the oil derrick, splattering mud on several other personnel.

We watched from under the tent, no longer sitting, but standing, pacing, and trying to see every action. We weren't that far away, but several people were between us and that monstrous fake oil derrick. After a while, we could see the EMT's as they came out of the rear of that fake oil derrick. Each man was holding one end of a wide, flat board. Someone was on that board and connected to an assortment of drips, bags, and other medical paraphernalia. The board was then placed on a gurney and the bags and drips were connected to poles and then loaded into the ambulance. With lights and sirens, they sped away from the crime scene.

For a moment in time, joy filled my heart—Vonda was alive. But when I caught a glimpse of her beaten and swollen face, fear clutched my heart and I had trouble breathing. From where we stood beneath the tent, my vision was limited, but still I could see her battered face. Who knew what the rest of her looked like. How had she survived this long? *Dear God, please be with Vonda. Protect her, heal her.* My fear for her future was so great that an incoherent prayer was all I could offer. I feared that she might not survive.

✎✐

Rev. Peppers followed the siren blaring ambulance as it carried Vonda to Tyler Trauma Center. Good. Our own Dr. Martha was on staff at that hospital and would most likely be part of the team to care for Vonda. It was the only thing that gave me hope as Judge and I drove back to Three Bridges.

I was worried about Judge. It was easy to see that this whole ordeal had been difficult for this craggy lawyer to deal with. I was never certain of his relationship—professional or personal—with the townspeople, and Maddie may have been a close friend. He was obviously saddened and badly shaken by her death.

I couldn't erase the pictures imprinted in my mind, those flashes of reality, as the EMT's placed Vonda on that gurney and readied her for transport to the hospital. Her face was featureless, just a swollen mass of bruises, unrecognizable as a face, just a swollen blackened blob. My heart was breaking for her pain, and Judge also seemed to struggle to control his emotions. Every thought of how she looked was accompanied by unanswerable questions: Who? Who did this horrendous thing? What kind of person could do that—I didn't even want to consider the possibilities—but really there was only one person to be considered.

Another downpour hit as soon as we were on our way. The rain was bad enough, but we were almost pushed off the roadway by two oncoming TV news vans, rushing to cover the news. We drove on for a few miles closer to Three Bridges and met another set of trucks with satellites and blazing logos advertising yet another television station. The rain no doubt would hamper their coverage, but I really didn't care. We would survive without this horror being transmitted into the living rooms of our town. The average citizen may want to know all the details, but personally, I had seen much more than I wanted to.

I drove as close as I could to the porch when I reached Judge's house and then helped Rosalie to get him inside. He was as shaken as if he'd lost a close family member. Again, I wondered what sort of relationship he had with Maddie Wallace. Was she only a client, or was she a close friend? One thing was certain and sure—Judge kept many secrets.

The few short blocks back to the bank seemed to take forever. I wasn't anxious to go back to business as usual. I needed time to myself. My nerves were frayed and I wanted to sort out my emotions, to think about the things I'd experienced.

I needed to examine my feelings for Vonda. She had been a co-worker but never a friend, and I felt so ashamed. Would I ever have a chance to be her friend?

The rain was pounding even harder. If I parked my car in the back I would certainly get soaked walking to the front door of the bank. The only option that I could see to avoid a drenching was to park on the street in front of the bank.

I was going the wrong direction to park into the angled spots, but that didn't stop me. I made something akin to a U-turn and took the first available slot, about four spaces away but still in front of the bank. I parked next to a pearl white Cadillac. Mrs. Watson must have driven over from Tyler.

I made a mad dash through the downpour, covering the fifty or so feet as quickly as I could, nevertheless I was drenched. I practically threw open the heavy oak doors and stood in the vestibule, dripping water all over the marble floor that was eighty years old.

"Get in this bank, young lady! Oh my, I'm afraid you're going to catch your death. Come on back to my husband's office and let's get you cleaned up."

I was being herded into Jeff's office by his mother, and it was easy to let someone make a simple decision for me.

"Silly me, I know the office belongs to Jeff now, but he's hardly been here long enough to put his stamp on it. Come on now, Julie honey, we've got to get you cleaned up and dried out."

The compassion in her voice was my undoing. If Olivia had scolded me for making a mess on the marble floor, I think I would have held my emotions in check. As it was, I just fell apart, shaking, crying and in general, losing my composure.

# *T*hirty-Four

**In a heartbeat, I felt myself being pushed into Jeff's office** and soon felt his arms around me.

"What happened, Julie? What's got you so upset? You're scaring us, tell us what happened." He took me gently by the shoulders and then I was pushed into a chair and handed a box of Kleenex.

"They found Vonda, they found her in another storm shelter on Maddie's place. It wasn't very far from where Maddie was found—only a few feet—but in a different underground building. We don't know how they found her or who put her there, but it was awful."

To my embarrassment, I started crying again. Never in my life, at least since I recovered from the heartbreak caused by Ryan Daigle, had I cried over anything. But ever since he showed up in Tyler and then confronted me with the story about my mother, crying seems to be my response to everything.

My thoughts were aborted as a cup of hot coffee was placed in front of me.

"Drink this, Julie. Take a sip and tell us what you found. Is Vonda dead? Is that what has you so upset?"

Jessie had rushed in with the coffee and questions. I took a sip and shook my head, trying to regain control.

"She's not dead, but she looked so horrible. She was obviously beaten within an inch of her life. I don't know if she can survive those injuries."

Again, I was overcome with emotion, but tried to stuff those down with another sip of coffee. But everyone crammed into this office was waiting for more details.

"If she lives, who knows what the damages could be? She was black and swollen and looked so awful. I could see her face when they put her in the ambulance. It didn't look like a face, just a swollen black blob. I don't know how she could live through this."

"This is Wednesday afternoon. How long has she been down there, thrown away to die as if someone would throw out garbage? I just didn't know anyone could be so cruel—not even Odie Marshall."

I grabbed for some tissues and tried to gain control. The cup of coffee was clutched tightly but I was no longer drinking, only trying to draw some warmth from the cooling liquid. The July temperature was ninety plus degrees, but the rain and the emotions had left me cold and shaking.

Jeff and his mother were talking quietly in the corner, leaving Jessie free to ask questions and she did. "Tell me again where she was found. And who found her? Did Odie do this to those women? Where is that sorry son of a gun, anyway? I hope someone finds him before he harms anyone else."

I took a deep breath and began to answer. "There is an underground room built under that big oil derrick structure that R.J. put out there years ago. Thank goodness George Camp knew about the other room. He went down there and found her. Once she was found, everything happened quickly. The EMT's got her out and hooked her up to IV's and then left with lights and sirens. Rev. Peppers followed them, but like everyone else he was very upset."

I finally put the cup of cooled coffee on the desk and wiped my face with the tightly clutched napkin before asking for information—information that I should already know—but didn't.

"Vonda has no family that I know about. Do you, Jessie?

Do you know anyone?"

Jessie gave a brief shake of her head and I saw tears streaming down her face as she left for her teller's window. Even in the pouring rain, the customers of Three Bridges Bank expected service. Olivia Watson's concern interrupted my wandering thoughts.

"Now, Julie, Jeff and I think you need to take a hot shower and get warm and dry. Do you have a change of clothing here at the bank, or can I send someone to your house for something? I don't want you out in the rain again. I know Clarke always kept an extra shirt, or sometimes some golf clothes. Is there anything you can change into?"

"I think I have some jeans and maybe another shirt. I kept something casual in case I had to go to the farm, or when I have to work late on Friday night. Yes, I think I must have something in my locker in the back."

"Okay now, I want you to get in that shower in there and don't come out until you're feeling better. I'll bring your clothes in. Jeff has already checked and there are clean towels in the bathroom. You need to get under some hot water—it'll make you feel much better. When you come out, we'll finish this story. I'll see if I can rummage up a hair dryer."

My emotions were still on a rollercoaster ride and this unexpected kindness again brought tears to my eyes. I hurried into the small but elegant bathroom. I had been employed at this bank for more than eight years, but this was the first time I'd ever ventured into the private quarters for the bank president.

Dressed in jeans and a tee shirt, I calmly re-entered the office and sat before Olivia Watson. Before I could even think of speaking, the wife of my former boss—the mother of my current boss—once again took control of the conversation.

"Julie, now that you're dressed, I think it would be a good idea for you to go to the hospital in Tyler. I know you'd feel better if you were there. Jeff can take you in and Jessie and I will close the bank. Did you get your hair dried? I don't want you to get sick."

"Mom, chill out. She looks much better now than a few

minutes ago. Look, here's Cynthia. Maybe she knows something."

"Julie, is it true? Did they really find Vonda down there? What do you know?"

"I'm on my way to the hospital in Tyler. Vonda is in really bad shape. Cynthia, you can't believe how awful she looked. I just don't see how she's going to make it. Jeff is taking me to Tyler. Do you want to go with us?"

◈

We waited, we prayed, and walked the floor, and then the waiting and praying started over again. Dr. Peppers would frequently rouse himself from his quiet praying to remind us that God was in control of this situation and only God would determine the outcome.

Wait, pray, drink bad coffee, and walk the floor. Hours had passed, and time was a blur, and other people from Three Bridges as well as Leslie Phelps had joined in the silent game of hospital waiting.

Sometime later, Dr. Martha emerged from those ominous double doors bearing the words—"*Hospital Personnel Only.*" We all stood with uncertain expectations until she was close enough to speak privately to us.

"Hi folks, I think you can all relax a little bit. We've done everything we can do tonight. We've patched, repaired, and x-rayed everything and I think she's going to make it. In my years as a surgeon, I've never encountered such as this. That poor girl was beaten within an inch of her life. I believe God has a plan for Vonda, otherwise she would already be dead."

Martha paused, shook her head, and took a deep breath before continuing. She recited the list of injuries as skillfully and dispassionately as one reading a grocery list—but I wasn't fooled. This woman was keeping it together by the smallest of margins.

"She has severe bruising over most of her body and her face

will have to be surgically reconstructed in time. Broken ribs, broken hand, some bruising in the abdomen which may be severe. We'll just have to wait and see as the swelling goes down. Her left arm and leg are so swollen that we may not really know the extent of the damages. We've done X-rays, Cat Scans, and an MRI and didn't see any other broken bones, but there could be other things that crop up."

She paused to take a deep breath and looked at each one of us before she spoke again.

"Folks, right now, it's a watch, wait, and pray situation. And please pray for the nurses and doctors on this case. We may be professionals, but we have hearts also. Vonda's instinctive will to live has captured the heart of every medical professional that has come in contact with her. We all need your prayers."

I could see her exhaustion as she sat down beside us for a moment. "Rev. Peppers, would you pray with us? And I need you to do something else for me. I plan to spend the night here, so why don't you guys eat dinner and bring me something to eat please. I need something other than hospital food."

We prayed, and our small group increased with other people from the community gathering closer—Jessie Baker and her husband, George Camp and his wife, Vonda's friend, Leslie Phelps and her husband, and several customers from the bank. Even Rosalie had left Judge at home and at his request come to check on Vonda. There were several others that I knew only by sight, and everyone came out of concern. Bad news always travels fast through a small town.

With steps slowed by exhaustion, Dr. Martha left the waiting room through those same doors—"*Hospital Personnel Only*." I turned to ask Rev. Peppers if he would join us, but I didn't speak when I saw tears of compassion course down his face and then wiped away. He nodded to us as he walked away toward the chapel.

I'd never seen our pastor so overwhelmed with emotion. That vision will stay with me forever.

Sluggish feet conveyed us to the elevator and I felt an arm across my shoulder and was hugged in a warm and sympathetic embrace. I almost broke down again.

"Julie, how can I make this any better for you?" I had no answer for him, but was quite happy to rest against Jeff's shoulder until the elevator stopped.

We ate a glum and somber meal and then returned to the hospital with Dr. Martha's food. We wanted to hear some good news and were willing to wait through the night if necessary.

But we only waited until midnight. Olivia Watson put down her foot and demanded that we all go back to Three Bridges. She would take the responsibility of checking on Vonda through the night and would notify us if anything changed.

"It's late, and you're right, Mom. We should get on back. Julie, tomorrow morning, I'll open the bank. I want you to come in at eleven o'clock and not a minute before. And I have a witness. Right, Cynthia?"

We left the hospital but walked only a few feet from the entrance before our path was blocked by an entourage of media people and our esteemed chief of police, Cletus Stamper.

"That's them. They're with Vonda. That's our deputy mayor, Cynthia Bickers, our bank vice-president, Julie Trahan, the bank president, Jeff Watson. I don't know who the old dame is."

"The old dame" was the only one with any desire to respond to the crudely worded introduction. That didn't happen because Cynthia and I closed in on either side of Olivia Watson, placed our arms around the shoulders of this very angry woman and urged her forward while trying to avoid the small throng in front of us. Jeff bravely faced the group and spoke.

"I have a very brief statement. Vonda Sue Gunderson was rescued earlier this afternoon and is resting well in the hospital. Her injures are very severe but we expect a full recovery in time. Thank you."

Cynthia and I had pushed around the group while Jeff was talking and he hurried to catch up, pushing us to walk even faster until we reached the security of the parking lot. We located Jeff's car and Olivia was parked only two aisles over. We said goodnight to her and headed back to Three Bridges, back home.

# Thirty-Five

**Odie woke from a sound sleep. Dead to the world for only a** few hours or a for long time, he hardly knew. It wasn't dark when he checked into this out of the way place, and he'd not eaten supper, but still, he fell down on the bed and slept until a very loud banging sound woke him. Through the cheap draperies that lacked inches in closing, the early morning light was shining brightly. Morning, but which morning? He'd figured that out later.

A short, dark, and very rotund young woman who spoke little English was standing before him saying words that he didn't understand, but the message was clear. She wanted to clean the room. Odie held up his hand, asking for a few minutes to dress, and closed the door.

He dressed in yesterday's dirty jeans and shirt, pulled an equally dirty and unrecognizable baseball cap on his head and started out the door as the cleaning woman pushed her cart closer to his room. He was incredibly hungry, but he remembered some sort of café just up the road.

When he stopped in front of this café, he had doubts. In the bright light of day, this place was about as seedy as he could ever imagine. Hunger made him ignore the shabbiness and he ordered. The food was filling—good coffee, eggs and pancakes. He ate the meal without thinking about the kitchen it had come from—those things no longer mattered to him.

His attention was drawn to a figure standing provocatively in a doorway that led from the café to some other room. For a moment he ignored the woman. Denise was waiting somewhere, and somehow she would be found and dealt with.

He finished his breakfast and went to the cluttered counter that held a cash register. The bleached blonde wearing a very short skirt and equally tight tee shirt pushed herself through the doorway and came to take his money and then to make another offer. That offer was too good to refuse.

❦❦

Odie stopped by the motel office to pay for another night, hoping for another day of rest. Maybe if he could really rest, that would take the edge off his anxiety, and he would return to Three Bridges tomorrow. It really didn't matter what day he went back, his objective would still be in place.

A grumpy old woman sitting in the room adjacent to the small lobby struggled to her slippered feet, grabbed a cane, and came out to take his money. She accomplished this without dropping either the cigarette clinging to her wrinkled lips or the mid-morning bottle of beer clutched ever so tightly in the hand that didn't grip the walking cane.

The woman didn't hold his attention after he saw the television screen that covered most of the office wall. He watched in stunned silence as a group of people stood facing the camera. He recognized them all.

He stared at the television, trying to understand why a twenty-four hour news network was covering events in Three Bridges, Texas. Automatically, he understood that this couldn't be good news for him. This was trouble, but what was he going to do? Now he could only listen.

He listened as Jeff Watson spoke words that made the blood chill in his veins. Fear took control and changed his facial muscles into something like cold, inflexible marble. He tried to breathe normally, but his lungs seemed to be unwilling to respond. Without any doubt, Jeff Watson was speaking directly to him alone.

"Vonda Sue Gunderson will make a full recovery."

Odie didn't remember going back to the dingy room, but at the end of an hour, he was dressed. His few belongings were packed and stowed in his car. He forced himself to walk slowly and calmly, but wasted no time leaving the motel parking lot. His worst fears were about to be realized. Miss Maddie's body had been found. Vonda Sue Gunderson had been found—she was alive and expected to make a full recovery.

My morning was totally out of whack, an expression I had picked up from my father, but it was pretty descriptive of the way I felt. Too little sleep, too much coffee, and too little food because I hadn't bought groceries in a while. Finally, I settled for a handful of dry cereal, a glass of juice, and another cup of coffee. I twiddled my thumbs until it was time to report to work at the bank. I was unaccustomed to having so much free time in the morning hours, but eventually the clock ticked closer to 11:30.

Jeff was on the phone when I entered the bank lobby, so I spoke to Jessie then headed for my office. Before I even had time to check my emails, I heard the faintest knock on my door.

"Julie, do you know Alice Mae Rushing? She manages The Flower Box for Odie and she needs to speak to you."

I knew this woman only because she came to the bank on a weekly basis to make deposits to The Flower Box and I had occasionally taken those deposits. For Odie Marshall to hire someone to run The Flower Box had at first been a shock—until I realized that the man would much rather spend time with Miss Maddie than actually work. Shoving those negative thoughts aside, I stood to meet the woman.

"Thanks, Jessie. Good morning, Mrs. Rushing, come in and let's see how I can help you."

"First of all, it's Miss Rushing, but please call me Alice Mae. As you probably know, I've been managing the Flower Box for about four months now, maybe five. Mr. Marshall doesn't spend much time in the store anymore, just checks in now and then to deliver my paycheck."

She paused, twisting the old black handbag in her lap, rearranging it one way then another until she figured out what she wanted to say next.

"Anyway, I'm here because something isn't right. I don't know what it is, but something's different, something's going on. I haven't seen Mr. Marshall since Friday night before the festival. He stopped in the store and talked for a few minutes while I closed up. He seemed very nervous and agitated that I was still there. I reminded him that I hadn't been paid in a while, and he said he would leave the money for me."

Once again, the black purse was pummeled as she thought, and I forced myself to wait without asking questions. It was a difficult thing to do.

"He's always been pretty timely with my salary, but I haven't been paid in three weeks, and he didn't leave the money as he said he would. I didn't worry at first because this has happened once before when he was out of town, but now I'm worried."

She drew a deep breath, and tried to continue, but couldn't. Another twist of the purse handle seemed to give her courage to continue.

"This entire thing has put me in a bad situation. I don't like feeling this fear. I started worrying when I heard about Miss Maddie and then I worried even more when I heard about Miss Gunderson."

The woman was becoming almost distraught with anxiety. I asked if I could get her coffee or water. She gratefully accepted some water, drank a hefty swallow, wiped her mouth with work worn hands and continued.

"I've been trying to contact Mr. Marshall on his cell phone

and he doesn't answer. I thought about what I should do, and late last night I came to the conclusion that I cannot continue to work for that man, even if he is never around. I won't run his business any longer, nor do I wish to be associated with him in any way."

I was still processing this when she laid a bank bag, some papers, and the key to The Flower Box on my desk. Before I could ask, she answered my questions.

"The bank bag contains all the receipts for the past three weeks—minus my salary plus a ten percent bonus that I feel I deserve. I have everything noted. The papers are just miscellaneous pieces of mail and such, and obviously, the keys are to the store. I've left my cell phone number in case anyone needs to contact me. I'll be staying with friends for a while. If you could take care of these things for me, perhaps give them back to Mr. Marshall, I would appreciate it."

"Miss Rushing, why are you so anxious to leave? Couldn't you wait to see if Odie returns? Perhaps this could all work out and you are doing such a good job at The Flower Box."

"No, young lady, I'm frightened to death of that man. Even before hearing about those two ladies, I was more than a little uncomfortable around him. The man I saw the other night was not the man that hired me. He had changed dramatically. To tell you the truth, it was as if I could see the devil himself whenever I looked at Odie Marshall. I compromised my core beliefs and principals by working for that man. I should have resigned the last time I saw him, but I wanted to think it over. Well, I've given this plenty of thought, and know that it's time for me to leave. I can't work there any longer. Thank you Miss Trahan and God bless you."

Before I could get my wits about me, she was gone, leaving me staring into space and thinking about her words. In only a moment, Jeff's voice brought me back to reality.

"Julie, do you want to grab a late lunch across the street? Seems a little slow in here just now and maybe we could talk."

"Oh, Jeff, I think we have a problem. Let's go back to your office. I don't want to deal with this."

I gathered everything the Rushing woman had placed on my desk and he followed me back into his office. I definitely wanted to pass the buck on this one. We talked for a while and I repeated the conversation as best I could. After talking for a while, we agreed that the sheriff should be called—we didn't really know how to handle this, but felt that the sheriff needed to know.

I waited while Jeff called Jim Bolton and brought him up to date on the latest happenings in Three Bridges. The last question he asked the sheriff was brief.

"Has anyone seen or heard from Odie Marshall?"

I knew when Jeff started shaking his head that there was no news on that front. When the call was completed, we walked across the street to have lunch at City Café.

∽◈∾

Lunch wasn't a pleasant experience because we had constant interruptions. Everyone was asking questions about Vonda. Even people who didn't know her personally were concerned.

Even more people wanted to get reacquainted with Jeff Watson who was now the most powerful businessman in Three Bridges. To his credit, he shook every hand that was extended in his direction. He was still the reluctant banker, but at least he was trying.

We finished our lunch and hurried back to the bank, waiting and praying for any news at all from Vonda.

∽◈∾

She was waiting—again. To Denise, it seemed that's how she'd spent most of her hours since she and Odie left Three Bridges. Now she was waiting to be dismissed from the hospital, and she was also waiting for Elbamarle County Sheriff's

Department to escort her back to Three Bridges.

The police department in this small town had been very thorough. When the 911 call was made, the caller relayed information that aroused the curiosity of one local policeman. He followed the story, found the tossed away cell phone and charger, and followed up.

The incessant and unanswered calls from an unknown number raised questions, and yesterday, they decided to ask Denise what was going on. She eagerly answered every question. When she mentioned that the caller was Odie Marshall, a call was made to Elbamarle County.

The questions from the local policeman changed.

"Miss Hougan, do you know a Maddie Wallace?"

"Yes, she was my employer until a few days ago. Why?"

It took a few minutes for everything to sink in, and it would be even longer for her to understand all she'd been told. Miss Maddie was dead.

She'd answered hours of questions and now she was going back to answer more. Finally, the deputy from ECSD entered her hospital room, and she expected to be handcuffed and led away. Instead, he had assured her that she was not under arrest. Rather, she was being escorted back to Three Bridges to assist the investigation. She thanked him and promised to do her best.

She couldn't prove that Odie Marshall had harmed anyone, but even she could add two and two and come up with the correct answer. When told about Miss Maddie's death, she knew he was responsible and that he had planned to use her for his escape. Then what? Would he have killed her?

Denise gave a mental shrug as she thought of her situation. On some level, she had always known that Odie wasn't really interested in her, but at the same time, being with him had been the most exciting time in her dull and boring life. A twinge of embarrassment made a brief appearance in her thinking, but she pushed it aside. No, she would not be ashamed of being with Odie Marshall—after all—she really couldn't expect anything more from life.

It was time to move on, forward or backward she really

couldn't say just now. When they returned to Three Bridges, she would help the investigation, then maybe start her life over somewhere else. Perhaps back in New Mexico in that small little cabin, or maybe somewhere else. Sooner or later, someone would hire her—she was, after all, an excellent chef.

# Thirty-Six

**He drove in circles, first one direction and another until he** calmed down enough to know that he had to go back to Three Bridges.

*"Vonda Gunderson is alive and expected to make a full recovery in time."*

Those words spoken by Jeff Watson on the cable news program still rang through his mind and echoed like a bad dream.

*How could she be alive, how? That last kick to the head should have killed a mule. Well, Vonda was as stubborn as a mule, and about as ugly, so that must be why she lived. How did she get out of the storm shelter? Someone must have found her, but who?*

Yesterday after he heard the television news, he went back to that seedy place where he had eaten breakfast, but sat at a bar in the next room. He drank and thought, and drank quite a bit more before he finally passed out.

This morning he drank enough coffee to push the hangover into a corner of his brain and then he forced down a breakfast that had no appeal. The thrumming hangover headache was replaced by nerves jangling with anxiety and questions that needed answers.

His only option became very clear. He was going back to Three Bridges and he would find out what was going on.

*Hey, why not ask Julie Trahan? The little know-it-all had plenty of answers anytime I went to the bank. She must have turned Maddie against me. That must be why Maddie shut down my money pipeline. Well, Maddie paid plenty for that, she gave her all. Maybe Miss Julie should do the same—that might actually be fun!*

The gas gauge indicator sounded and he began to pay closer attention to where he was driving. Very soon he would have to fill up this Mercedes.

*Oh dear Lord, why didn't I dump this car? Everyone in Three Bridges knows by now that Miss Maddie is dead. If I go back in this car, someone will call the police and even simpleminded Cletus Stamper will figure out that it was me. Got to think about this, gotta figure it out. Okay, Odie, you can make this work. Think.*

He filled the gas tank at the next convenience store and headed in the direction of Three Bridges with a plan. If he drove on the back roads, he'd have a better chance of not being spotted and in only a few hours he'd be asking Julie Trahan a few pertinent questions.

As he neared Three Bridges, the rain was coming down in sheets, but that was good. He could sneak into town without being seen. No sane person would be out in this heavy rain. It was getting late in the afternoon, Julie Trahan would be getting off work in about an hour. That was good. He would be the welcoming committee when she got home. Yes, his plan was set, and it was going to work.

Odie was headed south on Elbamarle County Road 380 and he had to focus on the road. He didn't want to miss his exit. The rain had stopped for a while, but now was threatening again and the afternoon was unnaturally dark. Must be another storm cell coming right on the heels of the one that had just passed.

Two miles later, he made a sharp right turn and drove only a few feet before the abandoned road became almost impassable from the overgrowth of bushes and trees. He didn't care what happened to this very expensive car, he had to get across Compromise Creek, and there was only one way to do it without being seen.

He remembered the town history well. He'd heard it countless times growing up around here, everyone had. This road had been built around 1880, and had been the only access to the town for about forty years. Sometime around 1925 or 1926, the town was hit with high winds and pounding rains that washed out both of the bridges into town. The flash flood did a lot of damage in a very short time, but within a few hours the creek was back at pool stage. Nothing else was back to normal however, the bridges were destroyed and strewn for miles. It took the state only a few days to start construction on a new road and a new bridge, the bridge that crosses Compromise Creek and connects to Main Street.

It took Odie about twenty-five minutes to navigate the abandoned road and it was well after five o'clock when he could drive the car no further. Trees had fallen and partially blocked the old roadbed, but he managed to drive over or around the rotting debris.

For a short distance, he drove through standing water where the roadbed had washed out, but just ahead he could see the remains of the old rotten bridge supports.

He parked Maddie's car and walked to the creek. And smiled. It was a really big smile and his lips seemed uncomfortable with the effort. Some enterprising souls had built a makeshift fishing pier and all he had to do was walk across Compromise Creek.

❦

It was raining again when I left the bank at four o'clock under strict orders from my boss to take some well-deserved "down time" to relax. He would bring supper and we would have time to talk about our relationship. I hoped that the closing went smoothly this evening.

We had added support to our weakened bank staff. Olivia and Leslie Phelps had agreed to work until this was resolved, but Olivia also brought someone else in to help. Ford Stokes, a former bank owner and friend, had agreed to pitch in and help for a few days. This little job he was working at was far below his former status. Ford had been owner and president of one of the more prestigious banks in Tyler and had only recently sold out to a major banking corporation.

I busied myself in the kitchen for a time, fussing with the table settings. I settled on a very casual set of colorful dishes with some chunky stemware and water glasses. One of my favorite hand-thrown pottery pieces would serve well for a centerpiece. I patiently waited until the rain stopped long enough for me to run out with clippers and snip off a few marigolds from the yard. I shook the rain from the tightly configured petals and then just stuffed them into the striated blue pot.

Everything was ready. I was pleased that Jeff was bringing supper tonight. I was looking forward to spending this time with him, hoping to figure out if we wanted a relationship. I wondered if I was brave enough to face all the challenges this would bring. I had to be willing to try. I had to learn to trust God to guide me through this, but tonight Jeff and I would talk.

It was getting late, but I still had time to curl up in my favorite chair for a ten-minute nap.

⤙⤚

Odie had crossed the creek, but wasn't as easy as it looked. The fishing pier was poorly made. Some boards were missing and others were rotted. With great caution, Odie moved closer to his target, one careful step at a time. After a few feet, the fast-flowing water in the creek was making him dizzy and even more unsure of his footing.

He took one step and nearly fell into the creek, but somehow managed to grab onto the rotting pier. From that point forward, he crawled. The rotten boards were dirty and laden with debris. When he reached the opposite creek bank, he sat down on the wet ground to regain his composure.

Why was this so hard? It was supposed to be easier than

this—he'd had it all planned out. Julie was only a few houses away from him. Nothing had gone as he planned, but he wasn't finished yet. He had one other message to deliver before he was caught. He couldn't plan for any other ending to his story. He'd be caught, but he had important work to do before that inevitable event.

He got himself together and began walking until he was only one house away from Julie's. Only one house, but these houses sat on very large lots, and this was one of the largest. He couldn't remember who lived here. It might belong to some weekenders, or to an old couple that might be at home. He couldn't afford to be discovered now, so he moved closer to the creek, seeking more cover. With his second step he slipped into a washout and slid all the way down to the creek bank, and was soon soaked to the skin.

It took him a while to work his way back up to the bank, and when he did, he was only a few feet from the old garage at Julie's house. He took no chances, but crawled through the grass until he reached the garage and stopped. He couldn't believe his eyes—a brand new Mustang convertible. Little Miss Julie was finally turning loose some of that money she inherited.

Maybe he'd get around to asking about the new car when he finished with his other business. The clap of thunder sent him to his knees and reminded him to be careful. He was so close to his objective. Maybe he'd wait a little while longer, to get a better idea of what was going on. He needed to be careful, he was so close.

Then he remembered the dog—where was that dog? Could he get into the house without rousing the dog? He looked around and finally saw a good-sized dog house under an old pear tree in the backyard. Yes, he could get on the porch before the dog could get to him. Finally, something was going right.

A fierce bolt of lightning hit something very close by and thunder followed within seconds with such force that the old windows rattled in their casings. It startled me from my nap and prompted me to pull out all available candles and a flashlight, just in case.

Grandmother had always forbidden me to use the shower in a storm but today I stepped in on faith—but showered hurriedly. I stepped out to the sounds of increased rainfall and intense rumbles of thunder. Candles on my makeup table were ready for use if we lost power, and there was still a small amount of natural light from a window to the left of where I sat.

With greater speed than I thought possible, I dried my short and curly hair, applied my makeup and dressed, except for my shoes. I started toward the closet and then remembered to grab a flashlight. The closet was big, with a tall ceiling, but the only lighting was from a multi-armed hanging light that was far more decorative than functional, and lately only two bulbs were burning.

I was looking for a pair of shoes purchased two or three years ago, strappy sandals scattered with small faux jewels. With the aid of the flashlight, I saw them on the top shelf. I dragged a short stepladder from the far corner of the closet and climbed. Just as I put my foot on the third step, the loudest clap of thunder I ever heard shook the house. Then the lights went out.

Something was wrong. An overwhelming stench had entered this closet. Sweat, stale and pungent sweat combined with other obnoxious odors. But that wasn't all that was wrong. I cringed as strong arms pulled me off the ladder.

# $\mathscr{T}$hirty-Seven

**Jeff thought this day would never end. He was anxious to** get to Julie's house and enjoy a meal and a serious talk. They needed to talk. He'd experienced only a few serious romances in his thirty-five years, but more than a few casual ones. He was tired of those brief relationships that usually ended badly and he was ready to find that special someone.

He smiled at the thought of Julie. Being with her this past week at the bank had opened his eyes and he was definitely attracted to her. Very attracted.

He locked the bank and walked across the street to pick up dinner. Henry apologized, but promised the meal to go would be ready soon, so Jeff jogged around to the bank parking lot, got his truck and drove back to City Café. It was Friday night but the weather was keeping the crowd away and leaving a parking spot directly in front of City Café. Jeff went back inside the café and waited for his order. True to his word, Henry had the meal packaged up in almost no time, but every minute he waited to see Julie seemed like an hour.

I was on the floor, and harsh hands held me as I struggled. I fought like a wildcat, but I was picked up and flung against the far wall, and before I could draw a breath, grabbed and slammed against the floor. Now someone was pressing me to the floor, the cold hard closet floor. I felt hands around my throat. It was hard to breathe and my ears began to roar, but I could hear Goldie barking ferociously and her nails hitting against the hardwood floor. How had Goldie gotten in the house? Why had she broken that hard taught rule that placed the house off-limits to her? Had she come to rescue me?

One rough hand was still grasping my throat, but the other hand was running over my body, tearing at my clothes. I struggled, but still my clothes were being yanked and pulled, and still those rough, angry hands wouldn't stop. I struggled harder, trying to kick him off, he brought both hands to my neck and began to squeeze so hard that I struggled to breathe.

The sound of Goldie's barking grew closer, and her hysterical barks matched my own fear as she came into the bedroom closet. My thoughts were erratic—*What is Goldie doing in this house? I've trained her to never come in—but she's here now. Oh Lord, did you send Goldie to save me? I'm here Goldie, in the closet!*

My world was beginning to swirl into darkness, and then I felt the warmth from Goldie's body as she lunged at the person trying to kill me.

When she lunged her weight against my attacker, he took his hands off my throat to try to push the dog away. Goldie moved back and then lunged again, growling deep in her throat. This time she grabbed my assailant and pushed him further off me.

I don't know where I got the strength, but I started scooting away, trying to put as much space between me and those hands that were trying to kill me and worse. But I knew I was safe. Goldie had my assailant in the firm grasp of her jaws—and she wasn't going to turn loose.

I was gasping for breath, my lungs hurt with the effort to inhale enough oxygen. I couldn't stand, but I grabbed onto the casings of the closet door, trying to regain my balance and for a second to utter a prayer, thanking God for my life.

Finally, I pulled myself from the closet and the next thing I knew, I was grabbing the door and forcing it closed. I leaned against it for a minute, trying to think how to lock the door, how to protect myself from whoever was in my closet, screaming for his life. Goldie continued to utter fierce growls and snarls. She wasn't granting this intruder any mercy.

I was afraid to move away, afraid to stay, and shaking with uncontrollable fear. Suddenly another pair of strong arms grabbed tightly and pulled me close, but this time it was in comfort

"Julie, honey, go to a safe room. Lock the door and call 911 if you can. I'll deal with this until help arrives. Go, get to a safe place."

At first I couldn't move. I never thought I would be so happy to see anyone—especially Jeff Watson—but I didn't want to let go. "Come on Julie, you're okay now. I need you to call for help. Call 911."

I did as I was told, and fumbled on my dressing table until I found my purse before locking myself in the bathroom. My shaking legs really couldn't take me much further. With fingers that trembled in rhythm with my shaking legs, I found the cell phone, punched in those numbers and waited for help to arrive. I could hear Jeff talking to Goldie, getting her to back off from my attacker. I heard thrashing, more screams from the intruder, and more growls from Goldie. I heard scuffling again, and then a very loud thump and then nothing. I waited, uncertain about what I should do next, but Jeff solved that worry.

"Julie, everything is under control for now—but stay wherever you are. You're safe, you're going to be all right. Stay where you are until you hear the police."

I sank back down on the floor, in the corner of the bathroom, and breathed a brief sigh of relief—and then Jeff called me again.

"Uh—Julie—can I borrow a pair of panty hose? Where are they?"

Panty hose—what was this man thinking? Whatever he had in mind, I wasn't about to let Jeff Watson or anyone else rummage through my dresser, so I hopped out of my hiding place and was almost blinded by Jeff's flashlight. I ran to the dresser and extracted a pair of freshly laundered black panty hose.

Jeff grabbed them and tried to lighten up the situation. He pointed the flashlight on his face and did a Groucho Marx imitation by rapidly raising his eyebrows and shaking my panty hose in the air. "Pretty fancy stuff to hog-tie up this crazy madman."

I laughed. I was going to be all right. And then I recognized the person on my closet floor. Odie Marshall. I fell to the floor with my head in my hands.

*"Oh, dear Lord, you saved me from death. Thank you for sending Jeff, thank you for saving my life. Lord I thank you that Odie didn't accomplish what he came her for, but Lord, why? Why would Odie Marshall want to kill me?"*

Jeff found another pair of hosiery and secured Odie's feet to the bedpost. He pulled me to my feet and we backtracked into the kitchen, but Goldie refused to leave the bedroom. I gladly left her to stand guard over the unconscious assailant.

We hustled around, lighting candles, picking up our dinner that had been dropped or thrown onto the floor—really just doing everything possible to keep busy. I closed the back door and wondered if I had forgotten to lock it after scampering out in the rain to cut those marigolds. Too late to worry about that now.

From a distance sirens could be heard, first our local boys and before long, more distant sirens that I assumed were from the sheriff's department. When Cletus Stamper walked through the back door, followed by his two "boys," I realized again just how close I came to losing my life, and I sank to the floor, shaking in remembered fear.

Jeff pointed toward the rear of the house where Goldie was still uttering intermittent growls, then sat on the floor beside me and pulled me into a comforting embrace. The storm was still raging outside, lightning flashed across the sky and the wind rattled the windows, but I felt safe with Jeff beside me.

"I suppose even Cletus Stamper can find his way back there and handle that. Come on, Julie, everything is okay now. This is all over. Let's just sit here until the sheriff arrives and then we'll decide what to do."

I didn't need a second invitation. I snuggled up in Jeff's arms and tried to figure out what was going on. Questions raged through my mind and then I started shaking again. What had made Odie Marshall go berserk? Why was Odie Marshall trying to rape me? Jeff hugged me tighter, murmuring comforting words in my ear.

⟡

The storm was no deterrent to my friends when the sound of the sirens stopped at my back door. Cynthia was not more than three minutes behind Cletus and his boys, dripping more water on my floor and screaming my name.

Jeff jumped up and led her to where I was sitting in the still darkened house. After being assured that I was fine, Cynthia jumped up and ran out of the kitchen, cell phone in hand. I knew she was calling for backup. Soon I was encircled by other friends—Marlene, Dr. Martha and sometime later, even Hortense. At Martha's insistence, I swallowed some supposedly mild drug designed to calm me down.

Odie Marshall was wheeled out through the kitchen and taken to the hospital. Goldie had given him some nasty and serious bites and Jeff had left Odie with a black eye, as well as good-sized knot on his head. The electricity came on just as we were leaving to spend the night at Anderson Farms, but I never looked back.

⟡

So much for the *mild sedative* my doctor friend gave me. I slept until noon the next day, and woke to see my sister Catherine standing beside the bed with a cup of coffee and some blueberry muffins.

"Wake up, Julie, time to rise and shine!" Those words catapulted back to my teen years. Catherine had always been an early bird and I had to be dragged from the bed. My brain was confused. I couldn't understand. Why was Catherine telling me to wake up? I struggled to open my eyes, and my sister was standing by the bed with a tray in her hand.

"What are you doing here? Who called you, and why are you here?"

"Drink some coffee, eat a muffin, then go shower. I brought over some clean clothes for you. When you do all that, we'll talk. Trust me on this, Julie, everything is okay. Everything!"

It took a while for me to drink the coffee and nibble on the muffin, and even longer in the shower, but finally I made it to the kitchen, and found a room full of people.

Catherine, Judge McGrath, and my brother Sydney were waiting in the big old farm kitchen, sitting around the table and waiting for me. I looked at Sydney and became even more alarmed when he rushed over to hug me.

"What's going on? What—why are y'all here? Catherine, this is about to make me very upset. Why are you here?"

"Sit down, little sister. Believe me, everything is good. Just let me tell this in my own way. You know I always have to start at the beginning." And she did, telling about her vacation, and how miserable she was. I tuned back in when she began talking about the surprises when she came home.

"There were these bizarre phone messages from our mother, and certified letters from Judge, and then finally a telephone call last night from Judge that demanded my presence here in Three Bridges today. I called Sydney and asked him to meet me. That's all I know except for this."

She pulled a piece of paper from her pocket.

"I copied this down verbatim, but I'll just hit the highlights. You might want to read it later, because it's just too weird. Our mother is married again—to a very wealthy prince. I'm ashamed to say that I don't know if I believe her or not, but that was the message."

I must have had my mouth wide open. I realized that I really didn't know my mother and sadly, I didn't want to. Only a short time ago, she had been living with my ex-fiancé. Another thing to push back in my emotional closet to deal with later.

"I've got that, but what did you mean about certified letters from Judge and a call and why did you drag Sydney away from his family and work? Explain that, please, I am still confused. Whatever Martha gave me last night has got my brain in a fog."

"Have another cup of coffee and you'll be fine, trust me. Judge called me after you were attacked and I called Sydney. We're your family, and you need us. Judge wanted me to know that Mother had left him the same message—along with a few other choice words that I will not repeat—but rest assured the lawsuit is over. Mother will not file suit to get any of your inheritance. "

I drank most of the second cup and nodded with relief. That was good. But what else was going on?

"The certified letters were from Judge and Maddie Wallace. Last week, just before she was killed, Maddie transferred twenty million dollars into a special account to be used to set up a clinic in Three Bridges. She named me as administrator along with our brother as chief financial officer for this venture. Judge has more of these details but Julie, it looks as if Sydney, his family, and I are moving to Three Bridges as soon as we can tie up all the loose details.

There wasn't enough coffee in the world to get me over this shock—it was so out of the blue.

"What—all of us together again? Great."

That was all I could say, so I just sat there with a stupid smile on my face, shaking my head. Sydney started laughing and looked at Catherine.

"Sis, I think she's still doped out of her mind. Why don't we take her back to Grandmother's house and let her sleep this off. You and I and Judge can spend the rest of the afternoon going over plans for this new clinic. When she wakes up maybe she will be the real Julie, not this person in la-la land."

Then everyone started laughing and I really didn't mind being the joke. Laughing was good.

# $\mathcal{T}$hirty-Eight

**It took longer than a few hours for my bruised body and my** equally damaged emotions to recover fully, but I made it. The week that followed Maddie's death was fraught with emotions and surprises. In a very solemn ceremony, Maddie Wallace was laid to rest one week after we discovered her body. Following the interment, we met at Judge's house for the reading of the will.

Just as Catherine had already told me, Miss Maddie left most of her estate to a trust that would finance the establishment of a clinic in Three Bridges. This would be a major undertaking that would require months of planning and even though Maddie Wallace had left an enormous amount for the project, Catherine said there were not enough funds to complete the project. There would have to be many fundraisers in the future and the details would take months to work through. We would deal with those issues one by one, as they were presented.

Catherine stayed with me after the funeral and we spent time just getting to know each other again and time planning the future. We talked about Mom and Dad and our life in Louisiana, and then decided to close the door on those memories and make new ones here.

Sydney went back to Lafayette, with a heavy load. He had to resign from his job, sell the house, and move his family. They would live with me at Grandmother's until they found the right house to purchase. I am ecstatic. I won't be alone in Three Bridges anymore. I will have a family again.

There was another very significant and equally surprising bequest in Miss Maddie's will. The Three Bridges Social Club received a sizeable endowment to continue our philanthropy. She had been our anonymous donor. We have no idea how she found out about our private endeavor to help those who needed help, but after thinking about it, I suspect she heard of this through Grandmother. They had been friends.

Of course the question on everyone's mind was—what happened to Odie Marshall and why? What happened to derail Odie? Why had he killed Miss Maddie and why had he beaten Vonda so severely? We had no answers, and during the week, my friends and family had gone over every detail of the happenings of last Friday night as we knew them. We talked about it several times, and finally my brain was able to wrap itself around the fact that Odie Marshall had intended to rape and kill me.

Even now, I can hear his angry tirade as he yelled out those awful words. His anger was raging as they took him out of my house, handcuffed to the gurney and then whisked away. He was kept overnight in the hospital but was taken to a psych ward early Saturday afternoon. Odie had completely lost touch with reality.

Every conversation between Three Bridges residents included speculation about Odie Marshall. Cynthia and I had questioned each other for days now.

"Julie, what happened to him? Everyone knew that he had a terrible temper—even though he tried to be nice, that bad temper was always waiting to explode—remember how he yelled at me?"

"Yes, I do. I guess he lived behind his public façade, hiding a deep-seated hatred for women by constantly seeking to find one he could control. As his world began to fall apart, so did his grasp on reality. He fell back into his comfort zone of anger fueled by hatred that went too far."

"Julie, do you think he'll ever recover enough to stand trial?

He should be punished for what he did to Miss Maddie, Vonda and you—he tried to kill you too."

And still the questions of *why* were unanswered. Odie didn't answer that question, and Vonda was unable to answer now—perhaps in a few weeks. If Miss Maddie had any answers, again, we would never know.

Denise Hougan was the only person that might have insight into these horrible events, but she had no answers either. She was interrogated by detectives from the sheriff's department and when they realized that she was yet another victim, she was asked to remain available for a few more days.

She had nowhere else to go, so Judge arranged for her to stay in her former suite at Miss Maddie's house. The house was a significant part of Maddie's estate, and as executor, Judge made the decision that someone was needed to take care of the property, and he trusted the woman to do just that. Denise had merely lost her way when she fell victim to Odie's charm.

Last night was the first time Jeff and I have had any time alone. Catherine finally smartened up and realized that something was going on between us and decided to join Judge for supper. Jeff and I sat in my kitchen and ate takeout from City Café. It was Thursday, less than a week from that terrible Friday night.

When the meal was over, we went back to the porch and cuddled up in the swing. I told him as briefly as I could about Ryan Daigle and my mother. He pulled me closer, kissing my cheek and uttering comforting words as I struggled with the terrible story. When I had no more energy for talking, he shared a few experiences from his past. When there were no more stories from our past, we both began to think about a future.

He cupped my face in one hand, and then traced the fading bruises along my throat and shook his head.

"You're quite a woman, Julie Trahan. Not big as a minute, but you're a survivor and one of the cutest I've ever seen. I heard every word you said when you talked about your past, and I'm so sorry those things happened to you."

For a while we listened to the night as we sat in the porch swing. And then Jeff spoke again.

"Julie, I haven't had any experiences that ended as horribly as yours did, and like I said, I've been in many relationships. I know now why none of those relationships worked out. Never in all these years has anything felt so right as what we have. Mom always said that God had the perfect woman for me somewhere and I believe with all my heart that it's you, Julie. You've gone through so much lately, I don't want to rush you into anything, but I believe I've fallen head over heels in love with you. I'm willing to go slow in this relationship if we can agree to let God direct the path we should take."

"I think we can certainly agree on that."

✧✦✧

It's Friday again, and tonight we're having dinner at City Café. It was unusual, but I arrived early this time, probably because I was accompanied by my sister Catherine who believed in being prompt. Cynthia, Martha, and Marlene settled in only a few moments after Catherine and I. In short order, we were joined by Jeff, Roger Peppers, and Judge.

It was only a little crowded as we clustered around the big round table and before long we were enjoying our typical Friday night fare. We ate the wonderful calorie-laden fried food with complete enjoyment. We ate to the accompaniment of conversation and laughter, true friends enjoying this unique friendship.

My mind was filled with awe and amazement at how so many things had taken place in such a brief amount of time. I paused to think about this as my friends continued to eat and enjoy the fellowship around us. I had a smile on my face, but my heart was very sober as I thought about how my life had changed so dramatically, and I thanked the good Lord above that I am still alive. Odie had definitely intended to do me mortal harm, but God protected me.

Vonda had also been protected, and certainly saved by the

hand of God. Her injuries were so incredibly severe. Martha told us that she was making excellent progress although she still suffered terrible pain from her injuries. So many broken bones in her face, and other bruises, and severe soft tissue damage to her left leg, but she would heal given time. Again, Martha said that God had watched over Vonda. There was no other explanation for her survival.

Rev. Peppers was spending as much as time as possible with her, far beyond the call of duty, but even he had taken time to be here tonight.

In a few weeks, we will begin the process of selling Anderson Farms, and if nothing goes wrong, that part of my life will be over. I'm walking away from that part of my past with no regrets, only appreciation for all the things that I learned there from my wonderful grandmother, and the tutelage of my good friend, Hortense Salazar. I'm walking away from Anderson Farms, but what am I walking towards? What is my future?

Jeff and I spent those few hours together over dinner last night, and decided whatever future we might have should be just that—the future according to God's plan.

He's leaving again in a few weeks, going back to Santa Fe to close out his business there. When that's finished, he'll come back to Three Bridges and take charge of the bank. I'm okay with that because I know that now he wants to be a banker in Three Bridges.

While everyone around me was laughing, talking and enjoying the food and friendship, my mind replayed the events of the past few weeks. I thought about how Jeff and I couldn't get along—seemed to clash over everything, but yet we've fallen in love. I thought about how much I loved Ryan, and what awful choices he and my mother made, choices that nearly destroyed me. Then, I thought of the love my father and grandmother gave me, love that was compassionate yet disciplined. I've thought for hours about Odie Marshall, wondering why I was his target, and I know that question will probably never be answered.

My mental ramblings were interrupted by the handsome

man sitting to my right as he leaned over and whispered in my ear. "Hey, Julie, finish your meal so I can take you home."

I smiled at him and felt a certain comfort by his presence. We finished our meal, ordered coffee and dessert, and when we were done, Rev. Peppers pushed his chair back from the table.

"Friends, I realize that we are in the midst of summer, not long after Independence Day, but allow me to end this time of celebration with a prayer of thanksgiving.

"*Our dear heavenly Father, we thank you for your blessings. We are thankful that you have protected two of your children. You saved Vonda and Julie from certain death and we praise you for that. We ask that you will keep your arm around Vonda as she struggles through this healing process. Bless Julie with a good future and, Lord, bless each of us here and let us continue to be thankful for your blessings. Amen.*"

If you enjoyed *Blueberry Fields*, the first book in the Three Bridges Series, please go to Amazon.com and leave your review on the product page.

Prairie Creek Christian Press
Ben Wheeler, Texas